High Plains Passion

Love on the High Plains: Book 4

Simone Beaudelaire

Contents

Prologue

Garden City, Kansas

April 1889

11:40. Sheriff Dylan Brody snapped his watch shut with a sigh. "Come on, son, it's time."

The somber sound of his voice broke through the agitated pacing of a dark-haired youth inside the jail cell, and he glared at Brody with a look that should have melted the bars and earned his freedom.

Damned shame. He's just a kid. His life of crime will be short... but not because he made a better choice. "You know the procedure, son. Turn around. Hands out."

The kid responded with a slew of profanity, clearly too young to understand facing death with poise or dignity.

And who says you'll do any better, old man? "Now, listen, Will," Brody said, "there's nothing left to be done. You had your chance. This is what you chose. Are you going to fight me?"

"No," Will snarled. "I don't have to. *They* will. You'll be sorry, but it'll be too late."

And for you, it's already too late, Dylan thought, but he restrained the brutal truth. *No reason to point it out now.*

Will turned his back on the lawman in what looked like a gesture of defiance and stuck his hands out between the bars. Dylan swallowed hard and fastened a pair of rudimentary handcuffs around the youth's wrists. Then, he unlocked the door to the cell and led the young man out.

"Want to cover your face?" he asked.

The only response was a rank curse.

Shrugging, Dylan grasped the manacle and led Will Blalock out into the dusty street. Jeering townspeople greeted their appearance with a racket of booing, hissing and clapping. Ugly words spilled from them.

"Murderer!"

"You know how many children you left orphaned, you little prick?"

"Crime doesn't pay, son. The Good Book says..."

Unlike his friends and neighbors, Dylan felt no such vitriol. While Will was, in fact, a murderer, he'd had nothing to do with creating orphans. That shooter had escaped, while this young man hadn't. Dylan knew the crowd wouldn't care about the distinction. They wanted a scapegoat on whom to vent their fear and grief, and Will had been inexperienced enough to get caught. So he would pay for his crimes—and those of his fellow train robbers—at the end of a rope.

The weather had turned dark and cold, common in a place with such an uncertain climate, and the wind nipped them through their clothing, aggressive as the words flying from the crowd that lined the streets. Dust billowed up into tiny tornadoes, swirling dead winter grass that had not yet greened up completely and tossing it into cursing mouths, reducing their abuse to choking gasps.

Thank you, Lord, Dylan thought.

At the end of the long, straight street, the rugged gallows stood ready to exact rough justice. Will's steps faltered, and he was forced to rely on Dylan's strength to keep him moving forward.

At the foot of the scaffold, a couple approached. The man—young, handsome and wearing a grim expression in place of his habitual, white-toothed grin—held arms with a tall and rather homely woman. She regarded the robber with sad aquamarine eyes.

"What do you want, bitch?" Will snarled.

Dylan gave the handcuffs a shake. *I'll tolerate his abuse towards me, but Kristina doesn't deserve it.*

She took no offense. Instead, tears streamed down her heavily freckled cheeks. She sniffled, her short, upturned nose wrinkling. "I had to tell you…" she sobbed. "To tell you…" Again, her voice broke, preventing speech.

"What?" Will demanded.

"Settle down, son," Dylan suggested. "It's her brother you killed. She deserves to speak her piece."

"I know that," the boy snarled. "Let me tell you this right now… Heitschmidt deserved what he got."

Kristina wept openly now. "I know that. I… had to tell you I forgive you. Go in peace."

Will stared. "That's it?"

Kristina is the best of us, Dylan thought. *What class.*

She nodded, words having finally failed.

"Would you like to say a prayer?" her husband suggested, hope flaring in his eyes.

Dylan shook his head. *He wouldn't talk to you the last time you came to see him, Pastor, or the time before that.* While he understood why Cody couldn't give up, he knew the effort would come to nothing.

"Pardon me, preacher man," Will replied in a sarcastic drawl, "but as it's your fault I'm here, I don't want no comforting from you."

Cody bowed his head.

Fool boy. It's your fault you're here. Cody may have tied you up, but if you hadn't been robbing that train, this wouldn't be happening. "Okay, folks," Dylan told Cody and Kristina, "you two move on now. You did your best."

"May God have mercy on your soul," Cody said in his soft Texas accent. "Repentance is in the heart. Remember, Jesus forgave the thief on the cross."

Will's response was another foul curse.

Cody blanched and fell back, allowing the grim procession to proceed.

It seemed the encounter with the pastor had galvanized Will's resolve. He mounted the scaffold under his own power, strode forcefully to the trapdoor and drew himself to his full height, leveling a defiant glare at the hissing, hollering crowd.

"William Blaylock," Dylan began in a sonorous, emotionless voice, "you have been convicted of the murder of Calvin Heitschmidt by a jury of your peers and been sentenced to death. You shall now be hanged by the neck until you are dead, in accordance with the law. May God have mercy on your soul."

Dylan glanced at Will and saw his mouth white and his eyes squinting. "Can we just get this over with?" the kid hissed.

Dylan nodded. "Any last words?"

Will slowly filled his lungs with air. He cleared his throat and spoke. "You were warned. You didn't listen. Now you're going to be sorry. This town will pay. My father will come and avenge me. Mark my words. You can take my life." His defiant tone wavered, then he steeled himself and pressed on. "You can win this round, but you'll never win the war. Never." He turned to Dylan. "You'll be first, Sheriff. You and the preacher man."

Dylan pressed his lips together, lowered a black sack over Will's head and drew in a deep breath. He scanned the gathered townsfolk until he locked his gaze with a pair of soulful, dark-brown eyes. While every other person stared at the condemned, Lydia's tear-streaked face remained fixed on Dylan's. He lowered his chin, acknowledging her with a nod and then turned to affix the rope around Will's neck, carefully arranging the knot behind the condemned man's ear.

"Vaya con Dios," he murmured as he stepped back off the trapdoor. Bringing his foot down solidly on the boards, he signaled to the unseen executioner.

For a breathless moment, the tableau of a man, a noose, and a crowd, all adrift on a windswept plain seemed to freeze, imprinting itself on Dylan's memory forever. Then the floor of the scaffold fell away with a thump. The rope hissed as it lengthened and then creaked as it reached its limit. Will grunted but didn't have time to holler. His noisy exhalation ended in a nauseating crunch that told Dylan he'd once again done his job correctly. *Hell of a thing to be good at,* he thought.

Chapter 1

July 1889

Bang

Lydia knew the time without having to look at the clock on the back wall of her sweltering kitchen. The constant slamming open and shut of the dining room door told her noon had arrived, and the lunch crowd with it, in search of repast after a morning hard at work.

Wiping her sweaty forehead with the back of one floury hand, she scooped up the tray of sandwiches from her preparation table and shouldered open the door into the dining room, savoring the relative coolness. *Well of course it's cooler. There's no stove in here.* She took the long way around the room, past the east side windows, which stood open in hopes that the movement of the hot prairie breeze would pass through as it billowed down Main Street, carrying with it the next load of dust. Residents of Western Kansas had to be tolerant of blowing dirt, especially in the summer. The breeze in no way felt cool, but at least it was moving. A sigh of relief dragged itself past her lips.

Arriving at the service counter, Lydia set the tray of sandwiches next to her cashier and general assistant, Esther, who began piling them on plates.

Lydia circled the room, her black boots clunking on the bare wooden floorboards. *Well, no surprise, I'm far from a small woman. I can't trip lightly along like Becky can... or could,* she amended with a grin. Her friend's increasing weight had added a decided thump to her normally feather-light steps. *Even at thirty-five, she was still a radiant bride... and her 'honeymoon special' looks good on her so far.* Suppressing a petulant internal whine that questioned whether she'd ever find what Becky had, Lydia concentrated on her work, rolling up her sleeves in an attempt to cool her sweaty flesh further.

By now, the regulars had become accustomed to seeing their plump, black-haired proprietress with the sleeves of her gingham dress rolled up above the elbow, but she caught some scornful glances from a couple of strangers at the table nearest the west window.

Inwardly, Lydia shrugged. *What do I care if these two catch a glimpse of my forearms? They'll get their lunch like everyone else, glances notwithstanding. It's too hot to fuss, especially when there's work to be done.*

She dusted her floury hands on her apron, raising a white cloud in the room, and circled, greeting all the patrons and those passing through by train. As she passed, she let them know the day's lunch menu. Lydia didn't go in much for choices. In the summer, lunch always consisted of a sandwich on one of the homemade rolls she baked fresh each morning, a pickle, a piece of fruit, and a drink: coffee, water, or buttermilk.

The fussy couple turned their noses up at her homey fare. "Come on, Marge," the man said. "We could have brought sandwiches from home. Let's try the hotel across the street."

With another glare at the proprietress, they exited. Lydia grinned. "Shouldn't someone tell them the nickname of the hotel?" she asked.

The other diners snickered into their cups.

"What do you mean, ma'am?" a stranger with silver hair asked her, wiping coffee from a luxurious, curling mustache.

With a laugh, Lydia replied, "It's true they have a menu and options, but they also have a reputation, with the nickname of Accidental Hotel, because if you ever got fed there, it would be by accident."

The man chuckled, his dark eyes twinkling.

Lydia winked at him and moved on. Once she had greeted all the customers, she and Esther began handing out the plates and cups, moving carefully around the room to avoid tripping on the loose boards that were beginning to poke up here and there.

A strong gust of sultry wind puffed in through the open window, ruffling the napkins on all the tables and sending several to the floor.

Young Billy Fulton scurried around picking them up. He was a conscientious lad, perhaps not the brightest, but well-intentioned, and Lydia liked him.

"Thank you, Billy," she told him, collecting the napkins from his hands.

He grinned, showing his missing front tooth.

Lydia grinned back. "Now take a seat," she urged him. "I know you're hungry. I made an extra-big sandwich, just for you."

Billy flopped into the spindly chair, which groaned under his substantial weight, and accepted the plate Esther brought him. He would be earning that extra slice of ham later, when he came back to sweep up.

The door banged open again, but this time the noise of heavy boots tromping across the floor added to its clatter.

Lydia froze, turned to look at the newcomer, and felt her face flush. "Hello, Sheriff," she said, trying to control the nervous tremor in her voice.

"Hello Miss Lydia," he replied, pulling off his black Stetson by way of a greeting, setting it on a table, and settling into a chair.

She hurried to bring him a meal, fighting to still the trembling of her hands. Setting the plate on the rough wood, she turned to leave.

He grasped her wrist.

Lydia gasped at the unexpected contact. The sheriff reached up a large, calloused hand and wiped at her cheek. His fingers came away white.

"Thank you," she said, forcing the words out above the pounding of her heart.

He released her wrist and she returned to the counter without another word.

"He's sweet on you," Esther said in a carrying whisper.

"I know," she replied, her face burning.

"And you're sweet on him too, ain't you?"

Lydia replied with a curt nod.

"Well then go get him, girl. Why don't you?" The old woman punctuated her advice with a cackle that drew attention.

"Let's talk about it later," Lydia suggested. "We have work to do." The first customer to finish his lunch, a burly farmhand called Rooster McGee, stepped up to the counter and dropped a handful of coins on the polished wood.

"These real?" Esther demanded, giving the man a suspicious and squinty-eyed glare.

His jaw dropped. "Yes, ma'am," he insisted, bewildered.

"Come on, Essie," Lydia urged her friend with a laugh. "It's been how many years since he gave you that plug nickel? He's a grown man now. Let's forget it."

"Thanks, Miz Lydia," the young man said, pushing sandy hair out of his eyes and stuffing his bedraggled straw hat back on top. Giving Esther a sour look, he scooted for the door. She cackled again.

"Stop flirting with the young men, you old hussy," Lydia teased.

Esther's chuckles turned to peals of surprisingly musical laughter. "I'll flirt when I want to," the old woman snapped. "One of us should be eyeing the handsome men. If it ain't gonna be you, well I may be old, but I ain't dead yet."

"You're a dirty old woman," Lydia replied primly, swiping a cloth over the crumbs on the counter.

"And you're a silly young prude," Esther shot back. "That sheriff is a fine figure of a man. I'd be swarming all over him if he didn't have 'Lydia's private property' stamped over every inch."

"Fiddlesticks. I haven't claimed a thing," Lydia retorted, her cheeks heating.

"And just why in tarnation haven't you?" Esther demanded. "You're not getting any younger. If I was you, I'd hurry up and claim him. Pull him into an alley if you have to... or are you holding out for a ring?"

It slowly dawned on Lydia that the object of their indiscreet conversation might just be sitting behind her, close enough to hear every word. Slowly, her belly fluttering to nausea, she turned... and found the café deserted. *Thank you, Lord.* "Dylan and I are friends," she said as she circled the room, collecting coins and cups from the tables.

"But you want more." It seemed, despite the mock argument having ended, Esther was not willing to let the subject drop.

Stomping down a loose board, Lydia turned to her friend. "I know," she replied, "but don't you think, if he's interested, *he* should approach *me*?"

"If he does, sure," Esther replied with a shrug, "but if he don't, you should. You're no shy little violet. Go after him."

"I might, eventually," Lydia replied, "but I'll be the one to decide when."

"When you've got one foot in the grave, most likely," the older woman muttered, opening the till so Lydia could drop the coins inside. Lydia pretended not to hear.

Letting the conversation drop, Lydia swiped the rag from the counter and worked her way around the room, flipping crumbs off the wood of each table with half-embarrassed, half-angry twitches.

Before she could work herself into a greater tizzy, the door banged open again. Lydia frowned as one of her least-favorite people flounced into the room in a flurry of blue taffeta. The new arrival's full pinks lips curled into a smile Lydia always thought of as malevolent. She sighed. "Good afternoon, Miss Jackson. How can I help you? Lunch is over, you know."

Ilse Jackson, resident gossip and all-around troublemaker trilled a flirtatious laugh, as though Lydia had said something funny, though there was no rich man anywhere nearby. *She must be practicing.*

"Oh, come now, Miss Carré, you know I never eat in here. We have a cook."

Poor thing, working for those overstuffed snobs, Lydia thought, turning her back as though to fiddle with the cash register. Out of sight of Ilse's sneering face, Lydia quickly crossed herself. "So, if you're not here to eat, why are you here? I've never known you to set foot in my café." *And thank the Blessed Virgin for that.*

"I have a proposition for you," Ilse replied, one eyebrow raised though it didn't cause the slightest crease in her perfectly smooth, perfectly white forehead. *Disgusting. She's like a china doll.* "This town has been run by the men for far too long, and it's about time we ladies make our mark. This isn't the frontier. We're a real town, have been for over a decade, and we need to assert our civilizing influence."

That's sure a whole lot of words that don't mean anything. "All right, Miss Jackson, you pose an interesting point. However, I'm not sure I agree that the men are completely in charge around here—after all, plenty of local businesses are run by women—but I'm listening." *Get to the point. I've been up since three this morning and I want to close down the café and rest.* Lydia bit her tongue to prevent bitter words from spilling out. Ilse might be an obnoxious brat, but as long as she was being relatively polite, Lydia could match her.

"I'm proposing we found a Ladies' Council. So many times my father has told me there's no money in the town budget for the activities and events I think are important, but if all the influential women in town pool their resources, we don't need to worry about what they think. We can do what we need to do regardless of their opinion."

"It's an interesting notion," Lydia said cautiously. *With her father running for mayor, it's no surprise he's keeping a tighter hold on the town's purse strings. His years as president of the town council aren't marked by generous spending anyway.* "Tell me more."

"I've approached all the wives and daughters of all the influential families in this town." She ran through a list of names, ending with a sour expression as she added, "And of course Kristina Williams and the Spencer sisters. You were last on my list."

Lydia blinked. "Well then. I'm not sure if I qualify as the daughter or wife of anyone influential, but I am quite certain I own the most successful female-run business in town."

"That's true. That's why I'm here." Ilse's lips puckered to lemon sourness. Lydia couldn't decide whether to smack her or offer her a sugar cube. "That and we need a place to meet. If you would volunteer your café… and maybe some refreshments, that would be appreciated."

"So, let me make sure I understand," Lydia replied. "You want me to volunteer my place of business and give away free food to an organization you aren't sure you want me in, that I haven't agreed to join yet?"

Ilse didn't even have the grace to look sheepish. She merely nodded.

"And what would be the items on the agenda?" Lydia demanded.

"Let me use the café and you'll find out. Next Tuesday. 3:00 pm, so you should be closed by then, right?"

"Yes, I close up at two. You know that." Lydia sighed. *I'm usually resting at that time.* "Very well. I'll let you use my café this once, and I'll even volunteer a few treats, but whether this becomes an ongoing thing will depend on how the meeting goes. Agreed?"

Ilse gave her a strange look, as though uncertain of Lydia's sanity, but shrugged her shoulders. "I suppose. See you then."

Ilse bustled out of the room in a noisy flurry of skirts, seeming not to realize she hadn't even had the courtesy to thank her host for the generous offer.

"Little brat," Esther commented from behind the counter. "Glad I wasn't invited. That busybody's up to no good, I guarantee it."

"I agree," Lydia replied. "I'm only offering in hopes of staving off some ill-conceived disaster that might affect us all."

"You're a brave woman, Lydia," Esther said fervently.

"Did you get any word?" Dylan blurted the second he rounded the doorway into the bank's office. Wesley Fulton's head shot up from the pile of paperwork he was laboriously inscribing, then he quickly tucked his pen back into the inkwell before it could drip on the pages. Rising, the young banker approached the sheriff and stuck out his hand.

"Hello, Sheriff. No, sorry to disappoint you. I sent Jesse a letter, but he roams so far it's hard to track him down."

"You *sure* he's a good candidate?" Dylan asked for the hundredth time.

Wesley raised one eyebrow. "Yeah, I'm sure. He's from here. He knows every man woman and child over five who lives in this town. He's also been in law enforcement for years. He's just the experienced small-town deputy you need." Then Wesley paused to ponder. "Well, if he gets the letter… and if he decides to come."

This time, Dylan's eyebrows rose. "He might not come?"

Wes shrugged. "He said he wasn't coming back. His sweetheart died in the cholera epidemic that wiped out half the town. That outbreak is the reason you're here, Sheriff. The reason Cody is here too, and Kristina—she would never have stayed if her mama had lived—but I figure, it's been five years. Time fades memories and pain. Maybe he's ready to face what he lost."

Dylan didn't ask Wesley whether he'd ever faced his losses. It seemed the young man had a penchant for moving on without reflection. *Don't judge. He may move his life forward too quickly, but you surely take too long.* Not wanting to cloud the conversation with unrelated thoughts, Dylan returned to his main objective. "So you sent a letter, but you have no idea if it will reach him, or when, or if he'll come when he receives it, or if he'll even respond? Wes, I can't wait on finding a deputy until your friend decides to answer, if he does. I can't keep watch over the whole town with only one deputy. Neither of us is getting any sleep and the jail goes unguarded half the time. I need a man now, not 'sometime'."

"I know, I know." Wesley held up his hands in apology. "I don't mean to make your life harder, Sheriff. I just think Jesse West would be perfect for the job. If you can find someone else, fine. Go ahead. I know even with the volunteer watches at night there's too much to do, but maybe he'll come. I hope you'll consider him."

"Wes, if your friend turns up, I'll talk to him," Dylan promised. "Even if I have already filled the position, there might be something else he could do around here, and I wouldn't mind having a lawman in town, but I won't wait on him. I can't. Okay?"

"Fine," Wes agreed.

Eyeing the dark-haired man, Dylan saw Wesley's handsome face settle into a pout. *He's been more miserable than usual lately,* he thought. *I would have expected, having married his childhood sweetheart, with a baby due in a few months, he'd be happier.* Of course, Wesley Fulton had always been a bit of a spoiled mama's boy, and if there was one person old Mrs. Fulton couldn't stand, it was Wesley's wife Allison, née Spencer. *Grumpy, displaced mother and grumpy pregnant wife. Maybe his scowl is justified.*

"See you later, Wes," Dylan said, stepping out of the cubicle into the main area of the bank. It seemed the young man's sour mood had rubbed off on him. *Or maybe it's the pressure to replace Deputy Charles. I wish I didn't have to, poor fella.*

An animated, well-modulated female voice drew his attention to the teller window. At first, a line of sweaty patrons obscured the view, but Dylan persisted, and sure enough, his suspicious dissolved into the reality of Lydia Carré making her daily deposit of the café's earnings.

"Thank you, Jack," she said to the young teller—one of many Fulton boys, a cousin of Wesley's.

"You're welcome, Miss Carré," the youth said, writing slowly on a slip of paper and then handing it to her. "Here's your receipt."

She accepted the scrap and tucked it into her reticule, an intricately beaded pouch in a soft shade of pink. *It's the same color as her lips,* Dylan realized. His face burned as he realized what a besotted reflection he'd just made. *Yes, I'm attracted to her,* he admitted to himself, not for the first time, *but...*

He let the thought drift away. Lydia, however, would not be allowed to do the same. "Afternoon, Miss Carré," he said in a rumbling undertone.

The words seemed to draw her eye like a magnet. "Sheriff Brody," she replied. That was it. No further words passed between them. None were needed. Instead, their intense connection flowed between their eyes. She drew in a deep breath, her nostrils flaring, and drew the lip he'd just been admiring into her mouth.

Dylan wanted to groan. Instead, he closed the distance between them in two long-legged strides and offered his arm. "Watch your step," he said, voicing what had to be the inanest comment in a century. "It's a long way down."

Despite the fact that she'd navigated the steep entrance into the bank every day for the last five years, without ever tripping once that he knew of, she took his arm. "Thank you."

Titters erupted behind them, and the burning in Dylan's cheeks intensified, but he ignored the spectacle he was creating, because the scent of Lydia Carré—of freshly baked bread, lily-scented soap, and something else he couldn't define but would know the moment he took it in, even if he couldn't see her—filled his being. He swallowed hard as the front of his trousers suddenly felt much too tight.

He heaved a sigh and led Lydia out the door, away from prying eyes.

The sunlight sparkled bright and hot outside the bank, transforming stuffy closeness into biting heat that seemed to have sprouted fangs and claws.

"My lands, it's hot," Lydia complained.

He glanced her way as he helped her off the bank's high porch into the dusty brick street.

She wiped a bead of sweat off her forehead and fanned her face with her hand. Her eyes narrowed, squinting against the painful brightness, and Dylan was charmed again by the sight of the tiny creases in the corners of her eyes. *No innocent young miss, Lydia Carré is all mature, enticing woman. I could wish she was mine.*

"It is," he agreed amiably, but the intensity of his tone drew her eyes to his again and another sizzling lightning bolt of attraction passed between them. The expression on her lovely face moved from untempered longing and desire to disappointment. *She wants you too. You know she does.* Unsure what to do with their mutual interest, Dylan firmly returned their conversation to the mundane. "I'll be glad when the heat breaks. Fall can't come fast enough to suit me."

"Me either." A wry twisting of her lips revealed her displeasure. She tugged at the collar of her dress to allow a hot, stale breeze in. "I love what I do, but even before the sunrise the kitchen is miserable."

Dylan tried to imagine, and his mouth turned down to mimic the curve of his mustache. "Sounds terrible."

She nodded. "Those crisp October mornings, I love warming the kitchen with the scent of bread and pastries. It's so lovely." They moved down the sidewalk past the church, where muted organ music roiled and bellowed. "My pumpkins are going to be spectacular this year." They paused in the meager shadow created by the bell tower.

"Mmmm," Dylan hummed as they began moving again. His mouth watered. "I dream all year about your pumpkin spice cake. Will you save me a piece when the time comes?" He pleaded, sounding like an eight-year-old kid and not caring. "It would do wonders for my pitiful supper."

They sighed in unison as a tiny cloud passed over the sun, momentarily killing the heat. "Why do you say pitiful?" Lydia demanded, groaning softly as the beating sun reappeared.

As he considered his answer, Dylan regarded the row of multicolored, single-story structures that made up the main street of town, interspersed with businesses. The steeple of the church and the Occidental Hotel seem to tower over the street. "I can't cook," he replied at last. "Usually after work, I'm so tired I fall asleep and burn it up. You don't want to see what happens to a can of baked beans after two hours boiling on a hot stove." He chuckled at the memory.

Lydia froze in front of her café and gasped. "Oh, Dylan, please tell me you're not eating canned food." The horror on her face struck him as far too significant for such a commonplace admission. *After all, how many thirty-something widowers* don't *eat canned food?*

"Almost every night," he replied, puzzled by her vehemence. "Why?"

She frowned, her chocolate brown eyes filling with disgust. "I grew up near the canneries back east. Sometimes the workers ate at my parents' restaurant. The stories they told." She shuddered. "I've heard things about those places that would make you sick if the food already hasn't. Please promise me you won't eat any more of that. Only accept jars from people you know personally, ones who know what they're doing."

Dylan patted her hand. The warmth of her overheated and sweaty skin still felt pleasant, despite the discomfort of the blistering July day. "I don't know what I should do instead, Miss Lydia. You're closed in the evening and the hotel is too expensive for everyday eating. At least for a public servant such as myself."

Lydia's frown turned to a guilty giggle. "If you ever get served anything, that is," she said, mocking the shoddy service for which the hotel dining room was famous. "What about the boarding house? I know June Fulton is a fine cook. We worked together on last year's Christmas potluck."

"I feel bad eating with her now that I have my own place," he replied. "She has all those mouths to feed, and she won't let me pay." *And her pleading looks drive me insane. June is a sweet woman, but five kids, including a grown son who's slow in the head and will never leave home? I just can't do it.*

Looking at Lydia, he knew it wasn't Billy Fulton, who despite being slow was one of the nicest people in town, or his three rambunctious younger brothers, or his sister born just a bit too long after her mother's husband's passing that made June beyond consideration. *I know what I want. I just don't know how… or even if I should try.*

Lydia regarded him with those soulful eyes, eyes that seemed to have seen things no sheltered young lady would understand. *An ocean of sorrow lies beyond the chocolate warmth. A river of pain. An endless pool of compassion. It would be so easy to drown.* Something about Lydia touched long-dormant parts of his soul. His maudlin thoughts snapped him out of the hypnotic whirlpool. *Damn it, man, you're a sheriff, not a poet.*

"It's kind of you to consider her well-being," she replied, a wry twist of her lip showing she was aware of June's flirting. "Now then, how can a civic-minded lady such as myself ensure our longsuffering sheriff stays healthy…"

"First of all," he said, a teasing grin toying with his lips, "you can get him out of the hot sun."

Lydia blushed and let her arm slip out of his, grasping his hand so she could drag him into the suffocating shade of her café.

There really is no actual relief from the summer, he realized. but although the air inside the café seemed to close in on him and steal his breath, the scorching sun no longer gnawed at his skin. He sank into one of the wobbly chairs. Lydia pulled one up beside him but remained standing. "Can I get you anything?" she asked.

"I'd be mighty glad of a glass of water," he replied.

She smiled at him, the curving of her plump lips carving a dimple into her right cheek. Her dark eyes crinkled in the corners. "Be right back."

Dylan settled into the rickety chair and surveyed the café for the millionth time. After taking breakfast and lunch there most days, he knew the interior by heart. Wide-open windows, normally sparkling clean but caked with dust from the recent heat and wind. Tables and chairs deliberately left in a rough state, sturdy enough to sit on, but self-consciously humble. A long, scarred wooden counter opposite the exterior door and beside the entry into the kitchen where Lydia had just disappeared. A heavy iron cash register gleamed, though not brightly, in its natural shade of metallic black. The walls had been whitewashed rather than painted and the floorboards sloped and curled up in the corners.

Overall, it looked like a homey eatery, comfortable for those who lacked pretention. Most of the townsfolk preferred it to the hotel, which was their only other choice apart from eating at home, and the passers-through who exited the noon train in search of sustenance sometimes complained about the shabby décor, but those who put up with it enjoyed a tasty and inexpensive meal, nonetheless.

The kitchen door swung open and Lydia stepped into the space. Their eyes locked and she paused, captured once again it seemed, by the potent lure of their mutual, if unexpressed, attraction. The doorway seemed to frame her, as though the vibrant, vital woman had become a portrait of herself, one Dylan could commit to memory.

Heavy black hair pulled into a huge braided coil on the back of her head, the sides curling and bending in the heat. Round, pale face with a few freckles across the nose and those arresting brown eyes framed with lush lashes and thick, dark eyebrows.

Yes, her nose had some girth and length to it. Some might call it big, but to Dylan, it gave character to a face that might otherwise be too beautiful, too angelic to be real.

Plump pink cheeks, one dented with a dimple every time she smiled, set his heart pounding. Full lips begged to be kissed, though he hadn't tried it yet.

The collar of her dress sat close to her slender neck, though he'd managed to catch a peek at her collarbones when she tugged it. And below… ah, below the perfection of a female figure in full bloom. Her bosom was large enough to bring him to aching readiness, just seeing it push out the bodice of her dress. Her narrow waist flared to round wide hips he would sell his soul to grab hold of, but though the long loose skirt gave no indication of what lay between her hips and the dainty black boots on her feet, he could imagine plump, soft thighs.

Dylan swallowed hard, but lacking enough spittle to accomplish the task, he choked. *Choking on air,* he thought wryly as the spell shattered once again.

She hastened across the room, deftly avoiding tripping over a loose board, and handed him the water.

He gulped and the cool beverage moistened his dry throat enough to end his coughing spell. Eyes watering, he regarded his companion in consternation. "Thank you," he gasped.

Lydia patted his hand. Her rueful smile spoke volumes.

Her fingers remained resting on top of his. *Is this the moment? Should I speak?* And then too many ugly memories welled up like water from a bitter spring and flowed over his words.

Lydia's open face shuttered and she removed her hand from his.

Be patient, sweet lady. Please, wait for me, Dylan begged silently. *There's a gulf you can't imagine between us and I'm trying to cross it, but it's hard. Life's been rough and my heart isn't young and fresh. It doesn't spring back.*

The tepid, grimace-like smile on Lydia's pretty face did nothing to reassure him.

Chapter 2

Lydia regarded her teeming restaurant and couldn't help smiling. The five years she'd spent in Garden City—almost six now—had been some of the best in her life. *It's an unusual town to let women do as much as we do here. My café. Kristina's church music. Becky's shop. When I got off the train at this stop and there was no lunch, I made a snap decision, and look at me now.*

Half a decade later, the train passengers who stopped in Garden had the opportunity to join locals for whatever she felt like putting on. Sandwiches, soups, casseroles and stews left locals and passers-through alike full and smiling, which in turn made Lydia feel like she'd made a small but positive contribution to the world. Breakfast had been a more recent but equally popular venture. This morning, farmhands, local businessmen and women and some overnight guests from the hotel sat slurping coffee and munching toast.

The young couple she'd just met—getting married and relocating to the town—scooted out to continue their preparations. Lydia turned to regard her café as excitement over the challenge of creating a wedding cake on no notice warred with happiness for this young couple and a pang for her own disappointed opportunities. *I can't help but wish my own suiter had half that young man's gumption.*

"What a lovely young couple," a masculine voice said from the door in a well-modulated tone and an Eastern accent.

"They are," Lydia agreed, releasing her moment of self-pity and turning her attention to her customer. To her surprise, he looked familiar. "You were here yesterday, weren't you, sir? I thought you were just passing through."

"Oh, no," he replied, twining a thin, waxed strand of a mustache between his fingertips and shaping it into a perfect, dandyish curl. A flawless triangle of a black beard completed the goatee. His hair, steel gray and slicked with pomade, contrasted with a pale face that seemed to be lined from pain rather than sun. "I'm relocating to this town. It seems like a nice place. I'm examining the situation to see if they have room for a new business."

"It is," Lydia agreed, "and pretty friendly to outsiders, though it's still a small town. I'm sure you understand what that means."

He nodded.

"So what will you be doing here? Garden isn't so big on industry right now."

He shrugged. "I have many years' experience organizing and running things, and I'm blessed to have plenty of savings while I figure something out."

"That is a blessing," she agreed. "When I came to town, I had a small nest egg, which I invested in this place. Would you believe it was once a stable? So now everything is just as it should be." *Well almost everything*, she amended silently.

The gentleman stretched his mouth into a considering frown, his mustache undulating on his lips like a canoe in the ocean. "Good to know that if a tenacious person puts in the effort, the town rewards them."

"Oh yes," she agreed. "At least that's how it worked for me. Good luck to you, Mr...."

"Mr. Blaylock," he replied. "Samuel Blaylock. You're Miss Lydia Carré, isn't that right?" He grinned, showing white straight teeth.

"Yes, you have that right," she replied.

"Thank you for the good wishes... and the delicious breakfast, Miss Carré. I'm sure I'll be back soon for more of the same." His gaze lingered on her figure before returning to her eyes, a wordless expression of interest.

No answering surge of attraction welled up in her, flattering though his regard had been. For years Dylan had been giving her the same look, and it no longer spoke to her. *Or at least, not from this fellow.*

He rose, dug some coins out of his pocket and left his meal payment on the table. Clapping a smooth black bowler hat on his head, he nodded to Lydia and exited the restaurant, his gait noticeably unsteady.

Lydia gathered up the dishes absently, tucking the coins into the pocket of her apron. Instead of thinking about lunch, though, her mind turned to men. *Dylan isn't the only man in town. I could find someone else if I wanted to.* Her heart fluttered at the thought, and she knew it for the lie it was. *I could find a man who wanted to bed me, no doubt, with this harlot figure. He might even care for me, but my heart is taken. As long as I hold onto hope Dylan might come around, it would be unfair to pursue anyone else.*

"You know," Esther commented as Lydia set the dirty plates on the counter and retrieved the coins from her apron for her assistant to tuck into the cash register. The black beast opened with a noisy clang. "That's one suave number, that newcomer."

Lydia shrugged. "Looks fussy to me. His mustache wax is going to melt, and then won't he look silly? I can do better."

"Yes you can," Esther replied. "I'm not suggesting you invite that undersized cripple upstairs."

Lydia choked.

Esther continued as though nothing had happened. "If you're seen around town talking to the fellow once or twice, it might convince your reluctant sheriff to speak up."

Lydia considered the prospect. "It's not nice to call him a cripple," she pointed out, "and it's really not nice to play with his heart. I don't care how big a dandy he is. People have feelings. I can see he's interested. I'm not, so it would be unfair to encourage him."

"Lord have mercy, Miss Lydia, you'll be single when you're old and gray at this rate. Do something before you end up as shriveled as I am and still alone."

Lydia smiled indulgently at her friend. "Your fate doesn't seem so bad to me. Anyway, I have enough on my mind. I wonder what kind of cake those two young folks would like for their wedding. Fruit cake takes too long, but some nice white cake would work, or a spice cake…"

"I'd say white," Esther commented. "You can decorate it with fruit or sugared flowers. It's too hot for spice cake. What would you have for your own wedding?"

In her faraway place, where she lived to create new recipes and improve old ones, she spoke without reflection. "Crystalized flowers on white cake with white icing. The peaches are delicious this year. Peach filling would be wonderful." She could visualize the two-layer white beauty, teasing the eye with flashes of sparkling, sugar-coated color. "For myself, I'd love to marry in the fall, with spice cake." Then she realized what she'd said and sucked in a gasp. *Don't start down that path, Lydia. Be thankful for what you have.* "I have to go get these dishes washed and get ready for lunch. Any idea when Billy's coming back?"

Esther nodded. "He's mighty sick, his mama said, but she thinks he's on the mend. Maybe a couple of days."

"Thank goodness," Lydia replied. "I don't know how long we'd get on without that boy."

Esther regarded her with a considering expression as she began counting the coins in the till. "You're a good woman, Miss Lydia. I'm thankful for you every day."

Blushing, Lydia carried the egg-stained plates into the kitchen.

Dylan had his feet up on his desk. He knew it was a bad habit, but he had no intention of changing it. Besides, he had a drunk Angus Fulton in the cell again, and antagonizing Wesley's most obnoxious cousin gave him a thrill.

"Can't you sit up properly?" Angus slurred, managing to sound hoity-toity and stewed at the same time. Dylan turned the page on his newspaper and ignored the whining voice, grinning to himself despite the news in front of him—or rather the lack thereof.

Train robbers aren't going to go to ground altogether. I don't know how many there were, but I suspect it was several. They wouldn't have been able to pull off so many heists with only the handful of men we caught up to last December. I wonder what happened to the rest of the gang. In spite of what Cody and Kristina said, the man Kris's brother killed was surely the boss of that operation, not of the whole shebang.

The door of the jail swung open and a stranger walked in. Young and blond, with a firm jaw and shrewd blue eyes, he scrutinized the jail. Then his lips pursed. "I'm Jesse West," the man stated. "I heard you might have a deputy position?"

Relief set Dylan's heart pounding. "Thank the Lord you're here, West. I thought I was going to have to deputize Billy Fulton."

"He'd do an enthusiastic job," Jesse pointed out.

"Yeah, but the poor kid is scared of guns. Anyway, West, your telegram and Fulton's endorsement have me intrigued. Tell me a bit about yourself."

"Well," Jesse began, "I've been working the last five years as a bounty hunter, so you can see I'm qualified. You need a deputy?"

"Oh, yes," Dylan replied. "We're in one hell of a mess here."

"So I understand," Jesse replied. "I'll be honest, Sheriff, I'm not too happy to hear my hometown is having trouble. What's going on?"

Dylan raised his eyebrow at the man's blunt assessment. "I'm not too happy myself, West. This is my town now too, don't forget. I need the help of an experienced lawman to untangle it. The whole damned mess started with a train robbery back in December. Kristina Williams—Kristina Heitschmidt and her husband Cody, our new pastor—were nearly killed, but those two brave folks managed to save a few passengers from the robbery. Her brother died that day."

"Wait," West interjected, "Cal Heitschmidt came back?"

"He was on that train," Dylan replied. "No one knows why, and he's not around to answer those questions anymore."

Jesse lowered his eyes, his shrewd stare turning sad. "He was like a kid brother growing up. I practically lived with the Heitschmidts. Bet James took it hard."

Dylan nodded. "If it wasn't for his wife, I don't know how he'd have gotten through."

"Wait, what?" Jesse now looked shocked. "What wife? James Heitschmidt's wife died… she died right before I left town"

"Sorry, I mean Rebecca. She and James have been courting for a while, and they got married last month. Another of the crazy things that happened around here was that her dress shop was firebombed. If James hadn't gone in there and pulled her out, she would have died. It was a diversion because the robber gang attempted to break one of their own out of the jail."

"My head is spinning. Hold on. So you're saying *two* violent acts have been committed against the people of our town, in addition to both Kristina Heitschmidt and Rebecca Spencer getting married. Where have I landed, the moon? What happened to the sleepy town I left?"

He turned to stare out the window into the dusty street.

Dylan gave him a moment to gather himself. At last, the youth returned his attention to the sheriff, his eyes skating around the room to take in the rough planks, the iron bars, the scarred desk scattered with newspaper. "Anything else?"

"Well, the robber we caught was hanged a few months back. He threatened the whole town with vengeance, especially Cody and me." *Another reason I should be careful with Lydia. These bastards are smart and tricky. I might not be around to love her much longer.* "Since his death," Dylan continued, his voice rough, "I've been getting threatening notes. All are postmarked Pueblo, Colorado."

Jesse sighed. "Well, if they're holed up in Colorado, maybe you have some time to regroup. Why do you need a deputy?"

"Because my last one was killed at the train robbery," Dylan replied bluntly. "Wade Charles. Hell of a thing. Left a wife and four little children behind. I hate to replace him, but I can't run this town with only one deputy."

Jesse lowered his head in acknowledgment of Dylan's damnable position. "Well, I'm here if you need me. I need a more stable job."

"Well now, hold on, West," Dylan protested. "I need to know more about you. I know your friends can vouch for your character, but what about your work? After the excitement of the open trail, why on earth would you be in a hurry to settle down? Apart from train robbers, policing this town is pretty dull."

"I know," Jesse replied with a wry grin. "I met a girl…"

"Ah, the perennial story," Dylan teased, though honesty forced him to admit to himself that meeting a girl really did change everything. "Girls come and go."

Jesse grinned. "Not for me," he admitted. "Not anymore. Addie is special." He cleared his throat. "She's also in a family way. So ready or not, it's a settled town and family life for this bounty hunter."

Dylan bit his lip to keep from laughing. "Oops. Well, that I can certainly understand. You might want a stable life for your wife and kid."

Jesse nodded. "Once we get married, yeah."

"Oh HO!" Dylan exclaimed. "Sure you want to spread that around? This fella has big ears." He indicated the cell.

Angus gave him a dirty look. "I have per…" He belched. "Perfectly elegant ears. From my mother. She's from Europe, you know."

Jesse laughed out loud. "Angus Fulton. You still spreading that tale around? Know what I heard? Your elegant mother came from a whorehouse in Europe."

"You take that back, Jesse West, or when I get out of this cage, I'll…"

"You won't remember a thing," Jesse shot back. "You're soaked. Haven't you learned yet that you can't hold booze? There's no shame in it, you know."

"Shut up, West." The man sank onto the dirty bunk, swearing under his breath.

"Huh," Dylan said, impressed, "I guess you really are from around here. Is that true about his mother?"

"Who knows? I just say it to rile him up. Works every time," Jesse said, his eyes sparkling.

"I like your style, man. Okay, let's give this a try. You are planning to stick around for the long haul, right?"

"Of course," Jesse replied. "Thank you, Sheriff. I'm sure glad we were able to work this out."

"Me too," Dylan agreed, extending his hand to his new deputy. "So when can you start?"

"Can you give me a couple of days?" Jesse requested. "I need to marry my girl. It's pretty important. She's already showing, you know?"

"That's fair," Dylan replied. "Yeah, be sure you keep your lady happy."

Jesse nodded. "I'll get right to that. She's my priority now. I have to make sure she's okay." Then his cheeks darkened as though realizing he'd said too much.

Love, Dylan thought. *It's good if he cares for her. Life's too short to waste one moment of love.* Then he realized how many moments he'd wasted and firmly decided to change his line of thinking.

"Okay, West. Go take care of business. I'll see you back here in three days—not two, three, you hear? We'll go over basic lawman business, your duties, and the train robber case then."

"Thank you, Sheriff," Jesse replied. "See you then."

The young man's grin rivaled the sunshine outside as he clomped across the wooden floorboards and hustled out into the street.

Dylan sank into his chair and leaned back, laying his boots on the wooden surface of his desk again, this time crinkling the newspapers. His mind barely registered Angus' continued cursing and muttering. *Thank the Lord for sending me a deputy. Seems like a good one too. Things may be okay after all.* "Two days to marry his pregnant sweetheart." Dylan shook his head. "Kids these days. Good thing he loves her." That, of course, immediately turned his mind to his own stalled romance. *Maybe it's time to take your own advice, old man*, he thought.

He didn't realize it, but the concept brought a smile to his lips.

Chapter 3

Lydia had almost managed to forget that Ilse Jackson had volunteered her café for a meeting. This had eased her mind considerably and allowed her to indulge in her favorite activity—obsessing about the sheriff—but left her a bit under-prepared. That was why she found herself that sunny, blistering afternoon in July, rolling up little bites of fruit into flaky pie dough while her finally healthy helper washed the dishes.

"Are you better, Billy?" she asked the lad as she pinched the turnovers shut. Her damp hair stuck to her forehead and her sweaty dress clung to her skin.

"Uh-huh, yes, ma'am," Billy replied, splashing happily in the sink. Though his voice slurred due to his impairment, Lydia had long since learned to understand him. "I was awful sick, but I'm better now."

"I was so sorry to hear you were ill," Lydia told him with all sincerity. She brushed the turnovers with milk and sprinkled sugar on them. "I'm glad you're better."

"Thank you, Miz Lydia. I'm glad to be better and come back to work. Did you miss me?" He grinned, thick lips peeling back to reveal one missing tooth.

"I missed you so much, Billy," she replied, popping the turnovers into the oven and turning to the stove to freshen the coffee. *Why are you doing this? The oven should have been left to cool hours ago. Now the whole house will be hot all night. You need to decorate that wedding cake while the kitchen is cool, so the icing doesn't melt. Who cares what nasty Ilse Jackson has to say, anyway?*

She knew it was too late to argue, so even as she let her mind keep on whining, she set cups and plates on a tray and carried them into the dining room, ready to host this mysterious committee meeting.

A few ladies had arrived already. Allison Spencer Fulton, looking puffy and uncomfortable with only a couple of months left in her pregnancy, defied convention by turning up in a hastily altered blue gingham dress. Her sister Rebecca Spencer Heitschmidt sat beside her. Also expecting, Rebecca had no trouble disguising her own diminutive bump with a clever turn of the sewing needle, making a social necessity into a fashion statement. Third, at the table, Kristina Heitschmidt Williams looked svelte as always in a plain brown skirt and white shirtwaist, her strawberry blond hair escaping from a normally tidy knot. In the summer sun, her freckles seemed to have grown together in a mockery of a tan.

Lydia beamed at the sight of her friends. *No matter what nonsense Ilse has up her sleeves, these three will see reason.* She set the tray of dishes down on the counter, not trusting any of the wobbly tables to hold such a burden without tilting, and hurried over to her friends, greeting them with effusive hand-gestures. They rose to receive sweaty but sincere hugs.

"Allison, how are you feeling? Where's Melissa?" she asked the sturdy blond.

"Mrs. Fulton agreed to watch her." Allison's lips twisted at the thought of her mother-in-law. "I hate to think what that means they'll be doing all afternoon. Probably cleaning the parlor to her specifications. I left Missy napping. Maybe she'll sleep until I get back."

"Let's hope," Lydia agreed. She could barely reach across the expectant mother's belly to hug her shoulders. Then Allison settled back into her chair looking grumpy and miserable.

All her dreams came true, Lydia thought, *and none of it made her happy. Poor lady. Her husband ought to be horsewhipped and his mother tarred and feathered.*

Shaking off the thought, she turned to Kristina. Now here was a woman for whom none of her dreams had come true, and yet she glowed with joy. "How's Pastor Cody doing?" Lydia asked.

Kristina grinned, showing clean but crooked teeth. Her smiles turned her rather plain face radiant. "He's doing just great. He's wrestling with some tough scripture right now. Expect a wild sermon come Sunday."

"Will you have some wild music to go with it?" Lydia wanted to know as she squeezed the taller woman.

"I think so," Kristina replied. "I'll have to dig into my sheet music and see if there's anything fitting."

"I can't wait," Lydia told her. "We're so blessed. What other small town gets a concert every Sunday?"

Blushing Kristina wrinkled her short nose, setting her freckles rolling across her skin.

Last Lydia turned to her best friend, taking in Becky's radiant smile. *How much happier she looks. That serene expression she always used to wear never did convince me, but this smile comes from the depths of her soul.* "How's the shop?" she asked simply.

"Going well so far," Becky replied. "I'm having so much fun sharing space with James. Those robbers may have thought to demoralize me by burning my store, but so much good came from it, I don't even miss the space. Besides, I can sew anywhere my machine will fit. I met the most exciting new client yesterday," she went on, eyes sparkling as she shared the juicy tidbit.

"Who's exciting in this town?" Allison groused. "We already know everyone."

"Not everyone," Becky contradicted her sister. "You'll never guess."

"No, I won't," Allison agreed. "Tell me."

From the kitchen, the aroma of pastries wafted out into the dining room and Billy stuck his head through the door. "I think these are done, Miss Lydia."

"Okay," Lydia told him. "Now you hold on to that gossip for another minute and let me get set up for whatever nonsense Miss Jackson has in store."

Groans and eye rolls met her proclamation as Lydia hurried into the kitchen. A couple of trips had pastries and coffee set up on the counter awaiting the rest of the group.

She returned to the table with her friends. *It feels strange to sit.*

"Okay, Becky," Allison told her sister, "what's the gossip? Who on earth could possibly be exciting in this little whistle-stop?"

"Jesse West is back," Becky proclaimed.

Allison gaped at her sister.

"That's right!" Kristina agreed. "I saw him yesterday. He told me he's back to stay."

Allison looked from one woman to another. "The hell you say? Why hasn't he come to see me?"

Lydia replied. "He brought a woman with him. They're rushing around to get married as quickly as possible. I'm sure he had to start with what he'd need for a little wedding. Music, a dress for his girl, and food."

"Wait, you saw him too, Lydia?"

The chef nodded.

Allison scowled.

"But I'm sure you're next on the list," Becky reassured her sister. "You four were thick as thieves growing up."

"I know that," Allison snapped.

Wow, she's really in a bad mood today, Lydia thought, eyeing her normally cheerful friend.

There didn't seem to be anything else to say. Allison's sour expression killed any remaining desire to speak and at that moment, other women from town began meandering into the café, collecting refreshments and seating themselves at the rickety tables.

Ilse entered with her mother in tow, both turning up their noses at the shabby atmosphere and declining the food.

Snobs, Lydia thought.

"If everyone would settle down," Ilse said in a shrill, carrying tone, "we can get started."

The murmuring women stilled their gossip and turned to face the organizer of the event, who stood between the east side windows like a potentate, though even her blue satin dress seemed rather limp in the unyielding heat.

"Garden City has been officially incorporated as a town for more than a decade now," she began. "Remember our ten-year founder's day party?"

The women in the room turned to each other with puzzled expressions and began to whisper.

"I don't either," Ilse interrupted them. "That's because we didn't have one. I told my father we needed to do this. We're a town, a real town, not some kind of half-baked settlement, and we need to do things that town folks do. One of which is celebrating the day we became civilized." She looked around the room to see if she had everyone's attention.

She's not much of a speaker, Lydia thought, *but she does make a point.*

"It's women that civilize a town," she continued. "Men have too much work to do. It's the wives and daughters who make a place feel like home."

Nods greeted this pronouncement.

"But men, of course, also control most of the money, and so they think they get to decide what's in the town's best interest. I don't agree with their decisions about a lot of things, and I think it's time we as women take a more active role in shedding Garden City's frontier image. Dodge can have its famous gunmen and Wild West shows. We're Garden City. Doesn't that draw up a genteel image? Nothing to dodge here. No bullets flying."

Becky snorted and Kristina shuddered. *There are fewer bullets flying in Dodge City than here at this point,* Lydia said silently to herself.

It appeared facts didn't interest Ilse nearly as much as the point she was building up to. "So what I propose is this: by pooling our resources, women business owners and the wives and daughters of wealthy men can create a bit of influence. If we fight hard enough for what we want, we can turn this town into what it should be—a beacon of civilization on the prairie!"

Her impassioned words drew applause from a few of her most ardent supporters.

Toadies. That was a whole lot of words that didn't mean a darn thing.

"What exactly are you talking about, Ilse?" Allison demanded. "What are you proposing we do? Sit around and drink tea? Meddle in other people's business?"

"I hardly expected you to understand my vision, Allison Fulton," Ilse sneered. "You're practically a man yourself and only half as civilized."

"Well then," Allison said, hauling her heavy body from the chair and staring daggers at the other woman across the room, "I'll just take my 'uncivilized' self out of here. You're welcome to wallow in your usual horseshit without me."

Her uncouth words drew gasps and titters as she made her slow way to the door. Lydia couldn't help smiling. She wanted to leave too. Ilse's words gave her a bad feeling, but as they were stationed in her place of business, she felt compelled to stay. Settling back in her chair, she voiced the question Allison's tirade had raised. "So, Miss Jackson, you've made the theme of your presentation quite clear, but I'm still a little puzzled about the details. What kinds of activities do you think we should be pooling our resources to accomplish?"

"Uh, I was just getting to that," Ilse replied. Something about her face suggested a sneer, but Lydia wasn't sure if that was intentional or merely her habitual expression. "First of all, like I said, we haven't been celebrating our own town's anniversary. I think we should have a Founder's Day picnic and celebration every year."

Nods greeted this. After all, planning a party definitely qualified as civilized, and was something anyone could get behind.

"But this year we missed it since the actual date is in the spring. However, we can celebrate whenever we want to this year and move the celebration to the actual date next year. Does that sound agreeable?"

The ladies murmured in assent.

"How long do you think it would take to plan something?" Ilse asked, turning the conversation over to the group. The women began to chat at their tables, not sure how to answer the question but mulling it over, nonetheless.

Finally, the tables grew still again and Lydia, who seemed to have been appointed question leader, asked, "How long it takes depends on what we plan. A pot-luck picnic can be put together in a week or two, though I'd think we would want to wait until it cools off a bit. If you want something fancy with fireworks or a parade, that might take longer."

"Hmmmm." Ilse considered. "I don't think we should bother with fireworks at this time of year—we'd probably set the prairie ablaze—but a potluck doesn't seem like enough. What about if we organized some events and activities. Cooking and quilting competitions. Sack and three-legged racing. Maybe a kissing booth. Also some special foods. How long would it take to put that together?"

Again the women turned to talk amongst themselves. Finally, Lydia replied, "I think we could have that ready around the first Saturday in September."

Smiles greeted the words. Even Ilse lavished on her a smile slightly less condescending than usual. "Of course! I'll head up the decorating committee. Lydia, will you take charge of the food and cooking contests? Rebecca, you can make the prize ribbons. What else?" She tapped her fingertip on her lip.

"Don't worry," Rebecca said softly, "I'm sure we'll get it all straightened out. How about if we all think on it and meet next week with our decisions and assignments?"

Unable to refute the older woman's logic, Ilse acknowledged her with a nod. "All right, that's settled for now then. On to my next, and more difficult mission. You see, right here in this town, we are harboring the Devil. Pure evil and pure temptation."

She looked around the room, apparently gauging whether she'd captured their attention. The crowd of ladies sat in riveted silence, broken only by the creak of one of the uneven chairs as someone resettled her weight.

Oh, here it comes, Lydia thought, scowling.

"The good men of Garden City are being seduced away from their homes and families by the evils of strong drink and loose women, and we, the moral backbone of our community, sit by and do nothing."

She paused for breath while Lydia rolled her eyes. *She's been taking classes I suppose, to fancy herself such an orator.*

"I have here in my possession, a petition I intend to submit to the sheriff, the mayor, and anyone else with authority in this town, demanding to shut down the establishment known as Chester's Saloon. I expect all of you to sign it. I'm sure you'll agree."

Again all around the room women murmured their assent while Lydia seethed.

The meeting adjourned, the ladies rose and approached Ilse, eager to place their names on the damned sheet of paper as they made their way toward the door. Lydia tried to ignore them, gathering up the plates and cups and hauling them to the kitchen before returning to the dining room to see the few remaining guests out.

Damn it, now I'll have to talk to Ilse privately, and what a lovely mess that's going to be. I hope she has an alternate place to meet in mind.

As the assembly funneled out of the restaurant, the sneering, hated voice piped up again. "Oh, Miss Carré, you haven't signed the petition."

Lydia swallowed down her anger so she could respond calmly, though with each word she took a deliberate step forward. "Miss Jackson, I will happily head the food committee for your celebration. It's an excellent idea. However, no power on earth could compel me to sign that paper." Ilse's eyes widened as the larger, heavier woman approached her. She stepped across the threshold. Lydia advanced into the doorway. "Nor will I allow it inside my establishment again. So unless you want to meet elsewhere, I suggest you drop it, at least in my presence. Good day."

She shut the door and barred it, ignoring the immediate, loud knocking, and returned to the kitchen to wash the extra dishes generated by Ilse's brainstorm. *I hope I haven't lost every friend and client I have in this town,* she thought as she grabbed her scrub brush and set to work on the turnover crumbs. *Ah well. At least I have a project to keep me busy for a while.*

Dylan slipped into the church and took a seat in a pew near the altar. Lydia hadn't arrived yet, but he observed the other guests, curious who his new deputy had chosen to witness his special moment. Cody stood at the front, of course. Dylan felt no surprise that his gaze remained fixed on the balcony behind him, where, Dylan felt sure, his wife Kristina was providing the lilting piano solo that filled in the silence before the arrival of the bride.

Beside the pastor, Jesse held one hand in the opposite wrist as he nervously shifted his weight from one foot to another.

Sitting ahead of Dylan, James and Rebecca Heitschmidt sat as close as humanly possible, his arm resting on the back of the pew behind her shoulders, her arm squashed against his side. A glow almost seemed to emanate from the couple, so strong was their love.

Beside them, Wesley Fulton had his tiny, golden-haired daughter perched on his lap. Of his wife, Dylan could see no sign.

Silence fell over the church, like the intake of breath on the brink of a plunge into deep water. A soft swish of skirts told Dylan the pastor's wife was moving from the piano to her favorite instrument, the organ. Sure enough, the sprightly melody of *Jesu, Joy of Man's Desiring* spilled out of the pipes that lined the church behind his head, filling the sanctuary and spilling out into the street.

Another swish of skirts indicated all guests should rise. The tiny assembly obeyed tradition, turning to take in a small woman with dark auburn hair and warm brown eyes, her burgeoning figure swathed in a pale blue dress. Slowly she walked alone up the central aisle toward her man. The love she bore for him shone in her eyes.

Dylan glanced at the groom and saw that his nervous fidgeting had been rendered frozen in the face of the petite woman's loveliness. His gaze had turned to possessive affection. The sight stirred Dylan's heart.

Come on, man. All around you people are falling in love and getting married. How many years do you think Lydia will wait for you to make up your mind? You love her. You know you do. Don't keep her on tenterhooks. It's unfair. If you love her, tell her. Court her. Marry her. If you love her too much to marry her, let her go.

The bride passed Dylan and found her way to her husband-to-be, taking his arm. Cody began the brief service, of which Dylan was sure the couple heard nothing, as hard as they were staring into each other's eyes.

In front of Dylan, Rebecca leaned her head against her husband's chest. James tightened his arm around her as they returned to their seated positions.

Even as he spoke over Jesse and his bride, Cody's eyes kept straying to the balcony, as though affirming his own marriage vows.

Little Melissa Fulton squeezed her father Wesley around the neck, and he patted her back.

This room is full of love.

The door at the rear of the church opened slightly and closed again. Dylan could feel eyes boring into his back. He subtly shifted away from the arm of the pew and a moment later, Lydia's warm, full body slipped into the space. Without thought, he laid his arm across her shoulders, mimicking James' tender embrace. She inhaled sharply, then relaxed into the curve of his body. *She fits there.* He closed his eyes as the poetry of Song of Solomon washed over him in Cody's softly-accented voice.

Do you love her enough to keep her or let her go? Decide, Dylan.

In reality, there was no decision to make. The scent of her hair told him what he needed to know. The softness of her plump shoulders. The curve of her hip. He hugged her tighter. Despite the heat, she drew close to him.

Immersed in his woman, Dylan failed to notice the service passing, missed the music that ushered the newlyweds out of the church and even the exodus of the other guests. It was the sudden silence in the room that roused him from his reverie. He blinked to find himself alone with Lydia.

"Where did everyone go?" he asked stupidly.

"I think they've gone to James and Becky's for the reception. I was late because I had to take the cake over there."

"Ah, okay," Dylan replied. "I suppose they're expecting us too," he added. *Damn it, man, stop saying stupid things.*

"I don't think anyone is expecting anything," Lydia replied, "except to see Jesse and Addie eat cake."

"Is that her name?" Dylan asked, startled. "Jesse never told me. She's a pretty little thing, isn't she?"

Lydia smiled. "She's spunky. He's going to have his hands full with her. I like her a lot."

Rising, Dylan helped Lydia to her feet. "That makes me like him more. Not everyone is man enough to fall for a strong woman." The conviction in his own words fell on him like drops of fire. *I fell for her, but I never told her.*

Dylan walked Lydia out of the church, but instead of heading due south to the Heitschmidt home, he led her to the adjoining cemetery, under the shade of an apple tree with half-ripened fruit bowing every branch.

The sun penetrated through the limbs to dapple their faces with changing light. *Light like life. It never stays the same. Always in motion, nothing to hold onto, but the pattern has an undeniable beauty.* A golden triangle landed on Lydia's lips, calling his attention, and he lowered his head. His mouth caressed hers tenderly. After a startled moment, Lydia melted into the kiss, clinging as though the embrace contained the answer to every dream she'd lost.

Long moments passed as they lingered, lips caressing, in a public place in full view of the street. The beating summer sun no longer blistered with a fraction of the heat their long-denied passion generated. A stale, hot breeze ruffled their clothing and they finally broke apart as Lydia fought to keep her skirts in their proper place. Dylan made no move to step back.

She inhaled slowly, which did interesting things to her lush figure. "Why, Dylan?" she asked at last.

He frowned, eyebrows drawing together. "It's long overdue, don't you think?"

She dipped her chin then lifted her eyes to meet his again. "Of course. Years overdue. That's my question. Why now?"

The delicate arch of one dark brow drew his attention and he traced it with his fingertip. "A lot of reasons, I guess," he replied. "I've been regretting my dawdling for a while, thinking I was being unfair to you. I guess this wedding just brought it to a head." He gestured to a painfully new headstone off to their left. "Well, that and this."

She glanced. "Yes. Poor Deputy Charles. Just my age. What does he have to do with anything?"

"You know Jesse West is his replacement, right?" Dylan said, hoping to be able to articulate his swirling thoughts into something coherent.

"Yes," Lydia replied, her tone urging him to say something that made sense.

"Wade's death had the strangest effect on me. I've lived my whole adult life knowing that my job could bring about my untimely end, or that of one of my deputies. It's just one of the facts of law enforcement. For the most part, it didn't bother me. I didn't have anything so important I would hesitate to sacrifice my life for it. Well, shortly before the robbery, Wade and I were talking about this. He had a different perspective than me, and no surprise there, with a wife and four sons. He told me he'd happily give his life if it would make theirs safer or better. It's what a family man does, sheriff, deputy or otherwise."

"Okay," Lydia replied. He could practically see the gears turning in her mind.

"So I realized I had nothing like that and felt like my life was a bit empty as a result. And then he was killed in the way he was, and with everything that happened afterwards, well… We're at war, Lydia. This train gang is like a foreign army invading our territory."

"I know," she replied. "It's terrifying, but I still don't understand."

"Well, it made my decision even more complicated. When Wade died, his family had to leave. They had nothing left with him gone. The pension wouldn't have lasted a year with that growing brood. I'm glad her family stepped in, but I had to consider. If I spoke to you, if we… began courting, which is what

I wanted, what would you do if I die? I can't guarantee they won't get me eventually. There are a lot of them, most likely."

Lydia shook her head. "It would be completely different, Dylan. I'm not financially helpless. I can provide for myself. I don't need you to support me and I don't need a pension."

"I realize that now," he replied. "It took me a while. Your independence looks really good to me. But… Lydia, you do understand what I'm saying here, right?"

She raised an eyebrow at him. "At this point, all you've said—or almost said—is that there's attraction between us that has a romantic element to it."

He grinned, but with only a trace of humor. "Not going to take it easy on me, are you?"

"No," she replied, leveling him with a terrifyingly neutral expression. "You haven't taken it easy on me. For years you've snared me with hope and longing looks. You captured my heart and wouldn't let it go, but you wouldn't claim it either. I've more than earned a proper declaration, and I intend to receive one."

He sighed. "Fair enough." Bringing up one large, rugged hand, he cupped her cheek, marveling at the softness of her skin. She leaned into his touch. "I…" he swallowed. What had been easy to say at twenty nearly choked him at thirty-eight, and yet… *I do owe her this. Why would I even consider trying to get out of it?* "I love you, Lydia."

Her cool regard melted into a smile. "That's more like it. What took you so long, Dylan? Why was it so hard to claim me when you know full well that I love you too, that I always have?"

He shook his head. "It's a long story, and we're missing the cake."

"Forget the cake," Lydia replied. "I made the cake. I can make more. I can make one just for us. I'll make our wedding cake someday, most likely. Tell me the story."

Dylan made a face. "Did I ever tell you I was married before?"

Lydia blinked. "I'm sorry. Was it recent?" Then she paused. "No, it can't have been. We've known each other for five years. What happened?"

"I…" he exhaled heavily and clasped Lydia's hand in his. "I married young. I was twenty. She was only seventeen."

"What was her name?" Lydia asked, her warm brown eyes filling with empathy.

"Justine," he replied. "I didn't want to take over my Dad's store, so I became a logger. I cut pines up in northern Minnesota. Hard work, but I felt like such a man."

Despite Lydia's touch, which reminded him of the world around him, Dylan's mind went back in time. Back to a chilly, pine-smelling rock at whose base a rugged, sod-roofed structure barely large enough to be called a house sheltered his young family while he bent his back to provide for them.

"What happened to Justine?" Lydia asked, her voice floating on the cool air blowing off the lake.

"She was expecting. Didn't take long," he replied. "All seemed to be fine, even though she got so big. But when she delivered, something went wrong. She delivered without much fuss, but for some reason, the little fella only lived a few hours. The midwife couldn't tell us anything, and the doctor was nowhere to be found. The next day, Justine came down sick. Childbed fever, the midwife called it. I have no idea what that means, but it took her fast. I guess she didn't have to grieve our son long. After that, I didn't have much of a heart for logging."

He paused, swallowing hard as the image changed to the mounded earth under which his family lay, a rugged, iron-veined stone marking their place.

"Oh, Dylan," Lydia murmured, pulling him into her arms. He felt none of the Kansas heat, as it had been supplanted by the chill of his birthplace, far to the north.

"For a while there, I wanted to die, so I could be with Justine and the baby. We named him Isaac. Anyway, I became a sheriff's deputy, hoping to be killed in the line of duty, but it didn't happen. Instead, I found a new love."

"The law?" Lydia guessed.

This time, her words drew him back from the pine forest to the prairie.

"Yes, that's right. I learned to live for my work. I won't lie, Miss Lydia, I've found companionship here and there, sometimes with someone lonely, some times for pay." He regarded her face but saw no judgment there. "That stopped when I met you. For the longest time after Justine, I didn't know I could love again. You taught me how."

Lydia frowned, and he could see thoughts chasing through her mind. "That's a very sad tale, Dylan," she said at last. "I'm sorry it happened to you, but I still don't understand why it took you so long to speak. Many years have passed. I'm sure, if she loved you, she'd understand."

Dylan inhaled Lydia's fragrance—of bread and herbs—and then admitted the painful truth. "I don't want you to get with child. I can't stand it, Lydia. I like children, but I'm afraid."

Her lips compressed. "You're in luck then."

"What do you mean?" Too immersed in memory, Dylan struggled to comprehend Lydia's comment.

Her scrunched lips turned upward in a parody of a smile. "My parents died of typhoid fever when I was sixteen. There was an epidemic. I caught it too. Almost died. The doctors told me a long-lasting high fever like that damages the organs. I'll never conceive a child, so you don't have to worry about losing me that way."

He stared at her. *Never conceive? Never watch her struggle through the pain only to succumb?* He couldn't recall ever having such a profound sense of relief. "Life is uncertain, Lydia," he reminded her.

"I know," she replied. "The next breath could be our last. So you tell me, Dylan; what are we waiting for?"

Hope dawned like the sunrise. "Nothing. Not a thing. I won't waste another minute."

"Good," she replied. Her fingers traced the grizzled stubble on his cheeks, and she drew him down. "Kiss me."

Dylan obeyed the demand without protest and found her full lips just as sweet as he remembered. *Well, man,* he demanded of himself, *are you ready to commit?*

His heart responded with a resounding, "Yes! I want to kiss this woman every day for the rest of my life."

The answer satisfied him. "I love you, Lydia," he mumbled against her lips. "Will you be mine?"

"Of course," she responded, "I already am. I always have been, and in case you didn't know, I love you too."

He knew. How could he not? Her pleading eyes had told the tale for ages. Still, the words felt good, like a soothing balm on the sore places left by his first wife's passing, and that of his tiny son. He might never fully heal, but he suspected with Lydia's help, he could move past the pain and live fully again.

A wolf whistle shattered the embrace. They turned to see Cyril Fulton, one of Wesley's many uncles, regarding them with amusement. "'Bout time," the middle-aged man commented, "but don't you think you could pick a better spot? Sparking in the street ain't too mannerly."

"Go away, Cyril," Dylan growled. "I can tell by the way you're talking that a night in jail wouldn't be a bad thing for you."

"Testy, testy," the man replied, staggering off.

"He's right," Lydia said. "I guess, since we've been spotted, there won't be any way to keep this a secret—not that I want to—but if you had any doubts, it's too late. We're official now."

"I think we've been official for quite a while. Sounds like everyone's been waiting for this," Dylan replied. His words had the charming effect of turning Lydia's plump cheeks a lovely, glowing shade of pink. He touched his lips to one spot of color and then the other before leading her back out of the shade. Once again, the sun seemed determined to claw and rend the skin from their bodies in its unrelenting heat.

"Do we go to whatever's left of the reception?" Dylan asked his companion as they reached the street. He indicated to the right, south, where the Heitschmidt home awaited them. To the left, north, lay Lydia's café with her living quarters above.

"It might be better if we made an appearance," she said at last. "For one thing, getting caught kissing would be a minor scandal. If we didn't turn up somewhere public…."

"I see your point," Dylan replied.

"And besides," Lydia continued, "poor Addie's so new in town. I want to be sure she has someone on her side. Someone to ease her transition."

Dylan steered them right, and they moved quickly, though not quickly enough to prevent the late afternoon heat from drawing perspiration to every inch of their bodies. They passed through the main street of town, where one-story and two-story shops and homes competed in color schemes that did not coordinate with each other. One might be white with black shutters, the next green with a striped awning, and so on. The overall result was a cheerful hodgepodge of colors, sizes and patterns, made even more garish under the blinding sunset.

In Dylan's mind, so many houses so close together seemed crowded. He recalled the town of his birth, the large farms, the empty spaces clustered with trees and standing boulders. A town the size of Garden City no longer bothered him, but the few times he'd gone to Wichita or even Kansas City, he'd felt uncomfortably packed in. *Glad I'm here,* he thought as they passed the Jacksons' oversized, dark-blue home, its black-painted lacy gingerbread decorations recalling the coloring of the owner's wife and daughter: black hair, blue eyes. Even on a house, the palate seemed unwelcoming. Shaking his head, he grasped Lydia's hand more firmly. *Yes, there are people here I could do without—the Jackson women being at the top of the list—but I would put up with their snobbish ways a hundred times over for the opportunity to hold Lydia Carré's hand.*

At last, they arrived at the Heitschmidt home, which, though just as large as the Jacksons', had a welcoming feel about it. Decorated in a style Dylan attributed to James' German ancestry, the plain strips of wood decorating the exterior had a cleaner, less cluttered feel than fancy gingerbread. A broad, well-maintained porch greeted visitors and ushered them into a generous parlor where, at the moment, the tiny wedding party perched on various chairs and sofas, sipping iced lemonade and nibbling the cake Lydia had provided. The remains of the treat, placed on a sideboard that normally graced the dining room, had been a beauty, Dylan could see. The white vanilla interior practically glistened with butter, and a pinkish-yellow filling oozed between the layers, scenting the room with summer peaches. White frosting had crushed sugar like snowflakes clinging to its exterior, decorated with an arrangement of candied purple flowers.

"That's beautiful," he told her. She beamed.

"I wanted something elegant for the bride," she replied. "Just because a wedding happens fast doesn't mean it has to be pitiful or unattractive."

"I really appreciate it, too," the small, redheaded woman replied, approaching the couple. "You and Mrs. Heitschmidt really made my day special. I'll treasure these memories forever."

Dylan couldn't help but smile at the girl's sincerity. Her appearance made him think even better of his new deputy, who clung to her fingers, watching attentively to ensure she was enjoying their special day. The girl—*what's her name, Addie? Yes, Addie*—though short in stature, had the kind of firecracker personality that dared the ill-intentioned to try anything funny.

At the same time, something seemed to haunt her dark eyes, as though she'd seen too much and was trying to understand how to move forward. Even in the carefully cut gown, her pregnant belly revealed just how close the couple had come to disaster. And yet, Dylan could see the love on Jesse's face, and on

Addie's too. They adored each other. *I know how that look feels. I wonder when Lydia would like to take the plunge.*

"So glad you could make it," Becky said, every inch the gracious hostess, though the irony in her serene smile told him Lydia would be getting the teasing of her life when the two women found some privacy. He glanced at his lady and saw her beaming. *Oh well. Everyone's going to know, and everyone's going to weigh in, I guess.*

"Yeah, we took a small detour," he told the lovely blond, "but we made it in the end. Now, if it's all right with you, I think I have to try a piece of this cake. You know, see if it's up to Miss Lydia's usual standards."

Lydia laughed and swatted his arm. "It's better," she insisted immodestly.

"It is," James Heitschmidt agreed around his fork. Then he swallowed, his freckled Adam's apple bobbing. "I've never tasted a cake this good."

"Oh, go on." Lydia blushed around her smile.

"Better get some before I finish it," the store owner warned, moving toward them and resting his hand on his wife's shoulder. Becky grinned at him.

This is what life is all about, Dylan thought as he helped himself to a large slice of the tempting confection. *Friends, food, banter, and the love of a good woman. It doesn't get any better than this.*

After the bride and groom left, Dylan cornered Lydia on the porch of the Heitschmidt home. "Do you need help with anything?" he asked.

"No thanks, Dylan," she replied, "I'm fine."

"All right," he agreed easily. "I need to get back to work. I'll be extra busy for a few more days until Jesse gets started, but then I should have some free time, you know, to court you properly."

Lydia smiled, his words warming her deep inside. "I'd like that, though with my unusual schedule, we'll have to discuss what kind of courtship we can have. Oh, I'm so glad for this, Dylan," she added, her urge to gush overtaking her. "It's like a dream."

"This dream came true, sweet Lydia." He smudged his lips over hers, tickling her with his mustache.

A squirming sensation fluttered through Lydia's belly, along with a sensation of heat that seemed to radiate outward and downward. She bit her lip.

"I don't want to go," he murmured. "Now that I finally have you, I never want to leave."

"Soon, Dylan. We'll be together soon. I'll stop by and see you once I close up the café tomorrow, all right?"

He kissed her again. "Sounds perfect." Dylan's mouth grew hungry on hers, crushing her lips instead of caressing them. His tongue probed. She gasped, and it loosened her lips. He plunged in, claiming her mouth in a way she hadn't known existed.

At first, the wet penetration startled her. It felt strange and foreign, but her body, it seemed, knew how to respond. The squirming heat in her loins carried with it an unfamiliar sensation of moisture in the secret places she rarely thought about. She hummed, her hips arching unconsciously as she sought the relief of pressure against the spot. To her surprise, the seam of Dylan's trousers seemed to protrude more than she'd expected.

"Dylan?" she asked.

"I want you, honey," he replied. "I hope you won't insist on a long courtship." The strained, raspy sound of his voice, coupled with the insistent way he clutched her hips and pushed her against that overfull seam turned the squirming in her belly to nerves.

Dylan didn't press for an answer. Instead, he brushed her lips with his once more and, with a dip of his hat, left for the jail.

Lydia touched her mouth with her fingertips, wondering what exactly had just happened.

"Lydia," Becky called from the parlor's open window, "can you come here please?"

Grinning, and knowing a full accounting would be demanded, she returned to the stuffy indoors.

Becky stood guard over the remaining half of the wedding cake, while her husband hovered. "James, I'm not telling you again, shoo. This is Jesse and Addie's cake, and I don't want you keeping me up all night moaning about a belly ache."

"Rebecca," he whined.

"No, get, go on." She flapped her hands at her husband. "I want to talk to Lydia without you anyway."

"Oh my Lord." James rolled his eyes towards heaven. "The hens will be clucking."

"Be glad Cody wasn't here to listen to you taking the Lord's name in vain," his wife remonstrated. "You don't want him to take you aside again, do you?"

James made a face at his wife and stomped out of the room in a comically false display of temper. Lydia and Becky looked at each other and burst out laughing.

"Where is everyone else?" Lydia asked between wheezes.

"They traipsed right passed you, you goose, while you were sparking with the sheriff for the whole world to see." Rebecca wiped her streaming eyes with one hand. With the other, she held the little swell of her belly.

"Goodness, everyone's expecting," Lydia commented.

"I know," Becky replied with a sigh. "I'm excited, even if my sister isn't. Of course, when I only have two months to go and I'm big as a house, I might not feel quite so joyful then."

"I think you will," Lydia replied. "You and James have such a lovely relationship. I'm afraid Allison and Wesley aren't doing so well. Or am I wrong? You'd know."

"Let's sit," Becky suggested, indicating the sofa. The two ladies each claimed a spot by one of the upholstered arms.

Leaning on the soft fabric, Lydia turned to regard her friend. "What's going on?" she asked. "I know Allison hasn't been feeling the best lately."

Becky sighed. "She doesn't tell me everything either, but I get the feeling that marriage to Wesley has proven to be a grave disappointment to her. He's sort of… shaken after that nightmare of a first marriage he endured and now he's not at all like his old self. Allison doesn't know what to do, and now that she's nearly at the end of her pregnancy, she can hardly make herself try anymore. I think she's just taking care of Melissa as best she can and ignoring Wes because she can't cope with his weird habits and unaccountable moods."

Lydia frowned. "That's a shame, and I've heard from everyone how they always planned to marry. Why did he marry someone else? That never made a bit of sense to me."

Becky closed her eyes, her mouth twisting. "Gentleman's indiscretion," she replied. "Samantha was expecting Melissa. Wes couldn't deny the possibility she might be his, so he married her."

Lydia made a face. "Why on earth would a man bed down with one woman when he's practically married to another?"

Becky shrugged. "Young men do stupid things," she said, toying with the fringes on the edge of a small black pillow. "Young women too. One reason for everyone to wait to grow up a bit. Some of them move away from that nonsense and learn how to act right."

"Maybe a few," Lydia replied. "I don't have much faith in the male of the species. I've seen too much."

Becky's frown deepened. "So have I. If James hadn't come along, I think I would have been content to remain single. Love is a huge risk. You give your heart and…" she paused, bit her lip and then rushed on. "and then they leave you sad and alone, with everyone gossiping and pointing fingers."

"You know," Lydia commented dryly to her friend, "You're not making the most appealing case for courtship."

Becky smiled without humor, that serene, meaningless smile she'd worn for years and only recently allowed to turn genuine. "I'm not trying to make a case for anything. For those of us fortunate to have a skill, a trade, trying to snare a man isn't necessary. It's actually a blessing because then you can choose a really good man and move on if he proves to be a bad prospect."

"I don't think Dylan is a bad prospect," Lydia commented, reviewing what she knew about her suitor.

"I do," Becky replied. "He's kept you on a string for years. Watch him carefully for signs of waffling."

What? What's she saying? Becky's blunt advice roused a hint of defensive anger in Lydia. "I hardly think, after the internal battle he had to go through to get to this point, that he's going to back off. He seems committed now. Besides, this is Dylan we're talking about."

Becky's expression softened. "I hardly know the man. He intimidates me, but you know him better than I do. Do you think he'll marry you eventually?"

"He's hinted at it," Lydia admitted. "Though after this conversation you and I have been having, I'm not sure how I feel about that. What made you decide to marry after remaining single for so long?"

Becky rolled her eyes. "James rolled into my heart like a train," she said. "I fell hard for him long before he spoke, but once he decided what he wanted, he had me in a family way and hitched up in no time."

"Oh dear," Lydia bit her lip to keep from laughing. "Wrong order?"

"Completely." Becky laughed, a genuine laugh this time. "I didn't realize it until later, but…" she seemed to be counting in her head. "It must have been a good month before."

Lydia's thoughts chased down that avenue before she had a chance to reflect on them. Secure in the company of the least judgmental, kindest person she'd ever met, she dared to ask what she hadn't realized had been weighing on her mind. "What's it like, Becky?"

"Being with child?" the lovely blond asked.

Lydia shook her head. "Being with a man. I've heard things… seen things that make me wonder. I've never tried it…" her cheeks heated beyond the stuffiness of a July day. "It always seemed like something women have to put up with to make a man happy, but it isn't very nice."

Becky drew in a slow, deep breath, obviously considering her words. "I can be like that," she admitted. "Between you and me, there was a time… back when I was seventeen and engaged. We decided to experience… that, and it wasn't much of anything." She frowned and her own cheeks took on a pink hue, like a rose painted on a china cup. "Nothing at all, really. It was awkward and uncomfortable, though I didn't experience much pain. The pain came later when he abandoned me. I didn't think anyone would bother with me after that, not if they knew, and I didn't want to lie."

"Oh." Lydia reached across the sofa and patted Becky on the arm. "That's a shame. I'm sorry."

Becky shook off the unpleasant memory, and her grin turned naughty. "Don't be. James doesn't care, so all is well. Though I did get quite a scare when we accidentally lost control that one time. I thought I would lose him, but I didn't. See, that's how you know a true man instead of an overgrown boy. He stays around to honor his commitments."

"And now?" Lydia pressed, eager to hear more about the positive side of her friend's obviously happy marriage.

"Well, James convinced me from that first time on that he can be trusted with my heart… and also with my body." Her blush fired brighter but the smile on her lips spoke volumes. "Let me tell you, the right man, a kind, patient man, will make you forget every negative thing you've ever heard, seen or experienced. It's like nothing you can imagine until you've tried it. I'm glad James and I are married. Otherwise, I'd be a terrible hussy because I wouldn't be able to stop."

The burning in Lydia's cheeks threatened to set her ablaze. "Goodness," she said at last. "It's that nice?"

"Oh yes," Becky agreed with a nod. "If your Dylan is the man you think he is he won't let you down either."

Lydia bit her lip. "Strange. So strange."

"I know it must seem so," Becky agreed, "the way everyone acts, but it's as natural as life. It *is* life." Her hand stroked absently over the bulge in her belly where her child was growing.

The cycle completes itself. A man and woman love each other. They take each other in their arms and new life is created. The thought had never occurred to Lydia before, but in that moment, the transcendent beauty of it brought tears to her eyes. *I'll never bear a child, I'm not even sure I want to, but I do want to understand what she's talking about. It's nothing like what I've heard before.*

Lydia exhaled, releasing old thoughts and negative feelings to waft away in a hot, stale breeze that blew in the window. They swirled in the dust on their way out onto the prairie. New awareness dawned. *Dylan wants me. He wants to touch me the way James touches Becky. That's what it all means. That's what it's all for.* The idea lodged, but she couldn't consider it. *Not yet.* Reticence still warred with burgeoning desire, but she felt no urgency. *Maybe someday. We've only been courting a few hours.*

A ferocious yawn rose up out of nowhere, yanking Lydia out of half-improper contemplations. "Sorry. This is the time I usually rest. Early mornings when you have to bake bread for breakfast," she explained to her friend.

"Not a problem," Becky replied. "I could stand to lie down myself. Growing a baby is exhausting, and I'm no spring chicken, but please take the cake away. James is going to get awfully fat if he keeps picking away at it."

Giggling, Lydia collected her confection. The icing and flowers had already begun to wilt. *I'll wrap it up and give it to the newlyweds tomorrow.* "Bye, Becky," she said to her friend. "Thanks for the talk. It helped me quite a bit."

"See you tomorrow, Lydia," she replied. "Remember, we have another meeting of Ilse's infamous committee."

"Ugh," Lydia groaned. "I suppose I'll have to explain about that damned petition." She shook her head. "Fine. It needs to be done. See you then."

"See you." Becky waved as Lydia let herself out.

Chapter 4

Lydia carefully arranged some sandwich triangles on a plate, and then had to make a quick cursing grab as it nearly slipped out of her sweaty hands.

"Had to open your mouth, didn't you? Couldn't just make an excuse?" Muttering under her breath, she made her way carefully out of the kitchen into the dining room, where she placed the sandwiches next to the other plates, one piled with cut fruit, and the third with jam thumbprint cookies. "I should just forget about this group and let them find somewhere else to meet... and eat. Why am I contributing to this nonsense?"

Of course, it's too late now. She'd taken a stand and she would have to defend it. *And bare my soul to stupid Ilse Jackson.* Lydia sighed, inflating her full bosom to nearly obscene proportions, modest neckline or no.

This time, her friends didn't come early. Instead, the entire troupe seemed to arrive en masse, squeezing through the doorway two by two, ignoring the snacks Lydia had so lovingly prepared and taking seats around the dining room.

Ilse arrived last. Entering the room with the air of a displeased princess, she took her position of power and addressed the group.

"While I'm delighted to have received such support for my idea of a Founder's Day celebration, I must say, I was dismayed by the gauntlet thrown down by our most respected host at the end of the meeting. I've spent the whole week thinking of what would cause a seemingly respectable business owner of our town would deny such an obvious and helpful measure. The only answer I could think of was that, as a single woman, you must have no idea the harm these loose women wreak on marriages. Thus, I will chalk up your comments to ignorance, but I won't take no for an answer. You're wrong, Lydia Carré, and I expect you to admit it."

Lydia raised her eyebrows. Then she took a deep breath and spoke, choosing her words carefully to address the issue and not Ilse's sarcastic tone. "Let me start by asking a question. Should your plan succeed, should you close the saloon, what would become of the women?"

Titters and murmurs greeted her words.

"What difference does that make?" Ilse demanded. "I couldn't care less where they go so long as it's away from here." She snorted in derision. All around the room, women nodded, thinking no doubt of their own husbands and families.

Lydia nodded, her face hardening. "That's what I thought. All right then, I will not retract my refusal. The petition is a wasted effort because there is no law preventing a saloon from operating. You can pester the mayor, the sheriff and anyone else you like until the cows come home and accomplish nothing."

She considered them, saw the puzzled frowns, the considering expressions. Then she went in for the kill. "But that's not the real reason. The fact is, if enough people protest something together, something can be accomplished. My reason for refusing is that closing the saloon and sending the girls on their way is a cruel thing to do. Do any of you know any of those girls? Do you know their names, their ages, the reasons they do what they do? Or do you dismiss them as some kind of foreign creatures? They're not, you know."

She met each set of eyes. Some glared with outright malice. Others looked sad. The rest just appeared confused. *They're listening. That's good.* "There are seven of them. Most are under the age of thirty. Most of them feel they have no other choice. The truth is most women in their situation don't have a choice. Our society sets women up for this, and then takes great delight in taking advantage of them… or shunning them. I'm sure you can figure out who does what."

Some of the glares turned uncomfortable.

"What do you know about it?" Mary Miller, Ilse's best friend, sneered. "Do you talk to them?"

"As a matter of fact, I do," she replied. "I feel bad they get left out of everything, so if I have any leftovers, I take them over there, and I talk to them. Want to know what I found out? They're women just like us."

"Not like me," Ilse replied, her nose in the air. "I would rather starve than debase myself that way."

Lydia laughed in bitter irony. "What a stupid thing to say," she retorted. "You've never been hungry in your life. You throw a fit if the potluck is delayed for a long prayer. Imagine not eating for days… for weeks. Until you've experienced real hunger, you have no right to judge what others do."

Ilse fell silent, her porcelain cheeks flushed with anger.

Lydia ignored her, turning to Ilse's snooty young friend. "One of the girls up there is named Mary, just like you. She looks like you too. The poor thing was walking home from school one day and a boy assaulted her. Raped her, right there in the grass. Then he went on and bragged to all his friends about what a slut she was. Everyone believed him, even her parents. They threw her out. Seventeen with nowhere to turn. Another is called Julie. Julie's suitor convinced her to share liberties. Then he left. Then her parents died. With no prospects in sight, she ended up working."

Against her will, her eyes slid to Becky, whose story was so similar. The lovely blond was tracing the wood grain of the table with one hand, clutching the small swell of her baby with the other.

"The oldest of the 'girls', if you can call her that, is Ruth. She was a respectable married lady until her husband died. With three sons attending universities, she did what she had to do to fund their education. She hopes they never find out how she pays their tuition. Think, ladies. All these working girls have certain things in common. None of them has a saleable skill, and none of them has a father or husband to support her. Think about how fragile that makes a woman."

While most of her audience still looked confused, Kristina's expression had changed. So had Becky's.

"I'm fully aware that I'm blessed. My parents gifted me with a skill and over the years, I've been able to work by cooking, but I lost my family young too. I was only sixteen when the typhoid epidemic robbed me of my parents. That whorehouse, but for the grace of God, would have been my destination. And I can't help but think of Miranda Charles."

"Now you stop right there," Ilse hissed. "Miranda is a decent woman."

"She is," Lydia agreed, "but she's also a mother who loves her children. What do you think she would refuse to do if it kept her boys fed? She's fortunate her parents are able to help her because that pension wouldn't keep them alive a year. Kristina."

The pastor's wife met her eyes, looking nervous.

"You have a skill. With luck, you could use your music to make a living. You're blessed. Becky…"

"I can sew and sell what I sew. I could get by if I needed to." Lydia's friend scrubbed at her cheek. "I see your point."

"But surely," Kristina protested, "you can't mean to say you want them doing…that! Selling the gift God has given spouses to anyone who comes along. It's monstrous."

"I know," Lydia agreed. "I hate prostitution. It's wrong and it takes advantage of the vulnerable but closing the saloon won't end it. It will hurt those seven women. Several of them are saving up their profits to make a new start somewhere else. If we did somehow manage to shut down the saloon, it would force them to use their savings to relocate, unless, of course, you'd be willing to welcome them into the community."

The women began to squirm, no doubt imagining a lady of the evening sweeping up a store where their husbands worked or acting as a clerk in the bank beside a younger brother.

"I know I'm asking hard questions with no good answers," Lydia said. "I hate that by refusing to do this, I'm endorsing their suffering, but I believe I'm also shortening it. That is why I can't sign. It's cruel."

"She's right." Kristina rose from her chair. "Ilse, you need to scratch my name off that paper. I'm ashamed I ever suggested such a heartless thing. What's wrong with me?" She looked at Lydia, stricken.

"You didn't realize," she told the younger woman, "and why would you? Who thinks of these things? But I'm glad you understood."

The breathless silence in the room broke out into pandemonium as women began to quarrel among themselves. Some protested Lydia's view. Others affirmed it.

I got them thinking. That's all I can do. "Ladies, ladies," she remonstrated, drawing their attention back to her. "I believe we've dealt with this topic enough. We have lots of planning to do for Founder's Day. Let's plan."

Unfortunately, the genie could not be returned to the bottle. Angry over the unexpected turn of events, the women trailed out, Ilse leading the way.

Lydia stumbled to the counter, planted her hands between the uneaten trays of snacks and hung her head, breathing deeply.

A hand closed around her arm and Kristina's soft voice said, "Thank you."

Lydia nodded, not trusting her voice.

"It's hard to force people to think, isn't it?" Becky asked, "but I'm glad you did." She rubbed circles on the larger woman's back. "You were right, even if most of them will never admit it."

"I've offended too many people," Lydia said in a shaky voice. "I'm going to lose so much business I'll have to close up."

"No you won't," Kristina said wryly. "I bet you have the best week ever. Everyone will be coming in to see who else dared to show up."

Though she felt rather like tears, Lydia laughed. "How like most people that would be."

"It would," Becky agreed. "Also, you have at least two people on your side, you know."

"Make that three," another voice said from the vicinity of the doorway. Lydia, Becky and Kristina turned to see who had come in.

"Addie?" Lydia blinked several times. "What can I do for you? I hate to tell you, but the café is closed."

"I know," she replied. "I was out buying some supplies at the general store and a whole bunch of ladies came in. I heard a lot of pointless yammering that didn't add up, so I wanted to see what it was all about. I mean, what I was hearing sounded scandalous, but you were nicer to me than you had to be, and I like a good scandal now and again. Plus, that black-haired woman struck me as pretty obnoxious. How can I help?"

Lydia couldn't help but smile. "Would you like to join the cooking committee? Our town is celebrating Founder's Day. You can cook, right?"

The younger woman rolled up her sleeves. "Yes, ma'am. Put me to work!"

The three cells in the tiny jail all stood empty, which was just as well. Dylan's mind was so far from police work, he would probably have been chatting up whatever drunk happened to be on hand. Instead, he sat with his feet up on the desk, staring at the newspaper but not taking in a single word. His mind kept conjuring black hair out of the ink and soft fabric out of the paper. *Lydia. What on God's green earth took me so long?* Now the reasons no longer made sense to him. Only the third day of their official courtship, and he couldn't remember what life had been like before her kisses. *I don't want to imagine.*

The door swung open, hitting the far wall with a resounding crash. Dylan jumped and his chair tipped over, dumping him onto the floor.

"Sorry. Didn't mean to startle you."

Dylan rose from his undignified heap to greet Jesse West, who had just stepped in out of the blistering Kansas sun.

"My fault," Dylan replied. "I was daydreaming, but I thought I told you three days. It's only been two."

"I like to stir up trouble," Jesse replied with an unrepentant grin. "Actually, Addie wanted to spend some time with the women of town, and I think she was headed to see Miss Carré. I get antsy when I don't have enough to do, and that hotel room feels like it's closing in on me, so I decided to come see what's happening over here."

"You'll need a place of your own soon," Dylan commented.

"I know," Jesse replied. "Do you know of anything?"

Dylan considered. "There's one place, but I'm not sure what you or your wife would think. Wade Charles, my previous deputy, who was killed, built it for his wife and their sons. They were happy there, but..."

"I see your point. Addie is a pragmatic girl, but I'll have to run it past her. Still, a home intended for a family sounds like a good start. What was he like?"

"Wade?" Dylan considered. "He was a good man. At home, he loved his wife and wrestled with his boys. The neighbors complained about the noise of all their playing, but Wade pointed out to them that since he was a lawman, he wasn't going to arrest himself, and certainly not for noise, so they should quit fussing."

Jesse grinned. "I like the sound of him."

Dylan continued. "I think you would have liked him. Shame how things worked out. Here at work, he was cool and calm, always. No criminal, no matter how abusive, ever ruffled him."

Jesse appeared to be deep in thought. At last, he spoke. "I may be filling his position, but I won't be replacing him. I'm used to doing things a certain way. I know you're in charge, but following orders might not come too easy for me. Up to this point, I've been a free agent. Wanted dead or alive leaves a lot of room for interpretation."

"I suspected as much," Dylan told him. "I do expect, if I give you a direct instruction, for you to follow it, but I didn't hire you to be an automaton. I want your ideas. You may see things from a perspective I didn't consider."

"I hope to," Jesse replied.

"Take a seat, West," Dylan said, indicating the second chair, which he'd shoved into the corner to make room for his sprawling. "Show me what you can do."

Jesse grinned again and dragged the seat into position beside the sheriff. "So, tell me more about this train robber problem. What's going on?"

Dylan dug around in the drawers of his desk and brought out several newspaper clippings as well as notes written on heavy white paper in a small, precise hand.

"Last year this band of robbers pulled off more than a dozen heists. Mostly they robbed trains, but they also hit a few banks. They kept their faces covered and the victims never could agree on any descriptions."

"Most likely there was a large group," Jesse pointed out. "Robbing trains requires more planning than anyone realizes."

Dylan nodded. "That was my thought as well. Anyway, as time passed, they grew savvier, but also more violent. The last robbery was the worst. They killed several passengers on the train. It was only by the grace of God that Cody and Kristina got through unharmed."

"That was the day Deputy Charles was killed?" Jesse asked.

Dylan nodded, scowling into his mustache. "Yeah. Hit by a stray bullet, poor man. That was a pretty small group of robbers. We killed one outside, and two got away. On the train, one was killed—Cody said they called him 'boss'—and one was captured. A lot of folks figured the trouble was over..."

Jesse shook his head. "Not a chance. Unless they're super smart, really strong and motivated, I find it hard to believe an operation like that would be run by only a handful of men. I would guess the boss was in charge of that operation. A flunky, but a high level one, under the direction of a more powerful leader."

Wow. Dylan regarded Jesse with new respect. "You pegged it exactly. The one we captured let out that much. He said the real boss was his father, and if we didn't let him go, there would be hell to pay. He was right."

"So that's when they started targeting the town?" Jesse guessed.

"Yeah," Dylan agreed. "It's been all Rob and I could do to keep the streets guarded so incidents like the firebombing at Mrs. Heitschmidt's shop didn't become commonplace. That was the worst, but there's been quite a bit of petty mischief. Thefts, small fires, properties damaged. It was never enough to create all-out panic, but fear is simmering. We had to create a citizen's patrol to keep watch at night."

"Seems pretty quiet now," Jesse commented, scratching his golden hair.

Dylan nodded. "Something weird happened. I figured the violence would escalate, especially after the hanging, but it didn't. The harassment has virtually stopped, except for these letters." He indicated the stack of paper on the desk.

"They threaten all kinds of dire consequences, mostly to me, but a few to Cody. They're postmarked Colorado."

Jesse's face turned to an image of intense concentration. He lifted one hand and made a gesture Dylan couldn't interpret before cupping his chin, one finger tapping his lips. "Something happened to the operation. Something not related to this town. If they're reduced to writing letters and even the small-scale harassment has stopped, it stands to reason their gang got hit hard by something…" His eyes widened and he sucked in a noisy breath. "Could it be? It all fits."

"What are you thinking, West?"

Jesse shook his head. "It's a wild idea, Sheriff, but all the facts fit. Addie and I met in Colorado. We traveled across the southeastern part of the state. One evening we got attacked by some ruffian. We managed to put him out of our misery, but later on, I got to thinking. They'd been having problems too, but not with train robbers. Homesteads and farms were being looted and burned. I put together a posse and we rousted out a huge nest of criminals. Caught almost the whole crew. Only the leader and his flunkey got away."

"You think it's the same crew?" Dylan asked, startled. "What a coincidence that would be."

"It makes sense though," Jesse replied. "How many big operations like that do you think this area could support? There are no big cities anywhere around where criminals could hide in plain sight. Small towns are nosy, and the open prairie isn't a great place to set up camp. Too exposed."

"It does make sense," Dylan replied, his own thoughts churning through this new and unexpected angle. "It would also explain why small-scale harassment and escalating violence completely stopped and letters started arriving."

"Yes," Jesse agreed. "Most likely the only part of the operation left was the group harassing Garden city. When the gang got rounded up, he called in what was left to regroup. Now they're holed up somewhere… maybe Colorado? They keeping you simmering as best they can while they take stock of the situation."

"So the threat isn't neutralized."

Jesse shook his head. "Not as long as the real boss is around. If the boss really is that kid's father, he won't stop. Not until he's had his revenge. On the plus side, I got a look at the guy. It was over quite a distance, but I can give you a general description. Older man. Maybe near sixty. Gray hair. Short. Walks with a limp. His voice sounded… Eastern. Cultured."

"Jesse, I sure am glad I hired you," Dylan said.

Chapter 5

"She said, and I quote, 'not a chance in hell'." With a sigh, Becky sank into an armchair in Lydia's apartment. Lydia brought her friend a glass of cool water.

"I can't blame her," Lydia replied. "Poor Allison. She looks about big enough to tip over and roll away."

"I know," Becky agreed. "The bigger she gets, the grumpier she gets. I'm starting to understand a bit of why Wesley is in such a bad mood."

"Is this right?" Addie stepped out of the stairwell carrying steaming hot cake in two thick knitted potholders. "Don't take this wrong, Mrs. Heitschmidt, but are you sure your sister's not always in a grumpy mood?"

Lydia poked at the top of the cake with her fingertips and grinned. "Looks perfect. You're a natural, Addie."

The girl beamed. In the few weeks since her arrival, Lydia had made good her promise to take the younger woman under her wing.

"Call me Becky, please, Addie, and yes, I'm sure," Becky replied, answering the younger woman's question. "Why do you ask?"

"Well…" Addie inhaled and released the breath, so her shoulders bounced. "Jesse has taken me to visit her a few times. I don't know why, but she seems to have decided I'm no good. She's cold and… kind of mean." The young woman's pretty face twisted into sadness. "I don't know why. I mean, I know she's your sister and I'm sorry if it's unkind to say, but I think she hates me."

Becky frowned. "I'm sorry she made you feel unwelcome. It's not her way. Allison is a blunt, plainspoken woman. Always has been. But she's usually kind and accepting. For her to be rude… I don't know. I think it might not be you at all. Her life took an unfortunate turn a few months back and she hasn't been herself lately. I'll talk to her though. It's not your fault her mother-in-law is an evil witch or that her husband is a little… off-kilter, or that she's miserable with her pregnancy. I hope I don't become that grumpy when I'm a month from delivery." She ran her hand over the small swell of her belly.

"How far along are you?" Addie asked, changing the subject.

"Five months or so," Becky replied. "How about you?"

"The same, I'd say," the girl replied. "I like this part. I'm not sick anymore and I'm showing enough for it to seem real without being uncomfortably heavy."

"I completely agree," Becky replied. "I've heard this is the good part, and I think it's true."

The two women smiled at each other.

Lydia felt a pang knowing she'd never experience it herself. *Of course, I'll never have to be huge and miserable or suffer through morning sickness either.* The pang passed, and she retrieved the cake from Addie and set it on a small table. Though sometimes she wished for a 'normal' life, she had to admit she was doing well.

I own this building outright, no debt. The café below and this apartment above make a comfortable home and business. She admired the golden brocade sofa with dainty wood accents that faced her window and afforded a view of Main Street.

At right angles, a comfortable cushioned armchair where Becky now sat, her knitting in her lap as she chatted with her friends. Through a door behind her, her bedroom lay equipped with a bed large enough for two.

The second door, behind the sofa, led to the stairwell and down to the main floor. The third, across from the rocking chair, concealed her pride and joy. A fully equipped bathroom with a toilet that connected to the city sewer, properly connected and vented to prevent unpleasant aromas from filtering into her living space. *I'm so thankful they created the sewer and connected all the homes to it the year before I arrived, after that terrible cholera outbreak. It has made such a huge improvement for the whole town.*

Nothing about this life to regret. I have everything I truly need for life and comfort. I even, finally, have a romantic relationship with the man I love. I'm so blessed there's no room in my life for regret.

"…at any rate," Becky continued, "I'll talk to Allison soon, Addie. She isn't acting right where you're concerned. I don't think we're going to get her help with the founder's day food though. However, our committee of four, with a few teenaged girls Kristina recruited from the church, should be plenty to organize a potluck, serve ice cream, and man the pancake breakfast here at the café. I'd say we're set."

"I wouldn't have expected much from her," Lydia replied. "With Melissa to care for, and as close to delivery as she is, Allison has too much to handle already."

"Agreed. I'm so glad you decided to help, Addie."

"I'm glad to be included," the younger woman agreed. "I'm hoping to find my place in this town quickly since my husband has sacrificed so much for us to be here."

"You will," Becky reassured her. "Try not to worry too much about my sister. There are plenty of kind folks around here who are happy to have you."

"They're happy to have Jesse back," Addie mumbled, twining a strand of reddish-brown hair around her finger.

"They are," Lydia agreed, "and that's no surprise since they missed him so much. Eventually, they'll get to know you, Addie, and then they'll appreciate you for your own sake. It takes time, honey."

Addie smiled at Lydia. "I appreciate you both so much. Oh, and Kristina."

"Kristina is a treasure," Becky agreed. "She seems as much my younger sister as Allison. You've got her on your side as well. You're already on the path to having your own circle of friends to support you."

Addie's wistful smile turned genuine.

"We're glad to add you to the circle," Lydia said. "You fit right in as far as I'm concerned. Now then, how about we take this cake back downstairs and work on frosting it before it gets so maudlin in here, we all float away?"

The three women looked at each other and laughed.

"You should go," Jesse said, lifting his gaze from the sheriff's desk where all the evidence of the train robbers had been laid out in an attempt to see something new. "Take a day off and spend time with your lady. I can be on duty."

"Oh, go on." Dylan waved his hand and a newspaper clipping fluttered to the stone floor. He bent to retrieve it, his belt buckle digging into his middle. "I'm the sheriff. I'm always on duty. Especially when there's a public event like this. It's the perfect opportunity for our enemies to stir up trouble. Besides, you just got married. You should go to the party with your wife."

"I've got this," Jesse replied as Dylan placed the scrap of paper back on the desk. He rearranged the pieces and scrutinized them while he talked. "Addie's going to be running the ice cream station all day. She wants to meet folks. I'll stop by and check on her here and there, but she's fine. In the midst of everyone is the safest place for her. I've been hearing things about you and the café lady and I think, if you want her to know you care for her, you need to spend some time with her in public. Show everyone you're proud to be her man. Women appreciate things like that."

Dylan considered Jesse's words. "Are you sure? Don't you want to socialize with your friends?"

"I can socialize while on duty," Jesse replied. "Never know when an idle conversation might provide a clue."

Dylan grinned. "All right then. Hot damn, I don't know the last time I took a day off."

"And that's why you need this. Life isn't work, Sheriff. At least, not when you have a woman."

"Are you really giving me advice, son?" Dylan raised his eyebrows at his deputy.

"Hell yes. You may have a decade or so on me, but I've been married longer."

Not likely, friend, Dylan thought, but of course, Jesse couldn't know that, and he didn't feel like sharing. *Telling Lydia is one thing. That woman has been the keeper of my heart for years. This youngling doesn't need to know.* "More than a decade, Jesse."

The younger man shrugged unrepentantly. His grin turned impudent. "Then let this young fool offer some advice, you old donkey. Spend time with your lady. You won't regret it."

Dylan couldn't help but chuckle. "Okay, West. You don't need to twist my arm. I said I would go."

"Good."

Chapter 6

The church service ended with a rousing hymn, music bellowing from the pipes of Kristina's organ to spur the congregation to solidarity, faith and service. Then she clattered down the spiral staircase from the loft and joined her husband at the door. Cody slipped his arm around her waist and they shook hands one by one with each person who passed by. Hand in hand with Dylan, Lydia approached the young couple, smiling at their united front. At first glance, they appeared a strange pair. Cody's good looks contrasted with Kristina's plainness to a shocking degree, but the fire of passion burned equally in their eyes. They loved their work and each other with unwavering devotion.

"Ready for this afternoon?" Cody asked Dylan as they passed by.

"Wouldn't miss it," Dylan replied. "See you at the river in an hour."

As they stepped outside, the first thing Lydia noticed was a break in the heat. Yesterday, rain had pummeled the city in a mammoth gully washer. A night of breezy late-summer heat followed by a sunny day had dried out the grass, but the noticeably cooler temperature had prompted an impromptu plan on the part of the small circle of friends.

"It sure is a beautiful day," Dylan commented as they traversed the sidewalk in the direction of the café.

"It is," Lydia agreed. "Just look at the sky." She indicated the cerulean expanse above them. "Not a cloud to be seen. The sun is shining and yet it's not hot."

"I know. What a relief. Even the nights have been almost unbearable until today. Now that the rain has broken the heat, this should be a wonderful afternoon."

"I agree. Are you sure your other deputy is all right with being left completely in charge of everything while you and Jesse play around?" Lydia wanted to know. A cool breeze, redolent of the coming fall, ruffled her skirt and teased wisps of hair from her chignon.

"Yes, I think so," Dylan replied. "Rob might be the youngest, but he's tough. Nothing scares him. He's a crack shot and smart enough to point his gun in the right direction. Each of us needs to be able to handle things alone in case something happens to the others, and he might be only nineteen, but he chose this job."

Lydia ran her hand down Dylan's arm and laced her fingers through his. "I know, and if something bad happened to him, he chose that too. You all did."

Dylan frowned.

I know you don't like that. You want to be responsible for your men, but law enforcement is a kind of war, and everyone understands that. You put your life on the line for the love of the job, and it might cost you your last breath. She squeezed his hand.

Dylan squeezed back but did not speak. Lydia chose not to press. She'd made her point and didn't feel inclined to nag.

They arrived at the café, still in silence, and Lydia unlocked the door with the key from her reticule. It clunked when she dropped it back inside.

"What are you hiding in there, woman?" Dylan demanded.

She smirked. "Wouldn't you like to know?" Then, before he could grab her, she ducked into the dining room and ran, laughing, into the kitchen, where an oversized wicker basket awaited them.

With his longer legs, Dylan caught up easily. He grasped her shoulder and turned her to face him, backing her up against the door to the pantry and stepping up until his entire body was plastered against hers.

She lifted her face and met his eyes, only to be assaulted by a passionate kiss. His lips ravaged hers, his tongue driving into her mouth, pulling back and stabbing in again. It reminded Lydia of what she knew about the physical act, and she swallowed hard. She inhaled through her nose, drawing in the scent of Dylan. Fresh prairie breeze, plain hard soap and man… aroused man. She didn't need to have prior experience with that muskiness to understand what it meant. *He wants to do that with you.*

As his mouth claimed hers, as her body responded without the need for conscious thought, her mind drew up a confusing whirlwind of half-imagined vignettes. Of Dylan unbuttoning her shirtwaist. Of him hiking her skirt up her thighs. Of him rolling her naked onto her bed. An image of his hand lacing into her hair as he settled between her thighs made her scalp tingle.

She moaned and twisted in his grip. His hands tightened on her waist, trapping her even tighter against the wood as the fullness in the front of his jeans compressed her belly.

His lips left hers and trailed across her face to her throat, where he nipped the sensitive skin and made her shiver.

"Dylan, please," she whimpered.

"Please what, Miss Lydia? Stop… or more?"

His breath on her skin seemed to spark answering wetness inside her bloomers. She felt good and ached at the same time, there in that secret place, and so she didn't know how to answer his question.

"What do you want, Lydia?"

"I don't know," she burst out at last.

He chuckled and drew back from her, smudging her lips with a tender, un-demanding kiss. "How do you want to do this, honey?" he asked.

"Do what? Our courtship?"

He nodded.

"I don't know that either," she replied. The pounding of her heart began to slow now that his intense touch had eased. "Part of me wants to claim you for good."

His eyes turned to silver flame.

He leaned in, but Lydia blocked him with a hand on his lips. "But part of me is scared to take that step."

"Scared?" He pulled her into his arms in a warm embrace that had much less power behind it. "You don't seem scared. Your body knows what it wants."

Lydia nodded. "I feel that, I do, but it's a big step."

Dylan kept one arm around Lydia's waist. With the other, he stroked her cheek. "It not surprising if you're a little nervous. Never done this before, have you?"

"No, never," she agreed, eyes wide.

He nodded. "I figured as much. Try not to worry, honey. Despite what the old prudes say, making love is natural and enjoyable. If you can trust me, I can take us there."

"Are you sure you're speaking for me as well? I've heard things… seen things that make me think only men probably enjoy it." Lydia bit her lip, nerves and embarrassment twisting her face. *That's not what Becky said, and she would know. Kristina either. She doesn't say much, but she's never had a satisfied smile before Cody. Not to mention, as fast as Allison got in a family way…* Though she tried to reassure herself with logic, though her aching body urged her toward

Dylan, her overactive mind couldn't put the gut-clenching nerves to rest. "What if I hate being intimate?"

"You won't," he told her, "unless you decide ahead of time you will. Nearly every woman is capable of enjoying being close to her man if she is able to get out of her head and into her body. Listen, Lydia." Dylan raked his hand through his hair, making the luxurious salt-and-pepper mane stand on end. Lydia quickly smoothed it down, enjoying the sensation of the silky strands beneath her fingers.

"I'm listening, Dylan," she said. "I'm not saying I'm against it or that I expect a bad time. I'm just… I'm just nervous."

He kissed her forehead, her eyelids and the tip of her nose before settling in to claim her mouth again. *How many ways does this man know how to kiss?* She wondered as he tenderly urged exquisite arousal from her with delicate swirls of his tongue.

Again passion arose within her. Her treacherous body melted in his arms even as her overactive mind struggled to retain control.

He released her again. "You're going to be fine, I think," he said, poking out his cheek with his tongue.

He looked so smug, she swatted his arm. "I'm not going to make it that easy on you, Sheriff."

He didn't respond aloud, but the look on his face spoke volumes. Then he settled back into a more normal expression, combing his rumpled mustache with his fingertips. "All teasing aside, Lydia, how do you want to handle this?"

She stepped back out of his embrace and turned to the icebox in the corner of the kitchen, pulling out a bowl of chicken she'd fried the previous day, covered with a red-checkered napkin. She placed it in the basket before returning for bottles of lemonade. "I'm not sure what you mean."

"Well, hmmm." He took a moment to think.

See, smarty? How can I answer the question when you don't even know what you're asking?

"Of course the point of courtship is that we're seeing if we want to marry eventually."

Oh goodness, that was blunt. And yet joy bubbled up like a spring in her heart. "Yes, of course."

"So we can either plan a slow courtship of a year or more, or move a little faster," he continued.

Oh, that. Lydia retrieved the cherry pie she'd baked before services, ran a knife through the crisp pastry and gooey red filling, and topped it with a napkin before tucking it into the basket as well. "I don't think we should wait too long," she said at last. "We need to talk a bit about what our expectations are from…" she gulped. "From marriage. We need enough time to plan. I don't want to have a hurry-up event the way everyone else seems to be doing. It doesn't have to be the wedding of the century, but a little preparation goes a long way toward making a special day even better."

"Ah, that's some sound reasoning, my dear," Dylan said. He lifted the basket from the counter and hung it on the crook of his arm. The other hand he extended to Lydia. She laced her fingers through his, an act which always caused a thrill.

"So how long is long enough?" he pressed as they strolled toward the back door of the kitchen. Outside, a small garden contained no grass, only two small apple trees, their partially mature fruit already dragging down the branches, a small patch of green beans, two large pots filled with tomato plants and a third in which an assortment of herbs clustered and twined together. Near the back fence, vines crept along the ground, laden with pumpkins and other types of squash. The wooden boards that delineated the rear boundary of Lydia's property hung with grapevines. The sides were filled with climbing flowers.

"I've never been back here," he commented. "This is a pretty space."

"Nature is beautiful," she replied. "It's nothing but the practical means to equip my café, and yet it looks like the Garden of Eden. I only grow the roses for their beauty, and yet the apple trees are just as pretty. I'm so glad the previous owners of the building planted them. So are the pumpkins. Everything God makes has its own appeal."

He leaned over and kissed her cheek. "I had no idea you were such a philosopher."

She colored. *Was that too much? Girls aren't supposed to be deep thinkers.* Then she shoved away the thought. *That's an Ilse Jackson way to think. He already knows you're intelligent, an astute business owner. He likes you as you are, so don't pretend not to be his intellectual equal. If he has an issue, it's better to know ahead of time.* "I suppose you don't know everything about me yet, do you, Dylan?"

He stopped beside the gate leading into a small alley between her property and the rear of the houses behind. "It would take the rest of my life to know everything about you, honey," he said seriously. "That's a course of study I'm looking forward to more than you can imagine."

The heat of embarrassment faded, replaced by a warm glow. Emboldened by his tender words, she reached out to Dylan, capturing the side of his neck in one hand and drawing him down to initiate a gentle kiss. He allowed her to control the embrace. She tasted his lips with shy eagerness that left them both panting.

"I think," she said slowly, "that a spring wedding would be just fine with me."

"Spring?" he asked, disappointed.

"Yes, why not?" she asked as she opened the ornate wrought-iron handle on the gate and led them into the alley. They turned right and made their way into the street, hand in hand. The cooler temperature seemed to be holding.

"It's a long time, Lydia," Dylan commented.

She smiled. *He is eager, isn't he?* "Less than a year."

"How long do you think it will take?" he demanded. "How big an event are you hoping for?"

They reached the street and turned south. A cool breeze blew up behind them, teasing the couple with tantalizing hints of autumn.

"Not that big," she said. "My friends and their husbands would be sufficient."

"Heitschmidts, Fultons, Williamses. Who else?" Dylan asked.

"Um, Wests," Lydia replied. "What about you?"

Dylan shrugged. "My other deputy, Rob, I suppose, but I think you've hit the major ones. So that makes ten adults and four kids, three of them babies who aren't born yet. You really think that's going to take more than half a year to plan?"

Lydia laughed. "Are you in a hurry, Sheriff?"

"Oh yes," he replied with intensity rather than humor. "A huge hurry. I've wasted too much time already with my dithering."

"So you took too long to decide what you wanted and that means I have to truncate my dreams of a white wedding?" she asked, hiding her grin and pretending to be serious.

Dylan frowned, his lips following his dark brown handlebar mustache. "I guess, honey, if that's really what you want, I'll let you set the pace."

Good. He's willing to listen and not railroad me. He also, it seemed, was willing to pout if the opportunity presented itself. "Dylan, I'm joking," Lydia admitted. "I don't need that much time. Actually, October or November would be perfect."

The Sheriff's rugged face brightened. "That soon? Hot damn. That sounds much better."

Lydia couldn't help but return his smile. *I see we're on the same page.* "Yes, Dylan. Why not?"

"I love you, Lydia. I do hope you realize that. The reason I waited to speak to you wasn't that I was unsure of you. I just wanted to be certain what I had to offer was good enough for you."

"It is," she reassured him. "I already have a satisfying life, Dylan. I have my café, which I hope you won't ask me to give up so I can be some kind of house-wife. I don't plan on that at all. I have a home, friends, a place in the community. I'm not looking to you to provide for me, because I'm already providing for myself. I'm asking you to be my companion."

His fingers tightened on hers as they meandered south, passing the church and the bank on their right, rows of colorful homes on their left. The uneven brick of the street caught at Lydia's high black Sunday shoes, but her grip on Dylan's arm kept her securely upright.

"That means even more to me," he replied. "I like the idea that you chose me because you want me and that you're not relying on me to stave off desperation. It's a better way, and you don't need to worry about your café. I would be tarred and feathered and run out of town if it closed because of me. I'm not quite sure how we'll manage our time when you keep such early hours and mine are all over the place, but we'll make it work somehow."

"We will," Lydia agreed. "I'm sure of it."

They had reached the train tracks at the southernmost edge of town, and Dylan helped her over the rails, as though such a low obstacle might actu-ally prove to be an impediment. She didn't mind. Beyond the train station, the wide, wild prairie stretched out to the horizon, a sea of grass undulating in the endless wind.

Like a sliver of mirror, the river sliced through, meandering on its slow, steady course toward Wichita and all points east. The previous day's rain had done little to compensate for the ravages of a long, hot season, and so a long patch of muddy bank adorned the river on either side. In the rainy season, likely to begin in a month or so, the river would completely cover that mud and overflow, turning into a raging torrent. But today, it seemed only to add to the peaceful ambiance of a perfect summer's day.

As they approached the spot where they'd agreed to meet their friends—under a wind-twisted tree a few feet from the water—Lydia noticed they'd arrived last. Becky and James sat side by side on a blanket. He held her hand in his lap. The sun reflected on their hair turning hers to gold, his to copper. His freckles danced on a satisfied smile.

To their left, his back against the tree, Wesley scratched in a tiny notebook with a dull pencil. A splashing sound drew Lydia's gaze to the water, where Allison, looking heavy enough to topple at any moment, dabbled barefoot in a muddy pool with her three-year-old stepdaughter, Melissa. *That blond hair looks so much like Allison's, Melissa could be her natural child.*

Another blond man, this one young and deeply tanned, stretched out on his side on the blanket, providing support to his petite, red-haired wife. Lydia waved to Addie, who grinned in response. Her smile looked strained. *I'll get to the bottom of that.* Last, Cody and Kristina completed the group. The freckled, strawberry blond woman also sat cross-legged on the blanket. Cody lay with his head in her lap. She stroked his forehead.

"Oh, good," Jesse said, drawing attention to the new arrivals, "the food is finally here. I was wondering if the lovebirds had gotten so distracted by their cooing, we'd never get fed."

"Shut up, whippersnapper," Dylan replied congenially, grinning at his impudent deputy.

Wesley looked up from his notebook, nodded once, and buried his face in his figures again.

Allison and Melissa squelched their way back to the group, wiping their muddy feet on prairie grass as they went. "Hello, Lydia, Sheriff," the expectant mother said in a sad, weary voice. "Wes, can you put that away, please? Everyone is here now."

"Just a minute," he replied. "I'm almost done."

"I'm not waiting on you, Fulton," Jesse told his childhood friend. "I'm starving. Let me at that chicken!"

Lydia laughed at his eagerness. "Of course, Deputy West."

"Here you go." Dylan set the basket in the middle of the blanket and helped Lydia to a seated position in the remaining spot on its edge. He laid his arm across her shoulders.

As the group munched chicken and sipped lemonade, Lydia noticed the normal rapport she felt with her friends seemed absent. Becky and Kristina tried to keep up their usual friendly conversation, chatting about this and that, but with Allison glaring daggers first at her husband and then at Addie, keeping up their chatting became increasingly difficult.

Wesley eventually packed up his notebook, but he remained withdrawn from the conversation, focused on his food, not speaking. Allison also kept silent, except for the muted groan she released every time she shifted position. Her enormous belly seemed to get in the way of everything, even eating. After only a few bites of chicken, she set her plate aside. The lemonade sat untouched.

"Are you feeling poorly, Allison?" Lydia asked at last.

She nodded. "There's no room left in my stomach. I'm hungry, but when I eat, it gives me heartburn. The midwife says I should just nibble whatever sounds appealing and hang on. I only have a couple of weeks left. I'll be glad when this is over."

"Sounds terrible," Addie commented. "I'm sorry you're having a hard time." Her gentle tone could not have aroused temper in anyone.

"You're next," Allison snapped. "We'll see if you do any better."

"Allie," her husband admonished, speaking at last, "that wasn't called for. Look, everyone already feels sorry for you. Don't milk it."

"You have no idea what you're talking about," she hissed at him. "Men never do. Think this is easy, Wesley? Do I look like I'm having fun?"

"You look like you're whining," he replied. "What do you think, Jesse? Shall we leave the hens to their clucking and put a line or two in the water?"

"Sounds good to me," Jesse replied. "You don't mind, do you, Addie?"

Addie cast a nervous glance at Allison. "I don't mind. See if you can catch a fish for supper, okay?"

"I'll try." Without a moment's concern for everyone's eyes on them, he kissed her lips gently before levering himself to his feet. Fishing poles and a bucket of minnows rested beside Wesley near the tree. Under Addie's wistful gaze and Allison's vicious glare, the two men gathered their gear and headed off to the bridge that spanned the river, where they could sit and fish without getting all muddy.

"Would you like to go?" Lydia asked Dylan.

"Don't mind if I do," he replied. Like Jesse, he showed no compunction about touching his lips to Lydia's temple before joining the younger men, well away from the group and out of earshot.

"What about Cody?" Allison asked, eyeing her friend. The young pastor still lay unmoving, his head cradled in his wife's lap.

"He's out cold," Kristina replied. "Sometimes the Holy Spirit just sort of… takes him over. He loves it, and he always preaches the best sermons, but then he passes out afterward. I don't expect to see him move for at least an hour." She smoothed his dark hair back from his forehead and gazed tenderly on his face.

I love this group, Lydia thought. *They feel so free to be affectionate with their spouses in front of each other.* Then her eyes fell on Allison, who still looked angry.

Maybe there's such a thing as feeling too free. And yet, she was contemplating marriage, which was sure to be a life-altering event. As much as she loved Dylan, as long as she'd wished for him and pined for him and dreamed of him, there would be bad as well as good to joining their lives together.

Maybe he snores. Maybe he leaves dirty hankies all over the place. Maybe he hogs the necessary. Though insignificant, these minor irritations could certainly grow over time. *I have to face that life with Dylan won't be a fairy tale. We'll have disagreements, even arguments. There may be days when he would rather go fishing than spend time with me. When I would rather he did.*

The contrast among the various relationships spoke volumes. Allison, who everyone said had loved Wesley since they were too young to know what love was, had found marriage to be more problem than joy.

Becky, Lydia knew, had expected to remain a spinster. James had had other plans. Jesse and Addie's story Lydia didn't know, but the way they interacted and the pinched, nervous look around the petite redhead's eyes spoke of both joy and uncertainty. All was not yet perfect in their world, and Addie clung to her husband as though to shield herself from some unseen threat.

Lydia turned to Cody and Kristina and drew in a slow breath. Like her, Kristina was a professional. A woman with a passion and a place she'd made for herself in the community. Like Lydia, she didn't need a man to provide for her. Not really. She had allowed Cody into her life because they cared for each other.

Mutual need linked Allison and Wesley, and that neediness had tarnished their love, but for Cody and Kristina, working together, fulfilling their dreams with the support of the one they loved, the light of joy between them rivaled the summer sun.

That's what I want with Dylan. Lydia smiled. She could see it happening. She raised her eyes to the bridge, where the three men sat, their legs dangling over the boards, far above the dirty water. Dylan sat taller than either Jesse or Wesley and had the biggest muscles. Years of office work had left Wesley thin, and Jesse was one long, wiry string bean. Maturity had filled out Dylan's figure into the image of manhood. She bit her lip at the thought of how that barely-leashed strength had pinned her to the pantry door. His power both made her feel protected and frightened her.

He seemed to feel her regard and turned in her direction, flashing a white-toothed grin at her. She gave a little wave.

"How cute is that," Addie said. "I love how comfortable you two are together." Lydia's cheeks warmed at the compliment.

Allison muttered something under her breath that sounded decidedly hostile.

"You know something," Becky said mildly, "your husband has a point. You're not being your usual friendly self, Allison. What did Addie ever do to you?"

"I agree," Lydia added. "She's a nice girl and she's new in town. I remember when I first arrived. You, your sister and Kristina made a point of coming to my café, talking to me, telling everyone how nice I was and how great the food was. Why welcome me and not her?"

"So everyone's going to gang up on me?" Allison demanded, her lip trembling. "Kristina?"

The freckled face scrunched as she sought for words that would speak the truth in love. "I think, probably, that you've got a lot going on, and you aren't feeling your best. I can see you've decided Addie is to blame. You haven't given her a chance. I'm not sure what that's based on, though I'm willing to listen if you want to talk about it."

Seeming to sense the tension, little Melissa, her face smeared with cherry pie filling, jumped up from the blanket and ran to her father. He plunked her down on his lap and let her pretend to hold the fishing pole.

"Skittish little thing," Lydia commented. "She's never liked me either."

Allison heaved a huge sigh, and then whimpered, pushing against her belly. "Stop that, you. Come out, and you won't be so crowded, but there isn't any more room." Then she met eyes with each of the other women. Becky looked back steadily, knowing her sister might become angry, but would never abandon her. Kristina's face spoke of concern for her friend. Lydia let a bit of her indignation over Allison's unfairness show. Addie curled up, her arms around knees she had drawn toward her chest, trying to appear invisible, as though debating whether she should stay or bolt. The roundness of her belly transformed her defensive shape into a ball.

"Doesn't it bother anyone else that Jesse went out into the wild world and came back with this one? And her pregnant out to there, no less, but no sign of a wedding ring. Oh, no. They had to hurry up and marry before anyone could get to know her. That bothers the hell out of me. Lydia," she turned and their eyes locked, "you, I understand. You never knew Jesse. You only know how to be hospitable." Having exonerated her friend for perceived duplicity, she moved on. "Kristina, I'm surprised at you though. I know how you used to feel about Jesse."

Kristina smiled kindly. "Used to, Allison. It's been years. Yes, I was sweet on Jesse when we were seventeen." She shot an apologetic glance at Addie. "I dared to hope, when Lily passed away, that he might find me acceptable. But why on earth would I hold on to that now? Look at what I have. What am I supposed to regret that I would begrudge him his happiness? I want him to be happy, and I'm glad he turned me down."

She stroked fingers through her husband's dark, curly hair. "Cody loves me. I'm first in his heart. That's as good as it gets and much more than I expected. So, in honor of years of friendship, I affirm Jesse's choice. This is the girl who taught him to love again. I won't say a word against her. Not unless she shows me by some action that she's hurting our friend. So far, she seems to be helping him."

Lydia couldn't help looking at Addie. Her cheeks glowed with both embarrassment and pleasure at Kristina's kind words.

"Before you dig any deeper into that hole," Becky added, "if you condemn her for going to the altar pregnant, you'll have to condemn me too. Don't forget that."

"I would never condemn you," Allison said. To Lydia, she looked almost frantic.

"Then, Allison, how can you say a word about Addie? Things happen. They're married now. You can't deny he's happy, and she seems nice so far." Becky said gently.

"Allison?" Addie interjected. "I didn't marry Jesse to hurt you, and I have nothing against you. I'm glad he had wonderful friends growing up, especially you and Kristina. You two taught him how to listen to women. Most men don't know how to do that. I knew about you both. He told me so many stories. I was looking forward to seeing this town, to meeting his friends. This seemed like a place for a person to start over, with no one judging them." Her face twisted into lines of uncertainty once again.

I wonder what that means.

"A place to fit in and make a life. I wanted that. I had hoped his friends could be my friends. If you won't accept me, well, there's nothing I can do about it, but I hold no anger toward you."

Allison bit her lip. "Why do you have to be nice?" she demanded.

"Why do you have to choose her for a target?" Lydia barked, annoyed by her friend's continued nonsense. "Why not be angry with the people who actually hurt you? Start with your evil mother-in-law. Leave Addie alone if you can't be her friend."

Allison sighed. "I'm not apologizing until I have a better handle on how I feel about anything. It's probably best to give me a wide berth until after the delivery. I'm not in a good state right now."

"You're not," Kristina agreed. "I do feel sorry you're so uncomfortable, but it has been affecting your mood."

"I can't control it," Allison said. "I feel so horrible. My feet hurt. My back hurts. When I try to sleep, my hips hurt and my legs twitch. I'm never doing this again."

Becky stood carefully and approached Allison, embracing her. "I'm sorry, honey."

Allison smiled, though it didn't look any too genuine. Then, she eased herself onto her side and drifted to sleep.

"See, it was never you," Lydia told Addie quietly. "She has a witch of a mother-in-law and she's hurting. You just got in the way. It's not fair, but try not to take it to heart. Allison isn't usually unfair. I bet once her little one comes, she'll be nicer to you."

"Yikes," Addie replied. "I'm not sure I want to go through what she is."

"Unfortunately, we don't have a choice," Becky said, laying her hand on her own tummy. "It's too late now. At least we're prepared."

"That's for certain. Um, do I even have a mother-in-law?"

"No, honey," Kristina said. "Jesse's dad was killed in a farm accident when he was fifteen. His mama sort of wasted away a year later. He more or less lived with my family after that. They were good folks though. They would have liked you."

"Oh." Addie fell silent. They all did. The wind whispered through the shoulder-high grass, making it dance like ladies in fancy dresses. They waltzed and swayed, clad in gold and green, adorned with dusty blue and vibrant red blossoms, while huge, gaudy sunflowers watched the sky with single, sightless eyes.

A melancholy feeling reminded Lydia of when she was younger, of looking out of Boston harbor into the vast, gray Atlantic. Though her childhood had been happy, the sight of the undulating waves always drew her, tugging unrealized sorrows from the depths of her soul and tossing them on the sun-bright water.

Stretching out on the blanket, Lydia regarded the sky. Fat, puffy clouds floated overhead. Her mind shaped them into dragons, pirate ships and for some reason, a goat. She smiled as sleep crept up and claimed her.

"Do you think Lydia knows how to cook fish?" Dylan asked, lifting the fat trout he'd just snared so his friends could see it.

"Lydia can cook anything," Wes replied. "You're a lucky man."

"What?" Jesse interjected. "Allison can cook. She force-fed us cookies all along. They weren't bad."

"Allison is fine," Wes replied. "We eat well enough. It's Sam who wasn't." Then he stopped, eying his little daughter.

"Daddy made us dinner until Mama Allie came to stay," Melissa announced. "He makes good soup."

Wes gave the other men a look that dared them to comment. Jesse guffawed, but Dylan, who had been present to witness the young banker's nightmare of a first marriage, kept silent. *Bad cooking was one of Wesley's smaller problems.*

Gathering up their trout, the men returned to the blanket. It appeared Sunday afternoon had attacked the women with an unplanned nap. Allison lay on her side, twitching in her sleep. Becky snored softly under the tree near her sister. Kristina and Addie chatted quietly while Lydia sprawled on her back, eyes closed.

Dylan took a moment to study his intended's face. *So pretty. So soft and yet so strong. I'm glad she's accepted me.* He knelt, setting the fish in the grass beside the blanket, and kissed her cheek.

Lydia opened warm brown eyes and looked up at him, first with confusion, then with a soul-deep joy that touched him to the core. "The afternoon is waning, honey," he told her quietly. "Shall we go?" He extended a hand.

She grasped it but wrinkled her nose. "Something smells like a trout."

"That would be… a trout," he replied, triumphantly retrieving his catch and dangling it far too close to her face.

She recoiled from the slimy scales. "Dylan!"

"If I clean this…" he wiggled it provocatively, so it nearly touched her skin, "do you think we could have it for dinner?"

"If you clean it, I'll cook it with potatoes and green beans, but if you hit me with it, you'll be left in the street alone with your fish."

"And no one to cook it? What a shame. All right, all right." He withdrew the trout and hoisted Lydia to her feet.

All around them, the lazy afternoon party showed signs of breaking up. Despite their tension, Wesley gently helped Allison to her feet, and then took her arm. Melissa grabbed her hand and they headed for their home, closest to the picnic spot, on the far south side of town.

A little further on, the Heitschmidt family home waited to welcome James and his bride in established comfort.

The church towered over the center of town, and in the shade of its steeple the tiny, single-story parsonage would shelter Cody and Kristina. Though the space would never work for a family, for the couple, it sufficed, especially after the installation of an attic bedroom as well as an indoor privy and interior walls separating the parlor, kitchen and dining room.

"Where are you staying?" Lydia asked Jesse and Addie.

"The boarding house," Jesse replied. "I don't know what's best… houses are not in ready supply right now but building a new one would take time—too much time."

"I need something quickly," Addie added. "I don't want to deliver the baby there. I'd like to be somewhere… ours."

"I'm trying, honey," Jesse said.

Lydia could see the frustration on his face as the younger couple moved on. At last, only Lydia and Dylan remained lingering in the lovely late-summer day, as the prairie grass blew, and the sluggish river sloshed against the banks. Dylan picked up the basket and Lydia accepted the fish. Their free hands linked together almost without thought. Holding each other just felt natural.

The couple made their way through the length of Main Street towards Lydia's home and café. "I'm glad we went, aren't you?" Lydia asked.

"Oh, definitely," Dylan replied, "but Allison and Wes aren't doing well, are they?"

Lydia released a slow breath. "No. It's hard to say who's in worse shape. I didn't know Wesley Fulton when he was a kid. I've heard he was outgoing and fun, but as long as I've been here, he seemed so... fragile."

"That's true," Dylan replied. "I thought it might have to do with that first wife of his. She was a piece of work."

"Hush," Lydia admonished. "The poor thing wasn't right in the head. She couldn't help it."

"She couldn't help being simple," Dylan conceded, "and that might have made her kind of angry and hard to get along with, but she could help lifting her skirt for everyone. I know she knew better than that."

Lydia frowned. "That's vulgar, Sheriff." They had arrived at the café and she turned the key in the lock.

"It true though. Wes isn't a bad guy but being with that..." she glowered, and he continued, "that woman wasn't good for him, and now Allison's turned every bit as grumpy as Samantha was. I do hope it's temporary or the whole Fulton household might just implode."

They stepped over the threshold and Lydia led Dylan back into her kitchen. Removing a sharp knife from a wooden block on the oak countertop, she handed it to him. Then she retrieved the basket and began unpacking the dirty dishes, which she piled up in the white sink below a small window that overlooked her garden. She worked the pump and water sluiced over the chicken plate and the pie pan before she began rummaging in the cabinets and bringing out a copper pot. She filled it with water and poked the ashes in the firebox of the stove, feeding it a bit more fuel. Then she turned and began peeling potatoes.

Dylan took a seat at a small table stashed in the corner between the door and the icebox. A newspaper—a month old by the look of it—sat on the surface.

"Should I use this to wrap the guts?" he asked.

"Yes indeed," Lydia replied. "I was going to use it for pumpkin, but there will be more before then. The slops bucket is..."

"I see it. Over by the back door." He retrieved the pail and set it beside the table before setting to work filleting the fish.

"Save the head and bones. I'll make soup another day. You know," Lydia said, continuing the conversation, "If I had to have Mrs. Fulton as a mother-in-law, I might turn grumpy too. Do you have any family, Dylan?"

"Nope," he replied. A strip of trout skin plopped onto the paper. Lydia set the potatoes to boil and turned her attention to a bowl of green beans in the icebox. She quickly began snapping off the stringy ends. "Or well… I do, but I don't talk to them."

"Why not?" she asked. *That sounds important.*

"Dad died when he was only thirty," the sheriff replied, setting aside one beautiful white filet and flipping the creature over to extract the other.

"He ran the general store. We don't know what happened. One morning he just slumped over at the breakfast table and that was it. I was ten. Mama remarried pretty fast, to a rich man who didn't want some other man's kid underfoot. By the time I turned sixteen, I had moved to the logging camp. Mama had more kids by then, and I guess she thought it was okay to forget about her firstborn." The bitterness in his voice brought tears to Lydia's eyes.

"Oh, honey, that's sad. I'm sorry." She dropped the beans back into their bowl and took the five steps to where Dylan sat, resting her hand on his shoulder.

He leaned his cheek against her skin. "That was a long time ago, Lydia. I don't think about it much anymore."

What a lie. She kissed the top of his head and returned to her beans. She set a second pot of water beside the first and began her next preparation. Soon she had a cast-iron skillet heating to melt a pat of butter as she mixed up cornmeal and seasonings. Just in time, because Dylan arrived a moment later with two portions of trout. The moist surface of the fish grabbed the coating the moment she dropped it onto the plate.

Dylan looked over her shoulder. "I'm feasting like a king today." Then he returned to the table to gather up the unwanted portions of the fish and put the whole mess outside, setting the head and bones aside for soup.

Lydia sighed. *Every cat in town will be paying a visit tonight, I'm sure.* The sound of the sink told her Dylan was washing his hands. *I didn't even have to tell him. He's at least half-civilized already.*

She dropped the filets into the butter.

Dylan approached from behind and rested his chin on her shoulder. His hands closed on her waist. "Why, Miss Lydia. Can it be you're not wearing a corset?" He sounded shocked.

She rolled her eyes. "As hot as this kitchen gets, I'd faint if I tried, if not fall down stone dead. I need to breathe more than I need a wasp waist."

"Good," he replied. "You have lovely proportions." He slipped his arms around her middle, turning the clutch into a hug. The close proximity to her man set Lydia's heart pounding again. His thumb made a strumming movement in the vicinity of her belly button. Heat shot straight to her core. Leaving the food to its own devices for a moment, she turned.

"This is dangerous," he warned her.

"I know," she replied, wrinkling her nose and smiling. Her eyes crinkled in the corners. "You shouldn't even be in here."

"Don't you worry about scandal?"

Lydia snorted. "There's always some scandal. Once we're boringly respectable again, people will move on to the next one. I have more important things to worry about. Like not letting the trout burn." She tugged his head down. "Kiss me."

He did, lavishing her lips with wanton, tender caresses. His mustache ticked her face, enticing a giggle from her.

"Tend the food, woman," he ordered in a false growl.

"Yes, sir," she replied in a parody of submissiveness. Turning, she managed to turn the fish just moments before the golden crust turned black. "Dylan, can you please get me two plates from the cabinet beside the icebox?"

"Of course," he replied, releasing her with obvious reluctance.

"And I don't know if you're a temperance proponent, but I have a nice bottle of red wine if you'd like."

"I normally drink whiskey," he replied, "but today is worth celebrating. I'll join you in a glass."

She smiled. "Oh, are we celebrating?" she asked in a show of false innocence. "Just what would the occasion be? I'd like to know." She retrieved two long-stemmed glasses from the shelves above the plates and set them on the table. "These belonged to my parents, by the way. I've kept them all these years, which wasn't easy on the train from Boston, let me tell you."

"Yes, we're celebrating," he replied with a growl. "Don't you think our betrothal is worth a drink at least?"

Lydia retrieved a loosely corked bottle and opened it. The rich aroma of fermented grapes wafted into the room. She poured a generous portion into each of the glasses and admired its purple hue. *I'm getting better at making this.* "I certainly think drinking a toast to an engagement is worthwhile," she said, not meeting Dylan's eyes, "but I don't recall having received a proposal. We talked about marriage, but no asking ever happened."

Dylan's hands closed around Lydia's, plucking the bottle from her grip and setting it on the table. Then, still clutching her fingers in his, he sank to one knee. "Lydia, honey, will you marry me?"

Lydia bit her lip and nodded, her words choked behind a flood of tears that threatened to spill. She sucked in a shaky breath. Her joke had gone wrong—or maybe right—as his formal proposal warmed her from the heart outward. She tugged on his hands, urging him to rise. He followed her lead and she threw her arms around his chest and rested her head on his shoulder, just below his chin. He enfolded her.

Long moments passed as they clung to each other. *This feels so good. So right. My man. My love.*

Suddenly she couldn't wait to be his wife. The warmth of his body sank into her soul and told her something she hadn't known before. *There will be powerful closeness when we become man and wife. The joining of bodies symbolizes the merging of lives.*

His hand slid away from her back, cupping her cheek and laying his lips on hers in a kiss that simmered with tender heat.

She opened to a tentative touch of his tongue, deepening the embrace. *Shocking, how something everyone says is naughty feels perfectly right.* She closed her eyes, drinking in the potent blend of love and passion, and then sucked in a sharp breath. In sliding away from her face, his hand brushed downward, seemingly looking to wrap around her waist, but touching her breast. With only two thin layers of fabric between them, the touch could almost have been on her bare flesh. His hand froze.

She pulled back from the kiss and met his eyes, took in the startled, eager expression that had nothing to do with seduction or triumph. "May I?" he asked.

Lydia didn't know how to respond. She blinked, but the rest of her remained frozen like a block of ice in the blistering heat of the kitchen. Passion rose to volcanic as Dylan's accidental touch turned deliberate. He lifted the heavy globe, gently squeezing. The touch stimulated her nipple, setting off a sizzle of arousal like ball lightning in her lower belly. The little bud rose proudly in his hand. He stroked it with his thumb.

Frightened by the intensity in Dylan's eyes, Lydia drew him down for another kiss, shutting out the sight but making no move to push his hand away from her body.

Then the smell of butter growing almost too brown shook her loose from the embrace and sent her scurrying out of her beloved's arms to retrieve their dinner. She quickly plated the fish, added a spoonful of potatoes with butter and salt, along with a sprinkle of fresh herbs, and the beans. "Nothing like prosaic reality to spoil a tender moment," she said as she carried the food to the small table.

"That's for certain," Dylan agreed. He joined her, sitting facing her so they could stare into each other's eyes. *Like a pair of besotted fools*, Lydia thought. *Of course, he looks just as hooked as I feel, so that's not a bad thing.*

Holding hands across the table, they ate in silence. Words seemed to have fled in the face of such intense emotion, but it didn't matter. The meaning flowed between them, free and easy as water along a riverbed. Obstacles did not interrupt, nor could the power be contained. *I love you,* she thought.

The light of that love reflected in his eyes.

Chapter 7

"Any idea," Jesse asked, leaning down to examine the threatening letters from the train robbery, which were once again spread across the sheriff's desk in the jail building, "why they decided to celebrate Founder's Day in September? There are a number of dates they could choose, but not one of them is in that month."

Dylan reversed a letter with a newspaper clipping and frowned as the move provided no insight. *If only I could concentrate.* "Since when has Ilse Jackson let a little thing like a fact get in the way of her plans? Though I have to admit, mid-September is a fine time to have an outdoor event. It won't be so hot then, but the winter will still be a long way off."

"You're right," Jesse agreed, "much as I hate to give that little cat credit for anything. Hey, how about if we lay out these clues in chronological order. Try to establish a timeline."

"I know the timeline pretty well," Dylan said. "What would that accomplish?" Jesse shrugged. "Maybe nothing, but you never know."

"You do it," Dylan said. "I'm going to walk down to the mercantile."

"What's at the mercantile?" Jesse wanted to know.

Dylan arched an eyebrow. "Cans of peaches." Then he chuckled and dropped the stupid act. "I'm expecting a package in the mail, and James promised to hold it for me," he explained, reminding his friend that the mercantile was also the post office. "I want to see if it's there yet, nosy."

Jesse grinned and waved before settling himself in front of the desk and shuffling the newspaper clippings and threatening letters into yet another new configuration.

Outside, the brief respite of the previous weekend had ended in another gully washing thunderstorm, and then a third, until the sluggish river ran high and the sunflowers lay beaten and naked on the prairie. Following the storms, the temperature and humidity had risen, leaving the town once again sweltering under a blanket of brutal heat. Dylan wiped sweat from his forehead. "Lord, if you're listening, we'll be happy to take some fall weather any time now," he muttered.

As though in answer, a hot, stale breeze blew up, moistening his skin. He shuddered. It smelled like a cross between old horse barn, wet dog, and stagnant puddle. *Fall can't come soon enough.*

"Sheriff Brody?" An unknown voice cut through his thoughts and he turned to see an equally unfamiliar face… or was it? Something about the dark-haired, middle-aged stranger registered in his mind, but what was it?

"Yes, I'm Sheriff Brody. Did you need some help, sir?"

The man nodded. "I'm Andrew Fulton, Wesley's father. There's been… there's been an incident down at the river." He scrubbed at his forehead.

"Father?" Dylan drew his eyebrows together and stared at the man. "I didn't know Wes still had a father." *What did the story say? He ran off when Wes was a kid and that was what drove Wes's mother over the edge?*

"Yeah, I'm still around," Andrew replied. "I'll explain later. Right now, um, you need to come with me."

Dylan's furrowed eyebrows shot toward his hairline at the instruction. "What's going on?"

"Um, my… um… my wife; that is, Wesley's mother… she tried to get up to some shenanigans with Allison. Um, tried to kill her, actually."

"Oh dear Lord!" Dylan exclaimed. "Is Allison all right? What the hell happened?"

"Allison is all right. Walk with me, Sherriff. I'll explain."

"All right." Alarm and confusion left Dylan with no choice but to follow this near-stranger toward the scene of trouble.

Andrew led Dylan south down the street past the bank. "You see, we think Charlotte probably lured Samantha out onto the ice last winter."

The non-sequitur did nothing to answer Dylan's questions, but it did cause a knot of tension to tighten his belly.

"And she just tried to kill Allison, like I said. Allison gave birth this afternoon and Charlotte lured her down to the river and pretended to throw the baby in, hoping Allison would…"

"Jump in and drown? My word. That woman should be locked up in the looney bin. How's the baby?"

"He's fine. She left him at the house." They passed the edge of town and crossed the train tracks, still heading south.

"Well, that's good. And Allison? It couldn't have been good for her to be running around right after giving birth."

Before them, the river, no longer a lazy silver ribbon, now rushed and snarled, beating against the bridge and washing over the boards.

"Wesley is getting the doctor to check her out," Andrew explained, "but, uh… well, there was a scuffle trying to get Allison away from Charlotte and… well, Charlotte fell in the river."

Dylan blinked. He took in the rushing flood and then turned to the stranger. "Fell in?"

Andrew nodded.

"Is she all right? Did someone pull her out?"

Andrew's lips twisted to the side. "How? Come on, Sheriff. Who was going to risk that," he indicated the water, "to save a murderer? She's in there somewhere. That's why I brought you. I'm reporting her death."

Dylan heaved a sigh. No doubt, if Charlotte had gone under and not been seen since, this would be a body retrieval, just as Andrew had suggested. Movement in the vicinity of a tree that stood to the left of the water drew Dylan's attention. James Heitschmidt leaned against the rough and twisted bark, regarding the water with intensity.

"James?"

"Oh, there you are, Dylan. Thank goodness. I think I saw her, but I'm not sure." James waved in the direction of the bridge. "We're in luck. She seems to have washed up against the piling. Otherwise, there's no telling how far downstream she would have gone."

"So you're in on this too?" Dylan demanded, uninterested in James' commentary.

"In on it?" James snorted. "We were watching Melissa—Rebecca and I—because Allison was in labor. When Rebecca told me she'd sent for Charlotte Fulton and not the midwife…" he shook his head. "I need to have a word with my wife about that one. Wes isn't rational where his mother is concerned. Anyway, we got to the house and everything was covered in blood. We found the baby outside in the garbage pile. Whatever went on in there must have been really upsetting for Allison. We barely made it to the bridge in time to stop her jumping into the water after… whatever it was Charlotte threw in."

"I'm sure it was a cat," Andrew added. "She hates cats and kills them whenever she can."

"So no one was in on anything," James continued. "Charlotte orchestrated some kind of horrible death for Allison, and we got here in time to stop it. Look, there. Think that might be her?"

Dylan turned to the river and sure enough, a large gray mass bumped against one of the wooden supports of the bridge.

"Here." James extended a large tree branch, forked at one end. "Must have blown down during one of the storms."

"That's lucky," Dylan commented. "Rare to find a big stick anywhere within a hundred miles." He accepted the branch and cautiously approached the river. Water seeped into his boots and soaked his socks. He scowled at the squishy sensation but stepped onto the boards anyway. Reaching over the low railing and catching the object in the fork of the branch, he pushed it toward shore. The current fought him, but he held on, straining his muscles as he maneuvered the unwieldy burden.

"A little help, please, gentlemen," he shouted over the roar of the water. Andrew and James approached and regarded him with matching expressions of disgust. Then Andrew stepped forward into the mud and managed to snag their quarry in one hand, dragging backward.

After another moment of struggle, the drowned body of Charlotte Fulton lay face down on the shore.

"She'd hate this," Andrew commented. "She considered mud to be her personal enemy."

James nodded. "Poor woman. I wonder why she was so... loony."

"Hard to say," Dylan commented, heaving the waterlogged body over. "I guess it doesn't matter anymore. I do hope Melissa turns out okay."

He frowned at the unpleasant sight of the stern, bony face, now coated in river muck, staring at the sky, eyes wide in death. Her normally tidy gray hair had escaped its pins, torn loose in the torrent and springing in wild disarray around her head. "Nothing left to do now but ask Cody to plan the funeral. To think I just wanted to make a quick run to the mercantile." He sighed.

"Could be worse," James replied. "Last time we had excitement in this town, train robbers nearly blew up my wife. I'm not glad Charlotte is dead... but she kind of brought it on herself."

"I'll have to look into that, of course," Dylan told his friend. "It's not that I doubt you, but you know. Procedures have to be followed."

"Of course," James said. "I understand. Only, can you leave Allison alone for a while? She's been through enough."

Though Dylan knew he'd have to talk to the only eyewitness of the entire incident eventually, he nodded. *A while. I'll give her a while.*

"Oh, dear Lord! Are you joking?" Lydia demanded, staring at Becky in shock as they moved around the sweltering kitchen, preparing for the Founder's Day breakfast.

Her friend shook her head and whisked pancake batter in a huge bowl, shouting to be heard over the clanging. "The doctor says Allison needs to stay in bed for a good long while, but she should be all right. Mrs. Fulton passed, though."

"Poor Allison," Addie said, frowning. She bit her lip as she sliced bacon. "Do you think we should bring her some meals?"

"That's a wonderful idea, Addie," Lydia replied, shaking a pan full of sausages. "I think that would be perfect."

"But she still doesn't like me," Addie pointed out. "She's been ignoring me since the picnic. Do you really think it's a good idea for me to… push myself on her?"

"Yes," Becky replied promptly. She attempted to heft the bowl.

"Now stop that, you," Lydia insisted. "Tend the sausage and don't you dare lift anything heavy." She retrieved the batter and began ladling it into waiting skillets. "To answer your question, Addie, kill her with kindness. Allison isn't herself these days."

"So everyone keeps telling me. What is she like normally?" Addie demanded. No pan remained for the bacon, so she set it aside.

"Blunt, but not mean," Lydia said. "I hope you're not easily offended by cursing."

"Not a bit," Addie replied. "I've been known to let one escape now and again myself."

Lydia met Becky's eyes and found an expression matching her own. *They're just alike. They'll either become friends or hate each other.*

"Ladies, the folks out here are getting restless." James' voice cut through the clatter in the kitchen. "Any idea when the food will be ready?"

The bubbles on the tops of the pancakes had begun to set. Lydia started flipping them over. "Just a few minutes," she replied.

"Good," James replied. "You've got a line halfway down the street."

Lydia rolled her eyes. *Of course we do. Free food always draws a crowd.*

"Would you get out of here?" Jesse urged. "I promise, Sheriff, I have things under control. I'll run and get you if anything happens."

"Whippersnapper," Dylan muttered under his breath.

Jesse grinned, showing white, straight teeth. "Don't you think you've kept your lady waiting long enough? Go get her. Walk around and give Ilse and her cronies something to gossip about."

"It's not like we're keeping things a secret," Dylan replied.

"Nope, you're officially a courting, betrothed couple, and not a moment too soon. Now get moving."

Muttering and grinning, Dylan left Jesse standing under one of the few large trees at the edge of town, where he could watch the impromptu goings-on while remaining in the shade. Once again, the weather had turned hot, and a stale, gusty breeze teased the revelers. Skirts flew, revealing ankles clad in sturdy boots. Hats sailed away into the waving grass and disappeared.

The wind blew a ribbon of dirt into the mouth of a toddler who had opened in anticipation of a huge bite of his peach ice cream. The paper cone dropped from his chubby hand. He shrieked and began to wail. His mother regarded the mess with a sour expression, then scooped the little boy onto her hip and carried him away.

Dylan stepped out from under the tree and scanned the crowd. He couldn't see any strangers, anyone behaving in a suspicious manner at all. He edged past the milling throngs of revelers, intent on the ice cream booth.

Screams of laughter drew his attention to the left, where a crew of partygoers flailed and tipped over, tripping over burlap potato sacks as they hopped toward a yellow ribbon, intent on the prize.

At the kissing booth, Ilse Jackson reigned supreme, subjecting her friends to pimply-faced lads while she looked on, untouched and smirking. He shook his head.

He continued moving forward until he reached a table set up under a makeshift awning of hastily-stitched fabric remnants stretched over some left-over lumber.

Kristina turned the crank on the churn that kept the mixture of cream, honey and fruit rolling in a tumbler surrounded by ice. Addie sat in the shade, fanning herself with a piece of folded paper.

Lydia collected coins from her customers and allowed them to select paper cones, each with a scoop of the sweet confection inside. In the heat, ice cream melted quickly, running down chins to spot dresses and dribble onto trousers. No one seemed to mind.

"Miss Lydia," he said, drawing her attention away from the line. Her eyes met his and they both smiled.

"Sheriff," she murmured with a demure lowering of her eyelids.

"Oh my Lord," Addie complained, rolling her eyes in mock disgust. "The pigeons are cooing. I think I'll be sick. You two are sweeter than molasses candy and twice as gooey."

"If Jesse was here, we'd be saying the same thing about you," Kristina reminded her with equally false sternness.

"Let's see how calm Kristina remains when Cody comes around," Becky commented, approaching from the other side, one hand on her belly. "So, is that all the teasing you ladies had in mind? If so, I think we should send Lydia on her way."

"Yes, Mother." Addie rolled her eyes again. The ladies regarded one another for a long, silent moment, and then as one dissolves into giggles. Dylan couldn't help but smile along with them. *Looks like Jesse's lady has found her place already. Well, good. I suspect he lives and dies by her say-so. If she was unhappy, he'd leave. I don't want him to leave. He's a good kid, and good at his job.*

Dylan extended his hand to Lydia. She rose, handed her paper cones to Becky, and left the table area. Accepting Dylan's offer, they laced their fingers together and walked back into the crowd.

"She's so in love, she didn't even say goodbye." Addie's final teasing shot produced gales of laughter from the women.

Lydia's tawny cheeks turned pink, but only slightly. Clearly, their shenanigans didn't upset her. Instead, her hand remained tight in Dylan's, seemingly preferring, as he did, skin to skin contact over the more proper arm-in-arm escort. Her touch fired his blood as always. He angled a look in her direction and wanted to groan. Her dress skimmed over her ripe, luscious curves, hinting at the soft, soft flesh underneath. *The day is fast approaching when I can uncover and explore those curves. I can hardly wait.* His sex agreed, rising to the occasion with a painful throb. The rigid fabric of his jeans fought its expansion, leaving him aching.

"Darlin', when did you want to get married?" he asked gruffly. *I hope I can survive until the wedding.*

"Oh, I think mid-October should be enough time," she replied.

Six weeks. Wonderful. Definitely a risk of life and limb… well, one limb.

"Are you in a hurry?" Lydia asked, eyeing him curiously.

"Desperately," he replied in an undertone. "I love you, Lydia. You know that, but, at least for men, love has a physical component that doesn't like to be denied."

"Yes, I know," she replied. "The difficult part for women is knowing the difference between a man who wants to show his love with his body and a man who wants to indulge his body without love."

"You do know the difference though, don't you?" he asked.

"I know you're not using me to get your way," she replied. "I'm working on not being nervous about it… but really I think I'm working myself up more." Her cheeks flamed this time.

He looked around to see if their personal conversation in a public place had attracted any notice. No one seemed to be listening, so he returned his attention to Lydia and noted a considering expression on her face. *I wonder what my lady is thinking.*

She didn't expound, and they dropped the uncomfortable conversation for a more appropriate time, instead taking in the Founder's Day festivities. The sack race ended, and groups of people plunked into the grass, tying their ankles to each other for the three-legged race.

"Want to try?" Dylan asked.

Lydia made a face. "I'm far too clumsy for that. I'd probably break my leg, and yours too."

He chuckled. "I'll take that as a no. All right then. Do you feel like watching or moving on?"

"I vote for moving on," Lydia replied. "I'm glad people are enjoying the games, but they're not my favorite."

"Well then, my dear, what is your favorite?" he asked.

She slid her gaze to him, and her expression turned warm. "Spending time with you."

Why did I wait so long to claim her? "Shall we walk then? See what we see?"

"Yes, please," Lydia agreed.

It seemed the whole town had turned out for the celebration, even people who rarely left their homes. One elderly woman stood scowling on the edge of the crowd, her cane ready to whack any children that dared come too close.

Dylan led Lydia away from her, not wanting to take any chances. Somehow, the noise and excitement of Founder's Day did not capture Lydia's interests. She subtly shifted their position this way and that until they found themselves walking through town instead.

"Lydia?"

She shrugged. "I don't know. I just would rather spend time with you out here than in all that crowd."

"Alone, together? Woman are you trying to cause a scandal?" he demanded. They stepped out of the sun into the shade of the church's steeple.

"I don't care about scandal," she replied. "I've lived through enough not to worry if a few nosy busybodies tell tales."

"Have a care, darlin'," Dylan urged. "If enough people get to whispering, your café might suffer."

Lydia twisted her lips. "Unlikely, but I'll keep it in mind. Besides, we're on a public street. How much actual trouble can we get into?"

"Good point," Dylan conceded.

"We are, however, alone on that street," Lydia continued, taking the opportunity to step close to Dylan and rest her head on his shoulder.

He conceded with an amused grin, despite the heat, to cuddle his woman. His hands traced lines up and down her back, feeling the muscles developed by years of whisking, lifting heavy objects and pumping water. *I know men who are weaker.* Her strength reassured him. *This woman has made her place in a world that isn't keen to accept her. She can handle whatever comes her way.*

Even as the thought rolled across his mind, his eyes fell once again on the cemetery, on the fresh grave of Wade Charles.

"What?" Lydia demanded, lifting her head and following his gaze to the gravestone. "No, Dylan. Not this again."

"What?" he asked, pretending not to have been caught ruminating.

"At least be honest," she urged. "Listen, I know his death upsets you, and it's no surprise, but, Dylan, you are not responsible. You have to stop feeling guilty about it."

"I should have kept him, safe," he muttered.

Lydia's warm hands connected solidly with his face, not in a slap, but a grab, turning his head away from the visceral reminder of untimely death and back to her warm brown eyes. She looked exasperated. "You can't," she told him. "It's not possible. Dylan, you have to release the idea that you somehow failed him. He died doing what he loved. He died a hero protecting the town."

"He died leaving a wife and four sons," Dylan reminded her.

"I know," Lydia replied, "and it's terribly sad for them, but they're going to be all right, Dylan. Miranda is young and strong. Her family will take care of her until she gets back on her feet. She's not going to starve. She's not going to wither up and die. Women are not fragile flowers, you know. We have a core of steel. Think of the women you know. I realize you'd rather lock us all up in towers to keep us safe, but life isn't like that. We survive. No matter the odds, no matter the pain, we go on, and one day, the sun comes out from behind the clouds and we smile again. Miranda will too."

"Not good enough." Dylan scowled. "His safety was my responsibility."

"You're wrong," Lydia retorted. She sounded angry. "Completely wrong. His safety is the Lord's responsibility. I don't know why his time on this earth was so short, but if you take away God's responsibility and try to put it on yourself, you'll be miserable, and you won't accomplish anything either."

Dylan's eyelids drooped. "What good am I then?" he demanded.

"You help people," she replied. "How many people do you influence to make better choices? How often are you the hand of God to keep the peace and administer justice? It doesn't make you responsible for the whole world."

"I don't think I know how to let go," he muttered.

Lydia's hand left his cheek to slide behind the back of his neck. She pulled him down and claimed his lips.

"We have to stop sparking in public," he commented against her mouth. Then, in opposition to his words, he deepened the kiss, teasing her lips with the tip of his tongue.

Lydia sucked in her breath. "Come with me," she urged. Dropping her hold on his neck, she grasped his hand and led him back down the street toward her café, dragging them inside.

"Privacy?" he asked.

She nodded, but he noticed an unusual color staining her round cheeks. Instead of urging him to a seat in one of the café tables, she brought him through the double doors into the kitchen, and then, for the first time, up the stairs to her private apartment above her place of business.

"What are we doing up here?" Dylan demanded, regarding the shabby, cozy furniture. "This is probably not a good idea, Lydia."

"Oh, I think it is," she disagreed. She drew in a deep breath, and her uncorseted chest swelled, drawing his attention to the fullness of her breasts.

A strange hum sounded in his ears. "Lydia?"

"I'm inviting you to my bed, Dylan." She gulped, drawing his attention to her throat, where her pulse throbbed visibly.

"Why?" he demanded. "We're marrying soon. Why jump the gun?"

Lydia grasped Dylan's hand and led him into her bedroom, where she urged him to a seat beside her on the edge of the red crazy quilt that covered her bed. "For a lot of reasons," she said, answering his question. "Because I'm tired of being afraid of my feelings for you and waiting another two months won't help. Also, I think you need to feel more certain of my commitment to you."

"Lydia…"

She laid her fingers over his mouth, and the sweet scent of cinnamon and cream wafted over him. *My woman always smells like something good to eat.* The image of what her suggestion would entail floated up before his eyes; Lydia sprawled naked on the bed, her glorious curves bared to his perusal, to his touch. He would cover her body and… He shook off the image, but not before his sex could react to it. He grasped her hand and laid it on his knee.

"Our town is under siege, Dylan," she reminded him. "We might pretend everything is okay, but it isn't. Violence has arisen against us, and you're the most likely target. You remind me of that over and over. Wade Charles is dead, and those robbers will be coming after you next. There's no way to avoid the knowledge." Her eyes had turned sorrowful. "I would survive without you, Dylan, but I don't want any regrets. I hope you survive. I hope we marry and live happily ever after as the strangest couple in town. I hope all those things, but my life has been harder than you know, and I don't have the luxury of self-delusion. If Deputy Charles' death teaches us anything, it's that we don't know when the next breath will be our last. When his wife kissed him goodbye that morning, she didn't know he would never come home."

Ah, that reason. Put that way, what she suggested made perfect sense. *Or am I letting… my other head do the thinking? I want my woman—of course I do—and she's offering herself to me. Do I fight to be noble or do I go along with her request?* He wasn't sure what the correct course of action would be, so he remained still, holding Lydia's hand on his knee, and listened.

She bit her lip and he could see the color rising in her cheeks, as well as the unusual shininess of her dark brown eyes. *She's crying over me and I'm alive and well.* He lifted her hand and kissed her fingertips. The sunlight shining through the window cast rays of gold across her, turning her into a curvy, dark-haired angel.

"Are you sure?" he asked.

She nodded. "I've been thinking about this for a while, but our conversation today clinched it. I don't want to wait anymore."

"If anyone found out…"

"Everyone is at the festival. Did you see the deserted street? No one will know, and in two months it won't matter anyway."

"You're seriously damaging my nobility," he told her, his cheek curving into a half-grin.

"Let me destroy it completely." She leaned forward and claimed his lips, teasing him with the tip of her tongue. "See?" she said. "Every time we kiss, it's easier. It would seem to me that, if we want to have a beautiful wedding night, we get some practice in ahead of time."

"Practice?" Muddled by her kiss and his steadily-growing arousal, he fought to understand. "Do you mean you want to take some liberties, touch and kiss, so we're ready?"

She shook her head. "The whole thing, Dylan." Now her cheeks had turned to vibrant red.

"Do you understand what 'the whole thing' entails?" he demanded, aware of how sheltered virgins could be.

"I know, Dylan. I know it all."

Somehow, he doubted it.

He took stock of the situation. *Lydia, the woman I love, my future wife, wants me to make love to her right now. She understands the risks and implications and she has asked for this.* Some part of him still felt arguing would be wiser, and yet… his libido agreed with his woman.

"What's wrong, Dylan? Do you not want to?" Lydia's face had compressed into lines of worry.

"I do," he replied quickly. "I'm aching for you, darling. I just want to do what's best for you."

"Are we really going to get married?" she demanded.

"Of course," Dylan replied, "but we're not married yet."

"Yes, we are," Lydia replied. "Cody can say some words over us, but will those words really change our commitment to each other?"

"No," Dylan agreed, wondering where she was headed with this.

"Have you known anyone who married but their hearts weren't in it, and it was a disaster?"

"Allison and Wes," Dylan replied promptly.

Lydia made a face. "I think they love each other; they've just lost their way. Hopefully, when Allison is less grumpy, Wes will respond in kind."

"Pregnant ladies get grumpy," Dylan reminded his beloved. "It's uncomfortable and heavy. Usually hot, too. It's up to the man to show forbearance, not his own sour disposition. That never helps."

A tender smile creased Lydia's lips. "I guess you'd know, but we're a bit off-topic. The point is, marriage is made in the heart, not in the church."

"Now that I do agree with," Dylan replied, tugging a loose curl from Lydia's hair, and wrapping the soft strands around his fingertip.

"So while we need to stand up in front of Cody and do it properly, for legality and to observe the rituals and all, I don't think I could feel more committed you to than I do now."

"Make your vow then," Dylan urged. "Let me hear the words."

She looked into his eyes. The slanting sunlight illuminating her face highlighted her luscious skin but also called attention to the tracery of crow's feet in the corners of her eyes.

She's not a kid. She's a mature woman who knows what she wants. We're both old enough not to worry so much about silly rules, and no one is taking advantage. Still, the idea of speaking their promises to each other first made sense to him.

"I take you, Dylan Brody, to be my husband until death do us part." Her voice caught on the word death.

"I take you, Lydia Carré, to be my wife as long as we both shall live."

She smiled. "I like that one better."

"Should we seal it with a kiss?" Dylan suggested.

She nodded. "Oh, I think so, for starters."

They leaned together. For all their vows afforded them no legal status, Dylan could feel their gravity settle around him, as though the world really had changed, and brought him with it. Tenderly he claimed Lydia's lips, his hand cupping her cheek to hold her in place. Not that she needed any persuasion. Her arms around his neck provided another layer of connection between them. *We love each other. We belong to each other, but we're not one yet.* He realized, more strongly than ever, how wrong that felt. *Lying with Lydia won't be wrong. It will be perfect,* he realized. It's what they both needed, for their security, for their relationship. *Cody can legalize it soon, but she's right. He won't make us more married than we already are.*

Dylan eased Lydia back onto the bed and stretched out beside her, leaning up on one elbow before following her down. He claimed her lips again, still gently. *I want you, sweet lady, but I'm going to do this slow and easy.* The idea didn't sit well with his little friend, but he ignored the clamoring ache, intent on giving Lydia an experience she wouldn't soon forget.

Her fingers fluttered in the vicinity of her bosom and she began to release her buttons, one by one. Dylan gently parted the thin white fabric, even as she set to work on his own shirt. Soon the garments hung open, revealing them to each other. Dylan leaned down and lined the straight edge of Lydia's chemise with burning kisses. Her strong, capable fingers slid under his shirt, caressing his shoulders and upper back.

Heat flared between them, blending with their potent tenderness and powerful love to create the perfect sensation. Dylan nudged Lydia's chemise lower with his chin, eager to see the voluptuous breasts he'd been imagining. They more than matched his expectations, full and plump, like tawny pillows, crowned with thick brown peaks that tightened even as he watched, reaching for him as though requesting his touch.

He kissed one, enjoying her startled gasp. *You like that, darling? So much is still to come.* Opening his mouth over the tip of her breast, he shifted to cover her, leaning on his other arm to free his hand to cup and toy with the breast he wasn't devouring.

Lydia sucked in air and released it in a whimper.

"Feel good?" he asked her.

"Hnnnnng," she whimpered.

"That's right," he informed her. "Men and women make love because it feels good. Sure this is still what you want, darlin'?"

Lydia arched her back, thrusting the tempting mounds toward him. He chuckled. *I know you like to be touched, sweet Lydia. I bet it's only nerves that hold you back.* Her intrepidness struck him. *Nervous as any virgin, and yet she wants me to show her, to touch her. She doesn't want to be afraid, and she trusts me to help her past it.* He lifted her breasts and pressed them together, so he could nibble and suck her nipples easily.

She moaned.

"Good, Lydia. That's good. I'm so glad you like this."

"More," she urged, her hips squirming beneath him. "More, Dylan, please. I... I need... I want..."

"I know, darlin'. It burns, doesn't it? But the flame won't hurt you. Passion is meant to be shared, to be enjoyed, with someone who loves you."

He shrugged out of his open shirt and untied the tapes that held her skirt in place, rising to his knees to tug the garment away. Then Dylan stood and regarded his Lydia—his beloved—in her underwear. Only a pair of knee-length bloomers and a thin chemise, lowered to reveal what it was meant to conceal, remained between them.

He unbuckled his belt, opened his jeans, and then sat down on the bed to remove his boots. All the while he kept his eyes fixed on Lydia. She opened her eyes and sat up, releasing her shiny black hair from its hairpins and letting it fall to her shoulders and around her back.

"Oh, darlin'," Dylan murmured at the sight of her, "you look like a Greek goddess or some kind of nature sprite, with your hair loose and your breasts bare."

Her cheeks flamed. Then she reached for the hem of her chemise and drew it over her head. "And now?" she demanded.

Slowly, Dylan's eyes traced every curve from her smooth jaw to her graceful neck, her strong shoulders and thick, muscular arms, developed from years of whipping cream and kneading bread; the muscles covered in a layer of pillowy flesh. Her full breasts swayed as she moved, tempting him back to her arms. Instead, he moved to the end of the bed, unlaced her boots, and dropped them to the floor.

"You look like an angel," he said fervently. "Like everything a man could desire in a woman. Then he crawled up over her body until he could open the tie of her pantaloons. Inside, the roundness of her lower belly provided another cushion just designed to ease a man after a hard day.

I'll make you glad you offered, he vowed silently as he eased the garment over her hips and past her feet, dragging her stockings along. At last, naked together, he stretched out over her body again. She stiffened, but he soothed her with sweet kisses and naughty, enjoyable touches to her breasts, letting his hand sweep low onto her belly, though not quite low enough. *Not yet. Let her ask for it.*

Lydia clung to Dylan's lips, trying to drown her nerves in his sweet kisses. His mustache scratched pleasantly on her face. His fingers on her nipples sent jolts of pleasure straight to the secret place he'd just bared. *Oh, Lord. I'm naked. I'm actually naked in bed with a man. How can this be real? How can I actually be doing this?*

It was one thing to talk—even with embarrassing frankness—to her beloved about intimacy. To be stretched out nude in the bed… *Well, that's an entirely different kettle of fish.* Her body seemed to understand what it wanted, hips arching of their own accord, trying to grind her aching emptiness to that protruding part of him.

"That's it," he encouraged her, his lips moving against hers. "You're doing so well. Sure you want to keep going?"

"If you let me up now, you'll never get this far again," she told him honestly. "Finish it while I still have the nerve."

Dylan made a face. Rolling to the side, he stroked his hand down her body anyway, coming to rest on the nest of springy black curls between her legs.

Lydia squeaked.

"This will only work if you relax and let it. If you fight it, it won't be good for you. I don't want that. I'll stop and we can try another day."

Though her overactive mind wanted to leap at the opportunity to postpone, the heat of his hand sinking into her most sensitive places tempted her body beyond resistance. She wiggled.

"Lydia?"

"Please don't stop."

He chuckled. "Of two minds? Well, let's see which one is stronger."

He massaged the sensitive mound of flesh briefly before delving through to the place where she ached for him. His fingertips dipped between the folds, finding a hidden pool of moisture and spreading it. Lydia bit her lip. The contact felt strange, though she couldn't have said unpleasant. Then she shot bolt upright with a screech. "What in God's name was that?"

She frowned at Dylan, who was laughing softly. "Something good, honey. Something special a woman has to help her enjoy lying with her man. Looks like yours is extra sensitive. Lie back, and I'll show you what heaven is like."

He took her hand and eased her back onto the pillow. His free hand remained between her legs. Lydia took several slow, deep breaths, trying to will her heart to stop pounding, but to no avail.

"Let me kiss you, honey. I know this is intense and strange, but it's how we become as close as two people can be. Remember it's a loving touch. You'll get used to it. Even come to like it, I bet."

"I'm sure," she agreed. *Oh, I do hope he's right. Is this what those poor girls let men do to them? How humiliating. It's uncomfortable enough with someone I love.* "Um, Dylan, about that kiss?"

He laid his lips on hers as his fingers probed again, this time approaching that too-sensitive bundle of nerves from a different direction, one that lessened the intensity to something bearable. All her lady parts seemed to heat and swell at his touch, and warm honey pooled and spread. Strangeness and discomfort slowly gave way to pleasure and eventually to eagerness. As before, Lydia's hips seemed to have a mind of their own, moving in response to his touches, once pushing close, the next moment pulling away. She slipped her arms around his neck and distracted herself with kisses as he prepared her.

Something hot and tight clamped down in her belly, making her clench. Dylan explored that reaction, pushing one finger into her body. His thumb continued strumming as he probed in deep, pulled back, and pushed in.

"Almost there," he rumbled against her lips. "Almost there. Let go, darlin'. Let the pleasure take you."

What does he mean? It does feel like something's building, but wha...uh... "Ohhhhhh!" Lydia sighed as ripples of sensation seemed to spring from the core of her body, locking her muscles and tingling across her skin.

A shift in the balance of the mattress told her Dylan was moving, returning to his position covering her body. Still trapped in a storm of ecstasy, she paid little mind to him moving her legs, opening them wider and kneeling between.

That is, until he grasped her hand and drew it down, wrapping her fingers around something hard and thick. Her eyes flew open.

"Last chance, Lydia. Do we stop for today? You don't have to do everything at once."

She stared at her hand, wrapped around his jutting man-part. It pulsed against her fingers. She squeezed, drawing a groan from the depths of his soul. The sun had shifted, sending shafts of light and shadow across their skin like a tapestry.

"You belong to me, Dylan Brody, heart and soul. I'm ready to add our bodies to the list. Don't stop."

"You know how this works?"

She guided his sex to the opening of her body. "Is this right?"

"Just right." He sighed. "I love you, Lydia."

She fed the tip into her well. *I hope this doesn't hurt too badly.*

He pressed forward another scant inch, embedding himself in her, but not with any depth. She lifted up to meet him, and another inch slid home. He grasped her bottom. "Deep breath," he instructed.

She inhaled and he pushed forward hard. A sharp pinch told her the deed was done. *That's it?* Startled by the lack of expected pain, she relaxed. Dylan hovered over her, weight braced on his elbows and stared down into her eyes. "You all right?"

"Not bad at all," she replied, still stunned that the feared event had proven so easy.

"Good. All right then." He eased back and pushed in again.

Now, this is what I imagined. How did the girls describe it? A dirty old man between your legs, sawing away? Though the description seemed to fit, the actual experience didn't.

The pleasure on Dylan's face as he claimed her body filled her with pride. Perhaps because he was neither dirty nor old, but the man she loved, his thrusting was not a problem, but a pleasure.

Oh, or maybe it actually feels good, she realized. *I'll have to see next time when it's not so new and strange.*

Dylan groaned and a new gush of moisture seemed to signal the end of their first encounter. He relaxed on her, letting her lush body take his weight as she petted his back. *Interesting. Very interesting. I hope we can do this again soon. I think I want to learn more.*

Chapter 8

When Lydia bolted awake at her customary hour, well before dawn, she startled herself by feeling… fine. No discomfort. No regret. *Well, except for being alone when I want Dylan with me.* Here then, was the most compelling reason their marriage had to be sanctioned by church and law. Her man could sleep beside her instead of creeping out into the alley and hoping not to be seen. Stretching, Lydia rose and fumbled across the room to the table in the corner, where she lit a lamp. By its dim and flickering light, she made her way to the wardrobe and retrieved garments, dressing herself mechanically as her mind dwelt on the previous evening.

Once in the kitchen, she hummed to herself as she puttered around the kitchen, shaking flour onto the counter by the light of a lantern, portioning out starter, and then adding eggs and milk she retrieved from the icebox.

"Hoodle dang fol-de-dye-do," she sang aloud, mixing the sticky mixture with her fingertips until it began to come together.

"What a disheartening choice," a soft voice said in her ear. "Can't you sing a happier song that 'Sweet Betsy from Pike'?"

Lydia jumped with a squeal, flinging dough into all the corners of the room. "Dylan, dang nabbit, look what you've done!" she whined.

"Sorry, darlin'," he said sheepishly, wiping a glob from his mustache. "I wasn't trying to scare you, just to say good morning."

"What are you doing up so early?" she wanted to know.

"I haven't gone to bed yet," he replied. By the dim light, Lydia noticed the shadows under his eyes. "After I left here, some folks got into the moonshine and got a bit rowdy. They 'borrowed' some horses and went riding all over the prairie. Took me hours to round them all up. Damned fools."

"Where are they now?" she wanted to know.

"Singing *Danny Boy* in five-part harmony in the jail," he replied, his lips twisting into sour lines. "The lot of them couldn't carry a tune in a bucket."

Lydia rolled her eyes. "You do have the most glamorous job in town, don't you, Dylan?"

"I sure do, Miss Lydia." Then he grabbed her around the waist in an uncouth clutch and planted a wet smooch on her lips. "I'm heading home to bed, and I sure do hope I can sleep, but I wanted to see you on the way through. Are you doing all right?"

Lydia smiled. "Wonderfully. I feel… happy and naughty at the same time. Um, Dylan, how did you get into my shop? It's all locked up."

"You may have locked the café, darlin', but you left the garden gate open."

She squinted at the kitchen door, open to allow a cooling breeze into the sweltering kitchen. Sure enough, the far gate into the alleyway stood ajar.

"Well, I never," Lydia harrumphed, disgusted with herself.

"You never should," Dylan replied, turning serious. "All kinds of riffraff might see that and think it's an invitation. I don't want some dirty farmhand poaching my woman."

"No worries there, honey," she replied. "Anyone comes this way without permission, I have a collection of cast iron skillets and the arms to swing them… and don't even get me started on the knives." *Among other things I'd rather not mention.*

"You're strong and smart," Dylan said, "and I trust you can hold your own, but do be careful, won't you? I love you and now that I have you, I don't want to lose you."

The humor had gone from his voice, and Lydia recalled his sad story about his lost bride and child. *Insensitive, Lydia.* "I promise to be more careful," she vowed, slipping her arms around his neck and pulling him down for a more thorough kiss. Then she smiled against his lips. "Now, if you want to come in through the gate sometime when the café is closed up for the night, but before it gets too late for me, you might work out some kind of signal."

"I'll let you know to expect me, how's that?" he asked. "I'd say starting with tonight."

The thought of Dylan joining her in her bed again caused a flare of eager nervousness to ignite in Lydia's belly. "I think I could find my way to allowing it," she replied, "but only if you get some rest. You look exhausted."

"I am," he agreed. "See you later, darlin'. Maybe around seven, unless something comes up."

"I'll be waiting," she promised.

Dylan fell asleep easily and dreamed of pleasant things he wouldn't quite remember later until a loud pounding at the door shook him from slumber. He sat bolt upright in bed. Shaking off the lingering urge to sleep, he dragged on a pair of jeans he found on the floor and stumbled to the door. He yanked it open to see Jesse West standing on the other side.

"Put your shirt on," the younger man complained. "I don't want to go blind."

"If you don't want to go blind," Dylan quipped back, "keep your hands out of your trousers. You want to see me dressed, wait until I come to work. Don't roust me out of my bed. This had better be good, Mr. 'I can handle everything.' "

"I can," Jesse boasted, stepping over the threshold. Despite his teasing, Dylan noticed his eyes looked tight and the corners of his mouth crimped. "I just thought you might want to know about this." He lifted a sheet of paper and waved it in the air, creating a rustling sound that jarred Dylan's barely-awake ears badly.

"Quit shaking that," he grumped. "I'm getting coffee. Come on." He hobbled toward the kitchen, his feet aching. "So what the hell is so important, West? Did we get another letter?"

"Yeah," Jesse agreed, following Dylan into the tiny kitchen of his two-room home near the edge of town. It seemed the year had finally gotten the message that fall had arrived, as the breeze blowing through the windows had a decided bite to it. *It's about time. It's heading on towards October. Back in Minnesota, we might have snow by now, and frost every night would be no surprise.* Dylan grabbed his kettle and stuck it into the sink, pumping the handle until a chilly stream poured over his hand, most of it landing inside the metal receptacle.

"The letter is postmarked Colorado again," Jesse said, "but the content disturbs me."

"How so?" Dylan moved the two steps to the stove, set the kettle on the burner and opened the firebox to poke at the coals. They flared to red, so he added another bit of fuel and made his way to his kitchen table, where Jesse sat, elbows on the red plaid tablecloth, glaring at the message in his hands.

"It asks whether we enjoyed our Founder's Day celebration."

Dylan lowered his eyebrows. "That was yesterday. How the hell…?"

"Damned if I know," Jesse replied. "It's crazy. How could this even have happened?" He paused, tapping his lips again, his sign of deep thought. "Do you really think the robbers are holed up in Colorado? Wouldn't that be a little obvious?"

Dylan considered the idea. "But if they're not, why are the letters postmarked from there?"

Jesse scratched his head. "Mail travels. If the letters were sent to Pueblo from somewhere else, and an accomplice received them, they could send it from there. If it was someone local, no one would notice. Especially if it's a bigger city like Pueblo. Who would even pay attention to a local mailing a letter?"

"You might be on to something there, West," Dylan said, startled again by the astute reasoning of his new deputy, "but that gives us a new problem. They could be anywhere."

"Yes." Jesse's face turned grim. "Anywhere we don't want them to be."

"It's not a good sign," Dylan agreed. "At the very least, there's one operative here in town keeping the gang informed. At worst…"

"The gang is here, or at least nearby, and there's only one operative in Colorado receiving messages and sending them back here."

"Or some combination thereof."

The younger man nodded. "Here I thought bringing my wife home would keep her safe from the life I used to lead. Looks like we're no better off."

"Well, except, there's safety in numbers. A whole lot of people live in this town. Even if half of them are women and children, every man will fight to protect it. There's no way the gang can take the whole town."

"I know," Jesse agreed. "Even Billy Fulton would take up a gun if Miss Lydia or Miss Esther were threatened., but I'm not worried so much about the town as about what their next move will be. This is a taunt. They're teasing us, letting us know they're close by. In order for us to have this letter now, they must have sent it no more than a week ago. The details here…" he pointed to the paper, "were finalized at the meeting last Sunday, or so my wife tells me."

"So they're letting us know they're nearby," Dylan said grimly.

Jesse nodded with a frown. "They wouldn't take that risk unless they felt relatively secure, which means they must have more members, enough to cause a problem, and that means they're probably planning another strike. Remind me again what actual actions they've taken against Garden?"

"I wouldn't say the train robberies themselves," Dylan replied, thinking out loud. "That was their original mission, and they hit several between Colorado and Wichita."

"Right. How did they decide to focus on a town again, instead of going after more trains? That doesn't seem very lucrative."

"I'm pretty sure it's personal," Dylan replied, sucking in a lungful of air and releasing it in a noisy whoosh. Rising, he dumped a serving of coffee grounds into the press and poured water over it.

"Lay it out for me," Jesse said. "Yes, I've heard it before, but you never know when a retelling will provide something important."

"All right." Dylan splashed the strong, black brew into a blue-speckled tin cup and made his way back to the table. "When they hit the Wichita run back in December, Cody and Kristina were on the train. They somehow managed to distract the robbers and sneak a few people off, one of whom stole one of the robber's horses and rode back to town to get help. When we got there, we drove off the band. A few died, including one in the car with Cody and Kristina, and for some reason Kristina's brother Calvin. They rounded up a second, a young man, whom we took into custody. He was tried for murder and executed."

Jesse sat in silence, his face grim as the images seemed to be flashing inside his head.

"There was an incident mid-spring before you arrived. Some unknown person firebombed Rebecca Heitschmidt's dress shop and nearly killed her, but it was a diversion. He attempted to break the kid out of the jail. I stopped him, but he threatened the town."

"Okay, and I arrived not too long after that," Jesse said, putting things together.

"Couple months after," Dylan agreed, "but by that time the violence had tapered down to threatening, impersonal notes. Also, don't forget, the kid was hung before you got here. I was expecting major violence around that, but nothing happened."

"And I suspect that's because I rounded up the nest."

"Your guess does fit, which means the gang had severely reduced numbers, but that the ones left were probably still around here."

"Right." Jesse frowned. "So then, they've been nearby all along, watching us, and the boss, who has a personal vendetta against you, joined them after the roundup in Colorado."

"Yeah, well," Dylan realized, "if the boss figures out you're the one who broke up his gang, he's going to be gunning for you as well."

"Damn, this is bad," Jesse said. "What should our plan of action be? I don't like sitting here waiting. We know they're nearby. We need to find them before they come after us."

"I agree," Dylan said. "I wonder if we can take them before they decide to strike again?"

"Maybe send a telegram to Pueblo law enforcement," Jesse suggested. "See if they can figure out who's sending the letters. Press them for information. I know the sheriff over there. I can do it."

Now why on God's green earth didn't I think of that ages ago? I must be losing my touch! Sulking, Dylan mumbled, "That would be a big help, Jesse. Be my guest."

Jesse nodded. "Right away." He hopped from the kitchen chair, then turned back. "Dylan, keep your eyes open. I have an itchy feeling. Something's about to happen, and it's not going to be good."

"I feel it too," he agreed. "I'm glad you're here, Jesse. We all need to stay on our toes. Let's call in Rob and every able-bodied man in town and give them the information. We should all be on our guard."

"Agreed," Jesse said, a second before the door banged shut behind him.

Lydia scurried around the dining room, setting plates of eggs and toast in front of hungry diners. The train had arrived about an hour ago, and her café teemed with strangers. Locals slurped coffee and chatted while harried passengers eyed the door, silently urging her to hurry.

Lydia couldn't help smiling. *All feels right with the world today. I'm happy.* She served plate after plate of food, but her mind lingered on Dylan. On their relationship, the intimacy they'd shared. Their upcoming marriage. *I think I can make sugar leaves and color them with beet and carrot juice, and use them to decorate our wedding cake,* she thought.

A hand closed around her wrist, nearly knocking her off balance. She drew up short, frowning over a plate at the man she'd noticed before. "Can I help you, Mister?" she asked. "Did you need more coffee?"

"I would like to speak with you privately, Miss Carré," he said, his tone brooking no argument.

Lydia twisted her lips. "I'm busy, Mr...."

"Blaylock," he reminded her. "Samuel Blaylock. If you wouldn't mind, Miss Carré, this is important."

"Mr. Blaylock," she said, growing colder as he refused to heed her, "the call back to the train is in twenty minutes. These good folks need their breakfast, and then locals have been waiting patiently. Whatever it is will have to wait at least an hour. Now let me go."

She set the plate on the table in front of him and yanked her hand free. *Go starch your mustache, you bossy dandy. I have work to do.*

She stormed away, ignoring his angry muttering.

Working as fast as she could, Lydia managed to serve all the travelers in time for them to eat and pay before the 'all aboard' sounded. Then she served breakfast to the locals, but her mood had darkened. *Why let one pushy individual spoil the moment?* She asked herself. And yet, something felt wrong.

When the last of the diners wandered out, Lydia sighed as she contemplated the mountain of dishes waiting to be washed before she could begin preparing lunch. A cup of coffee called to her, and yet, the persistent Mr. Blaylock awaited.

"All right, mister," she said, standing out of reach of his grabby hands, and leaning her hip against a rickety chair at a nearby table. Her feet ached. "What did you need?"

Now that he had her undivided attention, the man seemed to deflate a little. He curled his waxed mustache around his fingertips. In the growing autumn chill, the points seemed to hold a bit better. "I... I just wanted to talk to you..."

"So talk," Lydia insisted. "I'm listening." *What's going on with this fellow?*

"Well, it's been a long, long time since I lost my wife, and..."

Oh, dear. That's what I was afraid of. "Sorry, Mister, but let me cut you off right there. I'm engaged to be married, and I'm really happy about it. There's no future here, so don't say another word, please?"

"I can give you a better life than he can," Mr. Blaylock said, his resolve visibly firming.

"You don't even know who he is," Lydia pointed out.

He shrugged. "It doesn't matter. I can provide a better life than anyone in this town—and probably most others. I have a great deal of money and the means to make even more. My wife would never have to lift a finger; that is, unless she felt like cooking something special. All I'd ask in return is to share a bed and provide me with a son. You look like a robust woman. I know you could manage it with no problem. Think of it, Miss Carré. It's every woman's dream."

"I think better might be a relative term," Lydia replied, thinking out loud, even as the pang of the knowledge that she would never bear a child for the man she loved brought a suspicious sting to her eyes. "I chose this life and I love it. I love my work. I love that I own this place and that I keep hungry people fed. I love that the man I'm marrying doesn't want me to give up the life I've built for myself. He affirms me. Sounds to me like you have some wrongheaded ideas about what 'every woman's dream'. I'm not that kind of woman. A richer life isn't necessarily a better one. I'm sorry if that disappoints you, Mr. Blaylock, but I won't lead you on. There's no future here." Lydia took a deep breath, her face heating with embarrassment, but her resolve unwavering.

The man had grown paler. She could hear his molars grinding. "I see," he said. "I see, well… I made my offer."

"You did," Lydia agreed. "I appreciate your interest. Now if you'll excuse me, I have work to do."

Without waiting for a reply, she stalked quickly through the dining room into the kitchen, where she found Esther washing the dishes and Billy wiping them.

"What's for lunch today?" Billy asked.

"Chicken soup," Lydia replied, lifting the lid on a huge pot of stock that had been simmering for hours. She grabbed a long fork from the counter and skewered two chicken carcasses. "I'll shred the meat and put it back in, along with onions, carrots and peas."

"Yummy," Ether said. "I love your soups, and it's the perfect day for it, with the chill in the air."

"Save me some," Billy begged.

"Of course," Lydia replied. "An extra big bowl and some buttered bread, okay, honey?"

He grinned.

Life as usual, and I love it.

Chapter 9

Dylan sank into a chair. With his missive to the men of town, everyone would be on guard against a stranger with a limp, but he wasn't sure they understood the threat. *Hell, I don't even understand it. What will they do next? More letters or something more active and dangerous? Who or what will they target, and when? If only Jesse had gotten a closer look, we might have a decent description at least.* A throbbing behind Dylan's right eyeball made perfect sense under the circumstances.

Jesse and Rob bustled in, guns hanging from their belts, their expressions grim.

Two stout young men, Dylan thought, looking them over. Jesse, though not tall, stood proud and certain, his eyes shrewd despite the yellow hair and slender physique that made him seem ineffectual. *He's the sort that can get the jump on anyone.* Rob, younger, taller and more muscular, having grown up on a cattle ranch, looked like the brawn of the operation, and he was. *Along with me in the lead, it's hardly enough to keep us all safe.*

"Did you send the telegram?"

Jesse nodded. "The Sheriff of Pueblo promises to look into it and get back to us as soon as possible. He's going to investigate who has been sending letters to here. Maybe he can tell us something."

"It's a start," Dylan replied with a sigh. "I don't know how much we can do without more information other than stay on guard. You might tell your wife, Jesse, to stay close to other people and not be alone too much. Are you two still at the boarding house?"

Jesse shook his head. "We actually managed to get Deputy Charles's house, like you suggested." He frowned. "Right on the outskirts of town. I might ask if she can stay with someone for a while."

"Maybe with Lydia," Dylan suggested. "Safety in numbers and all. Plus, she's right in the middle of town."

"Remember," Rob cut in, "Rebecca Spencer's shop is also right in the middle of town, and so is the jail. Both of them got attacked. No one is safe anywhere. Can your women defend themselves?"

"Addie can," Jesse replied promptly but volunteered no further information. *I wish I knew the answer to that question. Lydia has been alone for a long time. I assume she can, but I don't know for sure.* "I'll go see her and find out."

"Maybe you should just hurry up and marry her, so she doesn't have to sleep alone," Jesse suggested.

"But if I'm a target, wouldn't that make her more vulnerable?" Dylan asked, "Especially when I patrol at night." *Marrying Lydia now sounds good and foolish at the same time.*

"I don't think there's a good solution," Rob said. "Do what you need to."

Dylan nodded. "Okay then. Let's get out of here. Talk to our families and friends. Share whatever you have to, to make people wary. Safety first. Meet back here at nine in the morning. Jesse, you're on duty until ten tonight, and then I relieve you. We'll take turns covering the night until the situation is resolved."

The men all agreed with silent dips of the head. Then Dylan ducked out of the jail and turned left, headed north until he could see the shingle above the café. *I need to talk to her. Find out if she's safe alone at night, and what she wants to do.*

Fall deepened every day. The leaves on the few, stunted and wind-blasted trees flashed red and orange as they flapped in a chilly breeze. The grass on the prairie beyond the edge of town was growing yellow and brittle as winter drew nearer. Still, after the beastly heat of summer, the wistful dying time felt like a relief.

Dylan breathed in the fresh, crisp air and released it. *I wonder if Lydia is done cleaning up from lunch yet… if she can take some time out of her day for me. It feels like I need to hold her.* Though his body reacted to the thought in the obvious way, his heart also ached for the closeness only their lovemaking could bring. *I need my woman.*

He increased the pace, barely glancing around the quiet street before slipping into the alleyway that led to her back-garden gate.

In the hush, the wind whispered in his ear. Thinking of the robber gang, of not knowing where they would next turn up, Dylan realized he had not followed his own advice. His attention focused on getting to Lydia, he'd scarcely noticed the streets around him and had no idea who had been out, what curtains hung open so people could peer into the street, what shutters closed on secrets. "Some lawman you are," he muttered, glad no one had seen his single-minded concentration and lack of awareness.

"You've got that right, Mister Brody," an oily voice spoke into his ear, the sound accompanied by an ominous metallic click.

Lydia finished cleaning up the kitchen. She'd long since sent Esther and Billy home. *I wonder if Dylan will come to see me. I'd like that.* Though she didn't feel quite as enthusiastic about being bedded as she'd hoped, it hadn't been horrible, and all the kissing and touching and the closeness pleased her. *Yes, those were all very nice. I suppose the rest will come in time.* A suspicious tingle told her she might, perhaps, be protesting too much.

Gathering up the basin of dishwater, she stepped out the back door of her kitchen. *Despite the growing cold, it hasn't rained much. Better water the plants. I'll need to bring them inside soon, but the back looks so sad without them.*

The red bricks, which matched the main street of town, had grown dusty and several showed deep cracks. *I'll need to do some repairs in the spring, I see... maybe Dylan can help me.* She poured the warm, sudsy water on the tomato plant, though it probably wouldn't survive another week and had certainly stopped producing. *Keep it alive anyway. It's green still and has a nice, clean smell.*

She moved through the compact space to her grapevines. They hung thick with clusters of fruit. She plucked one and sampled it, smiling at the tart taste. *Another week and they'll be ready for pressing.* She sprinkled the water near the roots and moved on along the fence to the gate, which she unlocked, tucking the key back into the pocket of her apron. It clunked as it fell in.

Wondering if any of her nosier neighbors might be looking into the alley, she eased the gate open. *Maybe this isn't such a good idea. People see Dylan sneaking into my yard, they'll know what mischief we're up to.*

Though she recognized the validity of the thought, it didn't stop her from peeking out, just in case. Her heart and breath stopped as one. A figure in a black coat and hat stood before her, arm outstretched, holding an ugly black shape against the back of Dylan's head. Her beloved seemed frozen, but she could hear his sharp, shallow breaths.

"It had to be you, didn't it," a familiar voice with an eastern twang hissed into the stillness. The prairie wind caught the words and carried them to Lydia's ears. "You took my son and now you've taken my woman as well. It'll be a pleasure to kill you, Brody."

Lydia inhaled deeply, forcing her fears deep, deep down so her surface demeanor became calm, her hands steady. Reaching into her pocket, she slowly drew out a tiny, wood-handled derringer. The sunlight flashed on the shiny barrel, but her adversary didn't seem to notice. *This is one hell of a shot*, she acknowledged, *and I'm out of practice. Good thing they're so close. Lord, please don't let me miss.* She focused her attention solely on the slender, black-coated arm that clutched the black revolver. *I was never your woman, Blaylock*, she thought as she compressed the trigger.

The roar of the pistol drove Dylan to his knees, whether to dodge or because his legs simply gave out, he wasn't sure. He felt no pain, though the loud concussion had left his ears ringing. The stench of gunpowder and smoke filled his nostrils. *Am I numb? It doesn't hurt, but I don't want to die. I haven't had nearly enough time with Lydia, and she's still in danger.*

He breathed deeply, regret gnawing at him as he waited for something to happen. Pain. Unconsciousness. The ground beneath his cheek. But nothing happened. He opened one cautious eye and looked directly into the barrel of a small handgun. A wisp of smoke rose from the muzzle. Behind, framed against the back wall of her house, Lydia stood in the open gate. Dylan blinked and turned to see a black coat flapping as the person wearing it limped quickly between two buildings and disappeared.

He became aware of wetness on the back of his neck and lifted his fingers, then stared at the redness. "Am I shot?"

A sob broke through the ringing in his ears and then a loud clatter. The gun skidded across the bricks lining the alley and came to rest at his knee. Then Lydia hurled herself into his arms.

As Dylan's hearing cleared, his mind remained muddled. "What did you do?"

Lydia shook, sobbing on his shoulder, her two fists clutching his shirt.

He grasped her chin and lifted her face so he could look into her swollen, tear-stained eyes. "Lydia, we're not safe here. Go back inside your house and lock all the doors." He groped for her derringer and pressed it back into her hand. "Reload this. I'll be back." He kissed her lips and then lifted her upright, pushing her back through the gate and shutting it. He heard a fumbling clunk as she locked it.

"Stay under cover," he insisted. "We don't know how many there are or where they might be."

"All right." He could barely distinguish words through her sobs and sniffles, but he recognized the acknowledgment. Her boots clicked on the bricks as she made her way towards the house.

She'll be mad when I come back, but she'll be alive. That's the important part. If we're going to be married, she'll have to get used to coming second to the town's safety.

Pulling his gun from its holster, forcing his reaction down, Dylan raced in the direction he'd seen the criminal go. *With that limp, he won't be able to get far.* By the time he reached the aperture between the Spencer home and their neighbors, the Millers, no movement betrayed a person passing through or hiding. He crept past the large, white home, keeping his eyes glued on the unoccupied house next door. *This would be a great hiding place.* He dragged his hat off and peeked through the window to see a room filled with furniture covered in sheets. No footprints marred the dust lying thick on the wood floor. *I hope the Millers come home soon. This house has been empty too long.*

Carefully skirting the structure, he crept onto the porch and checked the door. Locked, and none of the filthy windows had been broken. *Seems secure. Now what?*

He scanned the street. To the right, a few more houses grew wider and wider apart, until, just past the Wests' new home, the town gave way to open prairie.

To the right, Lydia's shingle flapped and clattered in the unending Kansas wind. Further south, the hotel's towering height and the church's tall steeple cast shadows over the street. He could barely make out the train station at the far end of town.

A few people milled around in the street, hurrying from one building to another, clutching coats and hats against the cold. No one seemed disturbed in the slightest. Dylan grabbed the arm of a man whose upturned collar rendered him anonymous. The head turned to reveal the flat face of Billy Fulton. *Thank goodness.* "Billy, have you seen any strangers around here?" Dylan asked.

Billy seemed to chew on the question—or maybe his tongue—until Dylan felt like dancing in place. "Yes, suh," he said at last. "Black coat and hat?"

"Yes, Billy," Dylan replied, trying to stay calm. *He saw him. Thank you, Lord.*

"He went that way." Billy pointed north, toward the edge of town. Dylan scanned the horizon but saw nothing. *I'd better get help.*

"Thank you, Billy. That was really important information. Now, can you go look after Miss Lydia? A bad man came far too close to her."

Billy nodded grimly, seeming to understand the gravity of the situation, and hurried down the street toward the café.

"Well, shoot," Dylan muttered, turning away from his quarry and back toward the jail. "He was too close. Much too close. Who was that guy anyway? He seems familiar, but I can't place him. Of course, in this town that alone should be warning enough. And what on earth was he talking about, stole his woman? I haven't stolen anything."

"Of course you haven't."

Dylan started violently, surprised to find himself facing the desk inside the jail building, staring at Jesse's smirking face.

"If you stole something, Sheriff, I'd have to arrest you."

Dylan lowered his eyebrows. Then he sank into a chair, his knees no longer willing to hold him. "He's here. He got the jump on me. My number was almost up, West."

Jesse's grin faded. "Who?"

"The boss. He caught up with me outside Lydia's. If she hadn't pulled her derringer, you'd be finding my body come morning."

"The hell you say? Lydia shot him?" Jesse shot up from the chair.

Dylan dipped his chin. "I think so." He touched the tacky spot on his neck. "This blood isn't mine. She ran him off. Billy Fulton saw him heading north. Walks with a limp, he said. An old guy like that wouldn't be running robberies."

"Right. Behind the scenes. A limp, you say? Then maybe he is the same one I met up with in Colorado. He had a limp. Needed help walking, even."

"Maybe he has an injury?" Dylan speculated. "Maybe it's partially healed?" *How the hell would Jesse or anyone know the answer to that? Stop babbling, man.*

"Could be so," Jesse agreed, scratching the golden stubble on his chin.

"What's to the north?" Dylan asked. "Isn't it just open prairie?"

"Jesse! Jesse!" The door burst open and Rob pounded into the room, waving a scrap of paper in the air. He noticed Dylan and pulled up short. "Sheriff. Sorry."

"Don't be," Dylan assured him. He considered standing, but his knees assured him such a move would not be appreciated or successful, so he turned the chair around. "I was about to send Jesse to look for you. What do you have there?"

"The reply to Jesse's telegram," Rob replied. Despite being well over six feet, broad-shouldered and muscle-bound, Rob's demeanor revealed his barely twenty years. *He's just a kid. He shouldn't be here. Of course, I was no older when I started. Hope I don't have to bury him.*

"What does it say?" Jesse demanded, circling the desk and leaning against the far wall, below the tiny, barred window, so the three men formed a triangle. "Read it to us, Rob. Let's hear together."

The boy raked his fingers through his dark hair and opened the missive. "It's long. Says the sheriff of Pueblo found out who was sending the letters. A widow woman. She'd been keeping company with an older fellow, a stranger who'd taken up residence in the town. He hasn't been seen in weeks. According to the grocer, she'd been receiving letters postmarked from Garden City and sometimes Dodge City for quite some time, and then returning the next day or even later the same day and sending letters addressed to you."

"So she's just passing the message on?" Dylan surmised. "That fits." He frowned.

"That's not good," Jesse added. "Sounds like she's the only one there, which means whoever is left—not to mention whoever they've recruited since then—is somewhere else. Bet your boots they're nearby."

"I'd agree with the whole operation being nearby. Do they have the name of the older fellow?" Dylan asked.

Rob ran his fingers down the paper. "Sam Bly," he said, stabbing at the paper. It tore under his finger. He blushed. "Sorry."

"Easy, son," Dylan urged. "Okay, so we have a name, though I don't know any Bly. Do you?"

Both Rob and Jesse lifted their shoulders.

"And we know they're here. Bly must be the boss. He's also probably the man who just tried to shoot me."

"Sheriff, what?" Rob stared, aghast, looking younger than ever.

Hero worship. Damn it, kid, don't look at me like that. We're a team here. "I had a run-in with Mr. Bly outside Lydia's café. He pulled a gun on me. If Lydia hadn't intervened, I'd be dead now."

"What?" Rob's face twisted in consternation. "Lydia saved you?"

Dylan nodded. "Never underestimate a woman, son. They're a lot stronger than any of us knows when they're riled up. I'm not going to swear on it, but I think she might have shot the gun out of his hand... while he held it up to my head. It was a one in a million shot, and she succeeded. Not sure I could have done it."

"Oh, God. They're in love." The youth rolled his eyes toward heaven.

"It'll happen to you too if you live long enough," Jesse pointed out, though the barely suppressed smile lingering in the corners of his mouth conjured images of a pretty, pregnant auburn-haired firecracker of a woman, "and it's not bad. It's the reason we do this. Gotta keep the womenfolk safe."

"Except when they're keeping us safe," Dylan pointed out. "Now that doesn't go beyond these doors, gentlemen. You hear? They might insist I deputize her, and then who would bake the pies?"

They looked at one another and burst into laughter, chasing away the tension.

"So, did you get a look at the guy?" Rob asked, holding his guts as weak chuckles tried to escape.

"Sadly, no." Dylan wiped his eyes and combed his mustache with his fingertips. "He came up behind me, and I have to admit I was distracted. He was wearing a black duster and hat. Billy Fulton saw him running north. I was just asking Jesse what lies to the north because I don't recall anything."

"There are a few abandoned homesteads," Jesse said, thinking aloud, "a grain silo, some cattle grazing land. Not much. No cover to speak of."

"Right," Rob confirmed. "There are cities in all directions if you go far enough. Dodge is closest, though not that close. Liberal to the south, and a few farms to the east, but to the north… nothing but prairie until you hit the Nebraska border, and even then, it's not much. I heard you can go clear into Canada without running into a city."

Seeming to realize at last that he was babbling, Rob shut his mouth with a snap.

Jesse narrowed his eyes, not at Rob's words, but as though he'd thought of something.

"What's going on, Jesse?" Dylan asked. "What are you thinking?"

"There's one possible place, northeast of town. A pretty big soddie. I used to play in it as a kid. Kristina, Allison and Wesley would remember. We used to play sheriff and robbers in there. The structure is half underground and really overgrown. You have to know where it is to see it, and there were the remains of a barn too, as I recall. A small operation might set up camp there if they don't mind living rough."

"How small?" Dylan wanted to know. "How many people could hide out there?"

The sharp focus in Jesse's eyes faded until he seemed to be studying something Dylan couldn't see. "Eight or ten, maybe. Not much more than that, unless they set up camp in tents. Trouble is, there's really no way to scout it out. The grass is too brittle and noisy this time of year, and there's no elevation to get a bird's eye view. The only way to get to them would be a full-on attack, which would look awfully silly if there turned out to be no one there."

"I'll risk it," Dylan said grimly. "These bastards have been a thorn in our flesh too long."

"Agreed," Rob added. "They made it personal, but we're going to win."

"Let's think through this," Dylan urged. "If we're going to put together a posse and go against them, we need to know as much as possible. Damn it, I wish I had more to go on."

Jesse began thinking aloud. "They'd have to send someone into town for supplies and to mail letters. We have too damned many strangers running through this town every day. Do you recall anyone new?"

Dylan shook his head. "I can't think of anyone. Can you, Rob?"

"Not really, boss," the kid said, scratching his head. "Have you asked your lady?"

Both Dylan and Jesse turned to him. "What?" Dylan demanded.

"Well, she saw him. She shot him. Ask her if he seemed familiar."

Dylan turned blinking eyes on Jesse, whose jaw hung agape.

"Kid, you're a genius. Okay, can the two of you cover things for a while? I didn't leave things too well with Lydia. Before she drops me like a hot rock, I should probably try to make amends."

"No problem," Rob agreed, his face glowing over the compliment he'd received. Jesse nodded, a knowing grin on his face.

Dylan glowered menacingly at the younger deputy. "Whippersnapper," he muttered under his breath.

Jesse poked out his cheek with his tongue but didn't say a word.

Lydia regarded her companion with a raised eyebrow. "Sure you don't want to run on home, Billy?" she asked.

"Sherriff Brody told me to watch over you," Billy explained, sipping coffee from a tin mug.

Dylan, seriously. "I know, Billy. He's very protective, but I promise I can watch over myself."

"He loves you." Billy sat back in his chair.

Lydia's lips twisted to one side. *Do I have to melt a little at each reminder? I understand locking up and hunkering down, but Billy's a gentle soul. I'm as likely to need to watch over him as he is over me.* She regarded the young man as he began to crumble the crust on a slice of apple pie. *I hope Dylan shows up to relieve him of duty soon. Four years of employment, and suddenly my instructions no longer hold water. Men and their conspiracies.*

Lydia sighed. Exhaustion caused a faint trembling in her fingers. She desperately wanted to rest, but with Billy here, that had become impossible. *Doubt I'd sleep anyway.* The image of her beloved Dylan, a gun pointed at his head, would haunt her forever. *My bullet hit far too close. If he'd twitched, I would have been the one who shot him.* She set her rag on the counter and made her way to a wobbly chair, sinking onto it and helplessly replaying the terrifying moments over and over.

"Sheriff Brody! Sheriff Brody!" A female voice interrupted Dylan's thoughts as he made his way back to Lydia's café.

Damn it, man, wake up! Shaking off the myriad thoughts crowding his brain, he paused to regard Ilse Jackson sailing in his direction, her skirt billowing in the wind. Her friend Mary trotted along beside her.

Oh, Lord. What now? "Can I help you, Miss Jackson?" he asked, striving for graciousness.

"Sheriff Brody," she panted, scurrying up to him and laying a strategic hand on the swell of her bodice. Her fingers fluttered.

I wonder if she even realizes she's doing that. Flirting seems to come to her as naturally as breathing. "Yes, Miss Jackson," he said. *Hurry up. I have more important things to do than deal with you.*

She drew herself up to her full height and regarded him closely, waving a sheet a paper in her face. "The women of the town have created and signed a petition, one that we insist you look at right away."

With a sigh, Dylan grasped the sheet and removed it from her, then scowled as he read the title. "Miss Jackson, my task is to keep this town safe, not to interfere with the running of a legitimate and legal place of business. Sorry, but this means nothing to me." His eyes scanned down the page, taking in the name of nearly every wife and daughter in the town. "I suggest you call a town meeting. Now if you'll excuse me…"

"Sheriff Brody," she snapped, "the saloon threatens the safety of this town far more than any train robbers. It undermines families from within, with the temptations of drink and loose women. Even if a few people are picked off, the town itself would remain intact regardless of train robbers."

Dylan stared at the woman. *Ignorant little featherbrain.* "You couldn't be more wrong," he told her bluntly, "but I'm not taking the time to explain it. Drop off your petition at the mayor's office and see if your father wants it or call a meeting. Whatever you like. I'm not involved in it."

Dropping the paper in the street, he hurried on his way, ignoring her muttering.

Arriving at the door of the café, he knocked. A flash of color appeared at the window, and then he heard a skirt rustling behind the door a moment before it flew open, leaving him face to face with his woman. *She doesn't look happy.*

"Can you please come in and tell Billy to go home?" she requested. "He won't leave until you say so."

"Oh, sure. Sorry."

Lydia moved aside and Dylan stepped over the threshold, seeing the object of their conversation seated at the table, his face in a cup of coffee. "Finish up, please, Billy," Dylan urged. "I'm here now and I need to talk to Miss Lydia."

"Alone?" The young man smirked. "Okay. I took good care of her, Sheriff."

"Thank you, Billy, I can see that."

Billy gulped his coffee and shoved a piece of pie into his mouth before scooting for the door, giggling.

Lydia turned the key in the lock, regarding Dylan with a sour expression. "Was that really necessary? Didn't I just prove to you I can handle myself?"

Oops. "Sorry, honey. It was an impulse. Safety in numbers and all that."

Lydia rolled her eyes.

"Are you angry with me?" Dylan asked, schooling his expression to deep contrition.

Lydia's laugh sounded exasperated. "You don't look like a little boy, so stop making that face."

"What, this?" He blinked repeatedly.

She swatted his arm. "Silly man." Then she sighed. "Once I had a chance to settle down and think, I understood everything you needed to do, other than sending Billy in here. I'm not a dunce, Dylan. You're the sheriff. Of course, you have to protect the town, and of course that comes first. I would have preferred to blubber in your arms a bit longer, but I understood. Did you manage to catch Blaylock?"

Her words brought him up short. "What did you say?"

"Weren't you listening?" she demanded. "I said I understand…"

"No," Dylan interrupted, clamping his hand down on her shoulder. "The name, Lydia. Did you know that man?"

Her dark eyes widened. "He introduced himself to me as Samuel Blaylock. Older gentleman with silver hair and a starched mustache. Walks with a limp. He's been in town for a few months. Told me he was setting up a business here."

Dylan scowled. "Yes. The business of mayhem. Blaylock, eh? Same as that kid we executed."

"So he really was his father?" Lydia's knees wobbled, but she stiffened them.

"Looks like it. How do you know so much about him?"

She bit her lip. "He's eaten here a few times. Most recently he implied that he wanted a relationship with me. Of course, I turned him down. Not only am I already taken," she grasped Dylan's hand in hers, drawing it off her shoulder and lacing their fingers together, "but he was far too bossy and forceful for me. You know how independent I am."

Dylan nodded. "I love that about you."

"And that's why I love you," she replied.

He tugged her against his chest, smiling to himself when her arms slid around his neck. He rested his chin on her soft, dark hair. "Blaylock, eh? He called himself Sam Bly in Pueblo. I can't believe he told you his real name. What an arrogant bastard."

"He's taunting us all," Lydia pointed out. "Thinks we're a bunch of dumb country folk."

"Well, Jesse thinks he knows where the lair is. We'll be rounding up a posse as soon as we finish our plan of action. Can you describe Sam Blaylock to the posse? One thing we don't want is for him to get away."

"Of course," Lydia insisted. "I'll help any way I can. I came too close to losing you, Dylan."

Her arms tightened.

"You saved me," he admitted. Bending his head, he kissed her hair. "Did you really shoot the gun out of his hand?"

She shook her head under his chin. "I couldn't. It was too close to you. I shot him in the vicinity of the elbow. I knew he wouldn't be able to hold the gun or squeeze the trigger."

"Ah. What a shot though."

She shrugged it off. "I was lucky. I wasn't more than ten paces away. Good thing I've oiled the gate hinges recently. He didn't know I was there."

"It was still a great shot. I'm impressed, Lydia. How did you know how to do that?"

Lydia pulled back in the circle of his arms. "No, Dylan. I don't want to tell stories right now. You took care of your business, and you'll be riding into harm's way far too soon. Right now, you owe me. Come here."

She tugged on the back of his neck.

He met her lips in a kiss of aching tenderness. Lydia would have none of it. She mashed her mouth against him, slipping her tongue inside to tangle with his.

Passion flared in Dylan. The memory of how close he'd come to death, the fear he'd suppressed, the regret, all awakened in him, bringing with it a fire than threatened to consume him. *Lydia is like air. I can't live a minute without her.* His lips gentled on hers, maintaining the kiss but reducing the force.

Lydia wanted none of his gentleness. Her fingers worked the buttons on his shirt and slipped inside, touching his skin.

"I was so afraid," she murmured against his mouth. "I thought I was going to watch you die."

"Instead you saved me." He cupped her face in his hand.

"Dylan, I..." what she was going to say disappeared as he claimed her mouth again, slowly walking her backward toward the kitchen door. *The planning will have to wait. Right now, I need my woman and she needs me. This is the reason we have to fight.*

She reached behind her to manipulate the knob. The door opened. The stairs to her apartment waited just across the room, but they didn't make it that far.

Once out of sight of the big, plate glass windows that overlooked the street, the passion simmering between them suddenly boiled over.

Dylan backed Lydia against the wall, his hands lacing into her hair. Pins sprang loose and sprinkled unnoticed onto the floor. He felt Lydia's hands inside his shirt again, caressing his skin. She thumbed his nipples, sending a riot of tingles through his body.

Oho, my love. Two can play that game. He grasped the front of her shirt-waist and yanked, sending a shower of buttons to lie forgotten among the hairpins. Quick as a flash he unfastened her skirt, which left her clad only in a thin chemise and pantalets. Wanting to take in the sight of her bare body, he released her mouth and lifted the chemise over her head. "Ah, Lydia," he breathed, reverently running one hand over her plump breast. She bit her lip, her cheek darkening. *She's still so new to this, not used to undressing for her man.* He reached her nipple and bestowed a naughty pinch on the sensitive nub.

Lydia sucked in a breath.

"Do you want this, love? Do you want to make love again?" he asked.

She stepped close to him and boldly clasped his hand, dragging it inside her pantalets. "I'm aching for you, Dylan," she told him. "I need to feel you're real, every bit of you; that you didn't die and I'm dreaming this moment."

"I'm alive, Lydia," he reminded her, slipping his fingers between the folds to find her wet and swollen. "I'm alive and really here with you."

Her breath caught on a sob as he pushed two fingertips into her well, but inside the tight confines of her undergarment, he couldn't maneuver enough to accomplish anything more interesting.

"Why don't you take this off, honey," he suggested.

"Will you undress also?" she wanted to know.

He began unbuttoning his shirt. "Oh, yes. Yes, in a moment we'll be bare and pleasuring each other."

Lydia bit her lip and propped one foot up on a chair.

Dylan chuckled. In his hurry to touch her, he'd forgotten she still had her boots on.

They undressed quickly. Dylan raced through his buttons and ties, easily removing his clothing while Lydia struggled with a knot in the string that held her bloomers on. He reached out to her in time to slide the white fabric over the smooth curve of her bottom. She stepped free.

"Put your foot back up on the chair," he ordered.

She blinked. "Dylan?"

"Trust me, honey, you're going to like this."

Her face a mask of uncertainty, she raised one foot and braced her hand on the table. The move left her secret places exposed to his perusal... to his touch.

"Good girl. Stay just like that." Dylan stepped close and wrapped one arm around Lydia's waist, claiming her lips in a sweet, tender kiss. In contrast, the fingers of his free hand performed a wicked dance against her barely-tried sex.

Lydia moaned as he stroked, spreading her passion liquid over every fold of flesh. *Now easy does it,* he reminded himself as the approached the swell of her clitoris. *She's so sensitive.* With gentle care, he manipulated the tender bud.

He released her lips and lowered his mouth to capture the peak of one breast, rolling his eyes upward to take in Lydia's gaze on them. He made a great show of licking her nipple even as he slid two fingers back deep inside her. Now that the encumbrance of her garments no longer interfered, he could fill her completely, stretching her sex to prepare her for their joining.

"Oh, Dylan," Lydia moaned, her eyes locked on him.

"Like that, honey?" he asked.

She didn't respond, but the surge of wetness against his fingers told him everything he needed to know.

Feeling adventurous, he slowly kissed his way down her belly.

She drew in a slow, unsteady lungful of air as he approached his destination, but offered no protest. Nudging his fingers deep inside her, he kissed the tender center of her pleasure and then teased it with a swipe of his tongue.

Lydia whimpered, her fingertips scrabbling on the tabletop at the unexpected sensation.

He gave her no mercy, settling in to pleasure her with long licks, slow and gentle but insistent. His fingers eased back and surged in again.

Lydia sobbed and wriggled, her body clenching as her peak neared. A cry of ecstasy broke from her, her muscles locking.

Dylan held on tight with the hand on her back as she shuddered. Dylan eased his fingers from her and gently turned her body, so she had both hands braced, bending her over the table. He urged her to lower her foot so that she knelt with one knee on the chair, while still standing with the other on the floor. *I like that. Keeps her open.*

He'd ignored the insistent ache in his erection until now, but the sight of Lydia's bare bottom, and below it, the glistening pinkness of her womanhood, shattered his will.

"Take me in, darling," he murmured, rubbing his erection against her bottom.

She rocked her hips back in invitation. Dylan grasped his sex and sought her opening. In a single, smooth thrust he pushed fully into her body.

Lydia whimpered.

"Are you all right, darlin'?" he asked. "Do you feel any pain?"

Her dark hair tossed around her shoulders as she shook her head. "It doesn't hurt. It feels intense and... big. A bit overwhelming, but I don't feel any pain."

"Oh, good." He eased back and surged in again. The clenching tightness of her juicy well caressed him with wanton pleasure.

Dylan tried to take his lady slow and easy, but soon his gentle glides gave way to hard, powerful thrusts that rocked her forward and claimed every inch of her for himself.

Lost in the sensation of Lydia's luscious body, he almost didn't notice her reactions; that is, until she squealed, and her body locked down on him. The extra tightness of her second orgasm overwhelmed him, and he exploded with a roar.

Lydia squeaked as Dylan's deflating erection eased out of her. He sank onto the chair and scooped her onto his lap. She rested her head on his shoulder. The wood groaned at their combined weight but held.

Wow, it was different this time. Not just 'nice' but really intense, powerful. Did our crazy circumstances make the difference, or am I adjusting? Probably some of both. She had to admit that the physical connection of sex had been just what she needed to reconnect to the man she loved after such a frightening day.

"Do you have to go again?" she asked wistfully, trailing her fingers down his chest.

"Pretty soon, yes," Dylan admitted. "We need to round up the posse. We think we know where they're hiding, and it's close. Be careful, Lydia." His voice turned grim.

"All right, Dylan. I'll be careful, but you do the same. I don't want to lose you." She slipped her arms around his chest and squeezed him tight.

"I'll do my level best to come home in one piece, but you know I can't make any promises. These are deadly dangerous men and their leader has a personal vendetta against me."

"I know," Lydia admitted. "I'm not pretending otherwise, Dylan."

He shifted and the seat groaned.

"Um, do you think we might continue this upstairs," she suggested. "I don't think this chair will hold us much longer."

Dylan chuckled. "Come on then."

She rose to her feet, startled to discover her knees wobbling. *That was some intense loving.* Grinning, she gathered up her scattered clothes. "If I take this blouse to Becky to fix, she'll know exactly what happened and tease the life of out me."

"She has no stones to throw," Dylan commented.

"She's not offering any," Lydia replied as she mounted the stairs. Dylan ran a proprietary hand over her bare bottom, "but you can't expect her not to tease."

"Jesse would too," Dylan commented. "I'm awfully glad that young man has come to town. He might just make the difference."

"I'm glad to hear it," she said. "I like him a lot. His wife too."

They cleared the landing and proceeded directly to the bedroom. Lydia dumped her pile of fabric on the floor to deal with later and pulled back the sheets on her neatly-made bed. Stretching out naked, she reached for Dylan, and he joined her. She rested her head on his shoulder. He stroked one hand down her body inciting tingles as he brushed against her distended nipple. *I wonder if he's going to want more, once we catch our breath.*

Dylan chuckled quietly.

"What is it?" she asked.

"Oh, nothing. Just thinking of something that happened earlier."

"Tell me." Lydia rolled over and rose up on her elbow, staring down into Dylan's eyes. He toyed with the ends of her hair.

"With everything going on, that little featherbrain Ilse Jackson is bothering me with a petition…"

"To close the whorehouse?" Lydia asked bluntly.

He nodded. "Looked like every woman in town signed it. What I want to know is what you ladies think I can do about it."

"Wait, what?" Lydia crinkled her forehead in consternation. "I didn't sign that garbage. I refused. So did Kristina, Allison and a number of other women. I don't think it would have been more than half." Anger bubbled in Lydia's belly, supplanting languid relaxation and latent desire. "That little...." She snarled. "She must have forged our names. Ooooh, the next time I see her..."

"Whoa, darlin'," Dylan said, stroking her bare skin. "You didn't sign it?"

"Of course not. It's not just stupid, it's cruel. Those poor girls are doing the best they can to get by, but Ilse and her cronies want to take away their livelihood for the sake of their own personal discomfort."

Dylan's face scrunched and he looked lost. "You care that much about the fate of a few prostitutes?"

Lydia bit her lip. "Any one of us could end up like that," she said softly.

"I think there might be more to this story," Dylan guessed. "Care to share?"

Lydia closed her eyes and admitted the truth she had kept to herself for the last five years. *Please don't hate me, my love.* "I used to work in a whorehouse."

Confusion clamped down Dylan's features until he looked like a crumpled and shrunken version of himself. "But... wait, what? ... Lydia..." He stuttered to a halt, took a deep breath and tried again. "I took your virginity. How is that possible?"

"Well, um..." She sucked in a lungful of air and released it in a sigh. "You told me your story. I suppose you'd like to hear mine?"

"Please," he replied.

Lydia considered. *Is this really how I want to be spending my few precious minutes with Dylan? What if something happens to him...?* She realized that if—heaven forbid—Dylan did not return from his mission, she wanted him to know the truth about her. *And choose me anyway. Please, Lord, let it be so.*

"Will you kiss me once, Dylan?" she pleaded. "I'm afraid to tell you this."

"Do you think anything will change how I feel about you, Lydia?" he asked, his consternation resolving into tenderness. "I love you. That won't change, but I do want to know the truth about you."

She nodded. Lowering her face, she claimed his lips once, then settled back into his embrace. "I grew up poor, in a rough neighborhood of Boston. Both my parents were immigrants, my father from France, my mother from Italy. They met on the boat and were married before they arrived. They opened a restaurant and catered to sailors, factory workers and dockhands. It was a humble existence, but a happy one. I didn't mind. They taught me how to cook." She paused. *I'll never stop being grateful for that.*

Dylan's hand roved down her arm and he grasped her fingers in a gentle grip.

"The dockside area is a nightmare of disease, and when I was sixteen, typhoid fever made its way through. The population was devastated. We all got sick. My mom was the first to die. She was pregnant. They'd been trying so long for a second child." She pondered. "I think, when dad heard she was gone, he gave up. He passed on two days later. After that, I don't remember several days. Whether it was grief or fever, I'm not sure, but I survived. It took me forever to get my strength back, but I dragged myself out of bed far sooner than I should have and made my way back to the restaurant, only to find others running it."

"They just took it over?" Dylan demanded. "Shouldn't it have been your inheritance?"

She shrugged. "My parents didn't ever get around to making a will. I don't know how it came about that these new people had it, but they did. I mean, I contacted the police and they explained that these men had the deed, so there was nothing I could do about it."

"Dear Lord, Lydia. So you were left with nothing?"

"They were kind enough to let me take my clothing from my room." Lydia sighed. "At first, I tried to find a job in a restaurant, but I was a kid and had no work experience. Everyone laughed at me, said playing kitchen with my mama didn't make me a chef. I got pretty hungry for a while there. I was a chubby girl, Dylan, which is probably the only reason I'm still alive."

His fingers trailed over her ripe figure. "I don't know about chubby, but your curves make me dizzy, Lydia. I've always been a sucker for a full-figured woman."

She smiled. "Thank you. I wasn't chubby after surviving typhoid and then spending weeks trying to figure out what to do with myself."

"What *did* you do?" Dylan asked. "Where did you sleep?"

"I didn't sleep much," she admitted. "It wasn't safe. I met some other girls in similar predicaments eventually and we watched out for each other. A pack of girls is safer than a girl alone, after all. We stole food sometimes. Other times we would sew a hem or run an errand in exchange for a coin. As she spoke, in her mind rolled back over the years until she was sixteen again, her belly cramping with hunger, trying not to devour an entire loaf of bread she'd swiped from a market stall, but to bring it back to her friends. "We called ourselves the Lost Girls." She smiled without humor. "We shared whatever we had, no matter how small."

Lydia carried the bread into the alley where Edwina, Ruby, Beth and Rose waited. Grimly they divided the small portion into five equal pieces.

Ruby stuffed her whole piece into her mouth at once, nearly choking herself with it. Her dirty blond hair bounced as she gnawed on the dry bite of food. "This isn't working," she said, showering crumbs onto the wet and grubby ground.

Beth broke off a tiny morsel of her bread and nibbled it slowly, her blue eyes tearing. She smoothed her medium brown curls off her forehead. "You're right, but what can we do?"

"There's one option," Edwina suggested, tugging her thick black braid.

Lydia shuddered. "Do we have to?" Even as she ate, her empty stomach continued to cramp, answering the question before she could ask it.

"I think we have exhausted all our other options," Rose admitted grimly, shaking her head until her silky red hair slipped its pins again. "This hurts. I'd rather have food, wouldn't you?"

"Of course," Edwina agreed. "They say decent girls would rather starve. I guess I'm indecent."

"Me too," Lydia said staunchly. "At least we'll be fed. We'll stick together. Maybe it won't be so bad. Have any of you been with a man?"

"I have," Rose said. "It's kind of wretched—dirty old man sawing away between your legs—but if you close your eyes and moan once in a while, you can pretend you're somewhere else." She sounded so sad as she said it, Lydia knew she was lying to herself.

Still, their meager meal exhausted, they'd linked arms and headed to the waterfront of Boston, where, as in any large city, houses of ill repute popped up to ease the needs of weary sailors. Hearts pounding, breathing shallow, they knocked on the door. A frowsy, middle-aged woman eyed them with bored disinterest. "We're full up, girls," she said, her voice carrying the tones of Ireland. "If you go down three doors, I know they're looking for help. Just opened up. No cook. Just the owner, who tends the bar, and one skinny girl. They'll probably take you in."

"Thank you," Ruby said grimly.

Every step down the street felt to Lydia like molasses dragged at her feet. Still, the dilapidated building awaited, a light in the window. "I don't want to do this," she whispered under her breath.

"No one wants to," Edwina said, patting her arm, "but think of food. Hot, tasty food."

Though Lydia hated to admit it, her stomach still knew what she needed to do. "Do you think it hurts?"

"The first time does," Rose told her, overhearing their conversation, "but after that, it's not too bad. Remember, just imagine you're somewhere else. It's not like we have to do this forever. Save up your pay and move on."

"So, just for a while then?" Lydia asked.

The others nodded.

It didn't help. Her empty belly threatened to invert itself inside her. She wanted to beg Rose not to knock on the door, but the knock sounded nonetheless, and the door opened.

"What have we here?" a young man asked, stroking a dark brown mustache. Lydia found him handsome, in a rugged sort of way. His hair hung a bit too long, curling around his ears.

"We're looking for work," Edwina announced boldly.

"Is that right?" he asked, looking her up and down.

"Yes," Ruby agreed. "The lady down the way said you might be in need of girls to get your business started."

He smirked at them and suddenly he no longer looked attractive to Lydia. "I can't say any of you is a great beauty, and you all look a bit thin, but I guess beggars can't be choosers. Any of you know how to entertain gentlemen?"

"I do." Rose met his eyes with a challenging stare.

"You'll have to show me," he said. "In fact, consider this an audition. I need to be sure you won't change your mind when the paying customers turn up."

Lydia's breath caught and tears stung her eyes. Hunger warred with modesty.

"I doubt you're up to 'auditioning' all of us in one night. You look pretty hungry yourself," Edwina commented, her bravado masking her fear, but her hands trembled, nonetheless.

"Well, you're not wrong," he said. "I'm not a great cook. Any of you know your way around the kitchen?"

"I do," Lydia said, hoping she could delay the inevitable by making dinner. "Is there any food in there?"

"A little," he replied, "though I've put most of my money into refurbishing this dump. Why not see if you can make us all something worth eating?"

"I might." Lydia also tried for bravado but failed just as badly. "If there's anything to work with."

"Let's go then," the man urged.

"Wait," Rose said. "Do you have a name, mister?"

"I'm Joseph. And you girls?"

He led the way into the kitchen as they introduced themselves. Inside the room, Lydia stared in dismay at the grubby walls, floors and countertops, the rodent droppings in the corners, and the broken windowpane.

"This place is filthy," she exclaimed. "My mother would be horrified. Do you plan to serve customers out of this hole?"

"Who's your mother and why should I care?" Joseph asked.

"Her name was Stephania Carré. She and my father owned a restaurant near here."

"I remember that place," Joseph said, his eyes going soft. "Your folks had a great restaurant."

"They did." She swallowed hard.

"What happened?" he wanted to know.

"They died." Lydia stared at her hands. "They got typhoid."

Joseph replied with a grimace.

Turning away to hide her tears, Lydia grabbed a rag, sniffed it and flung it into a dark corner. Pulling a handkerchief from her pocket, she pumped water into the grubby sink and added soap, quickly washing up a pot and two saucepans and leaving them to dry as she scouted ingredients.

She picked weevils out of the flour, lit the sooty stove and warmed water. "This would be better if I had yeast, but for the moment..." The girls stared over her shoulders as she explained, keeping her hands and mind busy to avoid thinking about the future. "Tinned tomatoes are not much good either, but since they're here... Joseph, do you have any cheese?"

Within an hour, Lydia had created a hot and crunchy flatbread with spiced tomatoes and bubbly melted cheese. Joseph's other whore—a sixteen-year-old twig of a girl named Maddie—wandered down to share the repast. Then, Joseph collected Rose and left the rest of them alone.

Over the course of the next few days, Lydia cleaned the kitchen. New food arrived and she cooked. Meanwhile, the other girls 'auditioned' for Joseph, but when Lydia's turn came, he took her aside.

"Look, Lydia, I know why you came here, but I don't think it's going to work. You're too afraid of men, and not to be rude, but you're not that pretty. That nose, you understand?"

After a week of food, the thought of returning to the streets hurt more than the insult. "What am I going to do?" she asked aloud, lip trembling.

"How did you like cooking for us?" he asked.

Not sure why the words gave her a bubble of hope, Lydia answered, "I like to cook."

"Did you help at the restaurant? Do you know how to cook for a crowd?"

"Of course," she told him.

"Well, I can offer you a job as my chef, then. You agreeable?" his false casual answer told Lydia this had been his intention from the beginning, and the attack on her appearance had only been a cover, not that she cared. Despite the guilt his offer produced, she couldn't help but agree.

"I cooked," she explained to Dylan, as the memory faded and her bedroom returned to focus, "but I knew that cooking in a whorehouse was no better than entertaining the gentlemen. I would never have a work history, so like the others, all I could do was save money, and I did. Ten years I hoarded every penny, and then I set out on my own. I ended up in Garden City, bought a run-down horse barn and you know the rest."

She stared at the ceiling, unwilling to meet his eyes lest she see condemnation there. *A lot of people are willing to judge a woman because of her associations. If Dylan is one of them, I need to know.* "You see, I was willing to do what they did, and only luck spared me. Sometimes I wish it hadn't. I hate that my friends became whores and I maintained my virtue, at least physically. It seemed unfair, but that's how it happened. I worked at a whorehouse... as the cook."

Silence stretched out between them, pulled thin like a sheet of pastry, and she wanted to weep with the fear that their bond, which yesterday had seemed stronger than cast iron, might snap if she drew in the wrong breath.

Then, a warm, tickling sensation touched her ear. Hot breath exhaled. Teeth closed around the sensitive lobe. She swallowed but didn't move, her eyes tightly shut. A change in the quality of the light hitting her eyelids suggested a shape blocking out the sun that shone through the window. Dylan's heavy weight eased onto her, pinning her to the bed. Their hands remained locked together. His lips trailed across her cheek and sought her mouth. A sob escaped Lydia as Dylan ravaged her mouth with violent tenderness. She ran her free hand up his back and into his hair.

"My poor darling," he murmured into her mouth. "You must have been so scared. You're so brave, Lydia. Did you really think I would turn from you? Not a chance. If you'd had to entertain instead of cooking, I would have understood."

Tears streaked down her temples into her hair. Lydia opened her thighs wide to accommodate Dylan better. His sex had swelled to full tumescence and he eased it gently back into her. Lydia whimpered, her sobs merging into quiet pleasure-cries.

"I love you." Her lips traced the words across his as he plunged deep into her well, pulled back and plunged again. Every deep drive set her sex clenching and her skin tingling.

"You know I love you, Lydia."

Joy welled up from the dark places she'd forgotten she had, turning them to starry brilliance. *No matter what tomorrow brings, I will never forget this moment.* "I know you do, Dylan. We love each other. It's perfect."

She clung to him, one hand on his neck, the other locked with his as his luscious thrusting set her eager flesh on fire. Pure ecstasy radiated out to every limb, every hair until she felt sure she must be glowing with it. Her breath sucked in, and she released it with a soft sigh, the power of the orgasm too strong for screams. Instead, she welcomed Dylan's claiming and returned it to him. *Never will I feel this way again. This man is unique. We're one.*

Passion ebbed, and she half-drowsed, not aware when Dylan rose, pulled on his clothes and prepared to leave. She felt his soft kiss, heard him murmur, "I'll come back soon," and closed her eyes. He eased the covers over her naked body. His boots echoed on the floorboards.

Chapter 10

"What kept you, Sheriff?" Rob demanded, eliciting a shout of laughter from Jesse.

"Never mind about that," the blond man wheezed, scratching the stubble on his cheeks.

"That's right, never mind, you two whippersnappers. Jesse, what's wrong with your wife that she doesn't make you shave?"

Jesse only laughed harder. "She was still asleep this morning when I left, so I got away without the lecture on respectability. And watch who you're calling whippersnapper, old man."

"Very funny," Dylan groused, only half joining in the banter. His heart remained with his woman, tucked into that warm bed. "Lydia says the stranger is named Samuel Blaylock, which, I'm sure you'll agree, is pretty similar to Sam Bly. He's older with grey hair, a fancy mustache and a limp."

Jesse's laughter cut off as the gears in his analytical mind began grinding. "Sounds just like the fellow from Colorado. How interesting is it that I came all the way home to find a safer life for my wife and kid, only to find the same killer who tried to do us in the next state over?"

"That is something, Jesse. You have some luck," Rob said, perching his rear on the desk. Jesse paced across the room and leaned against the wall.

Dylan circled the desk and dropped into his chair, propping his feet up on the wood and deliberately knocking Rob off the edge.

"So, gentlemen, what are your suggestions? I know I'm the boss here, but Jesse, you grew up in this town, and Rob, you never left. I have deputies not only for backup but for feedback. How do we storm a stronghold on a flat, empty prairie without us all getting killed?"

"Bring a *big* posse," Rob replied immediately. "The more targets there are, the better everyone's chances."

Dylan nodded. *There's sense in that.*

"Come at them at night," Jesse added. "Deep night. Gives us the advantage. There will certainly be a watch, but a watch isn't the same as a whole camp milling around. Keep the lanterns as dark as possible. Communicate with bird calls."

"Who knows bird calls?" Rob complained.

"My wife," Jesse replied promptly. "She's been teaching me. Most people don't notice birds, but imitating a day bird at night is a form of communication. We should also go on foot."

"No horses?" Dylan frowned. "Being on the ground takes away an advantage, Jesse."

"Yeah, maybe, but it's quieter. Horses are big and heavy. They'll make a lot more noise crashing through the dry grass."

Damn, this kid is smart. I would never have thought to go on foot.

"That needs to be a really big posse," Rob pointed out. "If we don't have horses, we should have even more men."

"Everyone who wants to can go, I'd say," Dylan replied. "I think we might be surprised by what we find there, and I don't want to be outgunned. These are professional criminals and killers. We might have more men, but they're nice family men. Bankers, shopkeepers and ranchers. They have their families to protect, but that doesn't mean they know how to take a life. Who here other than me has actually killed a man, and won't freeze at the critical moment?"

"Not me," Rob said, "unless the hanging I attended counts against my credit. I swear I won't freeze though."

Hope not, Dylan thought.

"I have." Jesse met his boss's gaze with a cold, hard stare.

This kid never stops surprising me. So is this what he's hiding under all that humor? I'm lucky he's on my side. "That might be it then," Dylan admitted, "but I suppose such things are normal enough in a small-town posse."

"Yes, and don't forget, every man in this town will rise to the occasion, regardless of experience," Jesse reminded him. "They have wives and daughters, mothers, sweethearts and sisters who are at risk. No one will forget the way they fire-bombed an innocent woman's place of business in order to create a diversion. Another gang member, one who will not be any bother to us, tried to kill Addie over in Colorado..."

"And the rest thought nothing of slaughtering a train full of women and children," Dylan added.

Rob scowled.

"They've already proven themselves uncivilized and dangerous. We're not exaggerating that the threat to the town incorporates every man, woman and child."

Rob shuddered. "To think they've been lurking beside us for who knows how long, just waiting for their chance." He shook his head. "Let's take these bastards down."

"The hard part will be planning this without them finding out we're coming. We don't know if anyone in town is on their side. Once we call the meeting, we're committed," Jesse said. "No one can be allowed to leave once they know our plan."

"Well, then, we'll call them tomorrow at sunset. It's too late to start this now," Dylan informed them, looking at the low light beaming in the window. "So let's get this planned out and then head home. I'll take first watch since I've already had a break. We have to be on guard now."

"I'll stay too," Jesse volunteered.

Dylan shook his head. "Go let Addie know to keep her head down. She's a likely target since she's known to be associated with you. Rob…"

"I'm going home," the young man replied. "I have to let Ma and my sisters know to lie low."

"Good thinking."

"Will Lydia be all right?" Jesse asked.

"I think so," Dylan replied. "She was powerfully mad at me for asking Billy Fulton to watch over her."

The chuckle that greeted his pronouncement sounded more like tension than mirth, but what else could be expected under the circumstances?

After a few minutes resting, Lydia woke up to the scarlet sunset beaming onto her face. While normally late afternoon would be filled with a simple supper and readying herself for bed, this time energy bubbled through her. She felt wide awake, and now that Dylan had gone, angry.

"That Ilse Jackson is going to get a piece of my mind," she muttered. Swinging her legs over the side of the bed, she began rehearsing everything she wanted to say to that dishonest brat in furious, hissing murmurs while she washed the residue of Dylan's love from her thighs and slipped into clean, intact garments.

A deft twist rendered her thick, black hair presentable for public. Then she scooped up her reticule, in which her now-reloaded derringer resided, its weight a welcome comfort against all the cruelties of life. *I won't shoot Ilse. I won't, but I won't promise not to slap some sense into her. She needs it.*

Her thoughts trained on the woman who made everyone's life miserable, Lydia hurried out of the store and down the street, heading for the Jackson home.

"Lydia? Lydia?" A soft, female voice called to her, breaking through her intense concentration. She turned to see Addie West, her burnished hair escaping a demure bun, approaching her from the direction of the home she and Jesse had purchased.

"What can I do for you, Addie?" Lydia asked, not wanting to slight her friend.

Addie drew so close to Lydia, they were nearly touching. "Is it true about the sheriff?"

Addie's hushed alarm set off warning bells in Lydia. She answered in an intense whisper, "What did you hear?"

Addie drew in a deep breath and laid a hand on the now-unmistakable swell of her belly. "That he was nearly shot. That you saved him. That the robbers are moving directly against the town."

Lydia nodded grimly. "Can you shoot a gun, Addie?"

The younger woman dipped her chin.

"Then I suggest you make a point of arming yourself everywhere you go."

Addie's gaze hardened, revealing a core of steel Lydia had never seen before. "I'm never unarmed. Never."

Lydia nodded. "Good girl."

"Jesse told me a bit about these robbers. They have no respect for women or children. They are everyone's enemies. Watch yourself, Lydia."

"Of course," Lydia agreed.

Addie seemed to relax a bit. "So where were you off to in such a hurry?"

As Lydia opened her mouth to speak, a flash of movement across the street drew her eye. She turned and her face hardened.

"What on earth, Lydia?" Addie gasped.

"Remember when you came by the shop, after hearing rumors about a petition to close the saloon?"

"Yes," Addie admitted. "Some people have too much time on their hands."

"That they do," Lydia agreed. "How would you feel if someone added your name to such a document without your permission or knowledge?"

Addie made a face. "I make my own decisions."

"Exactly, and one decision I made was to have nothing to do with that petition. Excuse me a moment."

Leaving her friend, she stormed across the red brick street to the front of the mercantile. Inside, she could see Becky Heitschmidt working away at her sewing machine. The woman lifted her arm in a friendly wave, but Lydia, intent on her quarry, did not return the greeting. "Miss Jackson," she enunciated in extreme disgust.

Ilse's head shot up from the basket of purchases she'd just carried out of the mercantile and she frowned at Lydia. "Yes?"

"I have a bone to pick with you, miss." Peripheral movement revealed that Addie had trailed after Lydia and now flanked her, also leveling an angry, brown-eyed stare at the town's most annoying citizen.

"Can't it wait?" Ilse asked with a careless laugh, smoothing a strand of shiny black hair back under her blue bonnet. "I have to get these goods home. It does them no favors to be out in the cold."

"Sorry, Ilse," Lydia said, her words polite but her anger dripping from every word. "It can't wait. You crossed the line this time and I expect you to listen to what I have to say about it."

Ilse laughed, but in the face of Lydia's rage, it sounded strained. *Good.* "What on earth can you mean?"

"I told you I didn't support your petition. I made it perfectly clear I wanted nothing to do with it. For you to have written my name on it anyway was wrong. I'm mortified, and very, very angry. Have you ever seen what happens when an Italian woman gets angry, Miss Jackson? It isn't the cold rage your German brethren favor, and I don't care in the slightest about making a scene."

Uncertainty crept across Ilse's pretty, pouty face. She bit her lower lip and took a step backwards as though to flee.

Oh, I don't think so, you little brat. Time to face the music. Lydia inhaled a deep breath, ready to blast Ilse to kingdom come, but she never got the chance.

"Oh, no!" Becky shot to her feet, dumping a lapful of pinned fabric onto the floor. "James! James, are you there?"

"What is it, honey?" Her husband hurried to her and laid a hand on her back. "The baby…?"

The breath she drew into her heaving lungs shuddered. "There were men… strangers… in the street. Oh, dear Lord. They…." She stuttered to a halt, swallowed. A tear slid down her cheek. "Get the sheriff, James. Hurry."

"What? What happened? Rebecca, what are you saying?"

"They took them. Lydia, Addie and Ilse. The strangers took them away!"

James froze in place, staring into the street, which suddenly seemed eerily empty. Then he hooked an arm around his wife's waist and hauled her back, away from the window.

"James, what are you doing? Go get the sheriff."

"I won't leave you alone." He tugged her behind the counter and pulled out the shotgun he normally concealed there. "We're going together."

Keeping his arm tight around her waist, James guided his wife to the door and out into the street.

"So, you're saying the soddie in question is here?" Dylan touched a roughly sketched map Jesse had drawn of the unclaimed land north of town.

Jesse nodded.

"Wait, I know that place!" Rob exclaimed, suddenly overcome with exuberance. "One time I brought…" he trailed off, his face coloring. "Never mind," he mumbled.

Jesse raised an eyebrow at him. "Not much of a spot for a romantic interlude," he commented. "Don't you have any class, boy?"

"Let's discuss Sarah a different time," Dylan urged, not wanting to get drawn into a lengthy conversation about the sweetheart the boy pretended not to have. Rob's angry muttering changed to jaw-hanging shock.

"How did you…?"

"Later," Dylan insisted. "Jesse, stop teasing him. This is not the moment."

"Sorry," the younger man said, though he didn't look at all abashed.

"So we gather the men of town tomorrow at sunset and tell them…"

The door to the jail flew open with a resounding crash that rattled the windowpanes and set the bars vibrating. Dylan overturned his chair with him still in it. His head knocked hard on the floor and for a moment, tiny stars seemed to be circling.

"Now hold on a gol-durned minute," Jesse shouted loud enough set Dylan's head throbbing even harder than the blow had. "Have you lost your mind, Heitschmidt? You can't come in here with that! What the hell are you doing?"

Shaking himself, Dylan slowly rose to his feet to see James, one arm tight around his wife, the other cradling a shotgun.

Becky shoved herself back against her husband as though trying to hide. Tears streaked down her face and she sobbed so hard, she could scarcely breathe.

"What's happening?" Dylan asked, feeling sluggish and stupid.

"Sheriff! Sheriff! You have to come, you have to... Oh, Lord!" She brought her hands up over her face and wailed.

"What is it?" Dylan demanded. "James, you'd best point that thing somewhere else."

James let the muzzle of the shotgun drop to the floor. He leaned on its sturdy barrel as though for support. "They were here. The robbers. They grabbed women from the street. Rebecca saw it."

"What?" Jesse stepped forward, eyes wild. "What women? Who did they take?" His breath puffed between his lips like an angry bull. "What women?"

"Settle down, Jess," Rob urged. "Don't scare the lady. Miz Heitschmidt, who did they take?"

She drew in several gasping inhalations and scrubbed her hands over her face. "Ilse..." she gulped. "Addie..."

Jesse cursed vilely and didn't excuse himself.

"...and Lydia."

The stars returned, pinpricks of light floating around Dylan's head. He blinked to dispel them, but his knees gave way and he sank down, perching his rear on the desk for support. "Are you sure?"

She nodded. "I saw it. They were talking. Addie and Lydia looked mad. Then five men jumped out from between the mercantile and the bank, you know that dark little alley..."

Though he had to strain to understand over her endless sobs, Becky's words slammed into his head like a hammer. He nodded, feeling numb.

"One put a hand over each woman's mouth. One took Lydia's bag and threw it in the street, and they wrestled them back into the alley."

"Did you see which way they went?"

"I'm sorry, sheriff," James said, sounding anything but, "I wasn't going to leave my pregnant wife alone for a minute, nor was I going to take her anywhere near dangerous, violent men. We came straight here."

Though he wanted to be angry, he had to admit James had a point. *He's not a lawman.* "Gentlemen, our plans have changed. Get everyone you can find and meet me at the church in an hour. If I don't show up, carry out the raid without me."

"But..." Rob started.

"Robert Fulton," Dylan said in his lowest, coldest voice. "You are a lawman. Do your duty."

"Yes, sir." The lad gulped and then straightened.

"I'm going with you," Jesse snarled. The skin around his mouth looked taut and white. His fists clenched so tight, his knuckles popped, and his hands shook.

Dylan laid an unsteady hand on the young man's shoulder. "Focus, Jesse. We need your cool head right now. We have to round up the posse. Rob can't get to everyone fast enough. I need you to be the deputy right now, not a husband, okay? *You'll have a better chance of saving her if you do your job.*"

Jesse drew air deeply into his lungs. His hands steadied but the fiery fury in his eyes remained undimmed. "Go south," he barked at Rob. "Knock on every door. I'll head north."

As Dylan raced for the entrance, he barely saw Rob's nod.

In the street, the temperature had dropped from autumn pleasant to chilly, and the red light of the setting sun seemed to bathe the brick streets in blood. Long shadows cast by the buildings lay low and cold over the town, and every window stared like a malevolent eye. Dylan ignored it all. In front of the mercantile, the sight of Lydia's handbag drew his gaze. He reached forward and lifted it slowly, heart breaking as he felt the undeniable weight of her derringer inside. *She's unarmed.*

A basket of yarn, ribbon and licorice candy lay spilled nearby, the delicate reeds crushed in the shape of a man's boot. Dylan lifted his eyes to the dark, seedy alley, filled with dirt and bits of refuse, hoping against hope for some sign, but of course, there was nothing.

Slowly he made his way into the dim space between the two buildings, barely enough for two men to walk shoulder to shoulder. *How could they have forced three unwilling women down here? Of course, Ilse is no fighter. She'd probably go meekly and hope for a rescue. Addie might fight, but she's tiny. But Lydia?* He shook his head. *She's neither small nor meek. They'd better watch out.* Though he knew she would fight, he didn't know what the outcome would be.

At the end of the alley, a dim shaft of scarlet light flashed on an object lying in the dirt. Dylan stooped and regarded a shower of abandoned hairpins, some black, some red. *Good girls. Well done.* The pins lay on the ground almost in a trail leading… "North." Dylan heaved a sigh. *Either this is a trap and they're lying in wait to kill me, or they're taking the women to camp to hold them for ransom. Time to summon the posse.* "Please, God," he muttered under his breath, "protect these women until we can get there."

He raced through the growing darkness down the street to the church, where the steeple cast a cross upon the ground. A shaft of sunlight beamed through the bell tower, falling on Dylan's face. The bell tilted from one side to the other, its musical toning urging the congregation into the church.

He paused a moment, eyes uplifted, praying wordlessly for things he couldn't begin to articulate. Then, spurred by the urgency of the situation, he mounted the steps to the church and strode through the door, nodding at the sight of a room full of parishioners who awaited his instructions. At the rear of the room, Jesse paced slowly from one side to the other, muttering under his breath. His distress resonated with Dylan. *This reminds me too much Justine and our son—knowing they're in trouble and not being able to help. I hope for Jesse's sake that the outcome is better.*

Making his way to the front, Dylan found Cody in his usual spot, trying to calm the crowd, though lacking information, he struggled to rein in the hum of conversation.

"Reverend, if I may." Dylan, who had never passed further than the communion rail, strode straight to the pulpit without a second thought. An instant, nervous hush descended on the church. "Folks, before too many rumors get started, here are the facts. Mrs. West, Miss Jackson and…" He gulped. "…Miss Carré were taken just now by what we can only assume to be the band of train robbers who attacked Pastor and Mrs. Williams last December."

A murmur rippled through the assembled group. He could almost guess what they were saying. *Everyone loves Lydia. Everyone. Not to mention, Addie's expecting. Ilse is pretty in a way that makes men want to own her. This will arouse some powerful protective instincts.* "Friends, we were already planning to amass a posse tomorrow and go after these…" he cut off the expletive in the face of several women in the audience, "scoundrels, but with three innocent women's lives on the line, we have to do it now. My deputies and I think we know where they're hiding, but we need every man willing to point a gun with us, and we need to go right away before they have time to hurt the women." Grimly he squashed down the obnoxious little voice that pointed out how much time had already passed, and how much more it would take to get everyone armed and ready. *Can't think about that. Not if we want to succeed.* "We're going on foot. If you have a rifle, shotgun or pistol at home, go get it and meet me back here in half an hour." As one, the men of the congregation rose, their faces set in matching lines of grim determination and they all filed out.

A clatter of boots on metal treads revealed Kristina Heitschmidt Williams hurrying down from the choir loft. She raced to her husband and threw her arms around him. "Are you going, Cody?"

He nodded. "I have to."

She squeezed him tight, her eyes wild. "Come home again, Cody. Come home safe."

He kissed her lips. "I love you, Kris."

"Reverend," Dylan said, interrupting their tender moment, "if you don't have a weapon, I can lend you one."

Cody nodded, looking a bit startled. He gave his wife one last squeeze, smudged her lips with his, and turned to join the sheriff as they walked down the aisle and out the door. "Do you think they'll be all right?" he asked.

Dylan shook his head. "I hope so, Cody. I really hope so."

Chapter 11

Lydia sank her teeth hard into the palm clamped over it.

The cretin howled and shook his injured hand, fingers flapping.

"Let me go, *fils de putain*," she snarled in French, adding several expletives in Italian as she drove an elbow backward into his ribs.

Beside her, Addie kicked back hard with one dangling foot, driving the heel of her boot into her captor's shin. He dropped her onto her bottom, and her breath whooshed out. Both hands flew to her belly.

"Easy there, girls," a sneering voice spoke. Lydia glared at a powerfully built man with a shiny bald head and a luxurious mustache. "Just cooperate and no one gets hurt."

"Cooperate with you bastards? Forget it." Addie hauled herself to her feet and spat onto the soil in front of his boots.

"Such language," he scolded. "Do you plan to kiss your baby with that mouth?"

"She presents a good point," Lydia said, rage calming her to icy condescension. "There are only five of you. How far do you plan to get if we refuse to cooperate?"

"Oh, you'll cooperate," the man said, flashing tobacco-stained teeth. The sunlight cast a bloody red tone over them, and she shuddered. He pulled a pistol from his hip and aimed it casually at the side of Addie's belly. "She could very well live, but what about the kid?"

From her place, still pinned by a man using only one arm, the other clapped over her mouth, Ilse's eyes grew wide.

Defeated, Lydia lowered her eyes in submission. "Where do we go?"

Jesse led the way out of town, his lantern mostly dark, save a thin shaft to illuminate the path ahead of him, and another that fell on his face, rendering him visible from behind. The wind picked up, whipping through the tall prairie grass and sending it swaying in all manner of noisy rustles.

Dylan, his rifle cradled on his arm, moved close beside his deputy, longing to encourage him, to speak the words that would put Jesse's mind at ease, but he didn't dare. He had no way of knowing if they were true. *It might well be that Jesse doesn't arrive in time to save his wife. Saying otherwise would be foolish.* His stomach knotted. *Lydia too. She's strong and smart, but I wish she had her gun.*

"Should I make some tea?" Kristina asked, regarding her friends, who sat on the sofa in the parlor of the vicarage. Allison looked up from staring into the eyes of her tiny son. Then she propped the little boy on her shoulder and shook her head. Melissa, perched beside her stepmother, leaned her cheek on Allison's arm, her eyes closing.

"No thanks," Becky said in a shaky voice. "I'd probably be sick again." From her perch beside her sister on the couch, her hands rested on her belly, but not in the typical gesture one often saw pregnant women doing. Her face had turned deathly pale.

"I'm sure they'll be all right," Kristina pointed out.

"No you're not," Allison snapped. "Don't talk nonsense, Kristina."

"Take it easy," her sister urged.

Allison shook her head. "This isn't right. Something isn't right. Why can't I put my finger on it?"

Kristina sank into an armchair adjacent to her friends. "What isn't right, Allie?"

"Why didn't they kill them in the street?" Allison glanced sharply at the child beside her, and, noting Melissa had drifted off, continued. "If they wanted revenge by killing the sheriff's woman, why didn't they just shoot her?"

Kristina blinked. "I'm not sure, but what else could they want?"

"Ransom?" Becky suggested.

Allison frowned. "Not likely. They'd have to know that if they took the women, the men of town would be after them in force…" She trailed off and then sucked in a noisy breath. "Oh, dear Lord. They were counting on it." She shot to her feet. "We have to go."

"Go? Where are we going?" Kristina stared at her friend, confused. *The last thing I want to do is leave the house, especially in the dark. I already feel so exposed.*

"We're sitting ducks, all of us, alone in our homes and isolated. They didn't take Lydia and Addie to take them. They took them to lure the men away from the rest of us. Come on."

Her words caused Kristina's sense of unease to crystallize into outright fear. Her pulse began pounding in her ears.

"What are we doing?" Becky demanded.

"We're going to your husband's store to get every gun the men didn't take. Then we're going to round up everyone who will listen and get together in the church. There aren't many of us who can shoot, so we need to stand guard in a place where a few shooters make the most difference."

Becky gulped audibly.

Kristina's blood pounded in her ears. *Oh, God please protect the men... but please, protect us too.*

The horses thundered across the prairie, the rocking of their bodies mingling with Lydia's nerves until she feared she might either scream or vomit.

A quarter of an hour north of town, and then a sharp turn to the west, into the thin scarlet ribbon of daylight that remained visible at the edge of the unbroken horizon. There, a string of tents sat beside the remains of a cottage, its windows fallen in, cobwebs clustered thickly on the eaves.

The robbers reined their horses sharply and slid to the ground, bringing the prisoners with them. A crowd of rough, disreputable-looking men crowded around, poking at them and cheering. Then the mob parted, and a familiar figure limped through.

"Samuel Blaylock," Lydia hissed with displeasure. "What the devil are you thinking?"

He chuckled. "Should have come with me when you had the chance, Miss Lydia."

She snorted. "Not a chance in hell. I tried to be kind to you, Mr. Blaylock, but that doesn't mean I wanted to ride off into the sunset with you, and I'm sorry, but from where I'm standing, my café is much nicer than this band of ruffians in tents."

His laughter grew in volume. "This is temporary accommodations, my dear. Once we rid ourselves of a few unnecessary people, we'll move to a different location far from here, and set up a new life. My bride would live like a queen. Too bad that won't be you. I don't forgive easily, and a bullet in the arm is the last thing I needed."

Lydia raised her head higher. "I'm not sorry. You deserved to be shot. Besides, I have no desire to be a queen of crime, Mr. Blaylock. You've chosen the wrong side of this battle, and I refuse to stand with you."

His laughter gave way to a glower. "I can't imagine how that bumbling sheriff won your heart, my lady, but you're the one who's chosen the wrong side." He gestured, and the thug holding Lydia's arm tugged, urging her toward the decaying house.

"I'll go with you," a soft, sly voice spoke into the night.

"Ilse, you're crazy," Addie protested.

"No," the girl replied. "You are all crazy, standing by your notions of right and wrong. It's too late for that. Our only chance to survive is to cooperate. What do you say, Mr. Blaylock? Can your plans be altered slightly?"

"You're mighty young." He looked Ilse up and down. "People will guess you're my daughter, but no matter. Bring her to my tent. Lock up these other two in the house."

The pressure on Lydia's arm intensified until the man was nearly dragging her. Again, she considered fighting, but with a dozen armed men standing around, there didn't seem to be much point. She allowed him to lead her to the door and shove her inside, Addie close behind her. The door slammed shut and the key clicked in the lock, the soft sound growing in volume in her over-wrought ears.

From the choir loft, Allison regarded the sanctuary. Busy mothers tried to urge overexcited tots to lie down on the pews and rest. Babies wept and fretted. Nervous children whined and milled around the room. At the windows, a handful of women and the remaining men, most of them ancient, crippled or otherwise too impaired for the posse, had taken up a position near panes of transparent glass, weapons cradled in their laps.

She turned back to the window above the organ bench, staring out over the dark, silent town. The low glow of dim lamplight from below did not impair her vision. A gust of wind sent brown leaves tumbling down the empty street.

I've done all I can, so why do I still have this itchy feeling between my shoulder blades? What have I forgotten?

A soft step on the metal treads alerted her and she met eyes with Kristina. "Melissa is asleep," she said softly, "but I think this little fellow needs you."

She handed Allison's infant son over and the young mother sank into a choir chair and unbuttoned her shirtwaist. "Hope you don't mind."

Kristina shrugged. "Feed him." Allison complied as her friend continued speaking. "Anyway, do you really think they'll come against us?"

"I don't know," Allison replied. "I hope not. I hope, come morning, that the worst outcome of the night is some tired mamas and a bit of embarrassment."

"I agree," Kristina said. She took up Allison's post, gazing out over the town. "Don't the shadows look so much like creeping figures?"

Allison nodded. "I could have sworn they were, but when I studied each one, I found they were trees, or leaves, or a cat. But I still can't shake the feeling I'm forgetting something."

"No doubt it's just tension," Kristina replied.

"No doubt," Allison agreed, taking the opportunity to gaze into her son's face as he nursed contentedly, one chubby fist waving in the air.

"Do you think Lydia and Addie will be all right?" Kristina asked. "Oh, and Ilse, of course."

Allison closed her eyes. "No."

Kristina inhaled through her nose. Her breath caught halfway through in an unmistakable sob. "With God all things are possible."

"Pray, then," Allison suggested. "Even if the men find them, the odds are against them being unharmed,"

Kristina acknowledged the statement with a long moment of silence. "Will the men be all right?"

"Kristina, you know I don't know," Allison said softly as she switched her baby to the other breast. "Most likely some will, and some won't, and all we can do is leave them in God's hands and hope for the best. I'm pretty sure there are a whole lot more of our men than there are robbers, so that's in their favor." Allison studied her son again. "If something happens to Wesley, and to me, will you and Cody take the children? My parents are old, and my sister has her own baby on the way now, so..."

Kristina didn't chide her. "Of course. You don't even have to ask me that."

She's the best friend anyone could ask for. I'm so blessed with my friends, my parents, my sister… even my husband is so much better now. Please, God, don't take them away. Let us get through this safely and help me remember what it is I'm forgetting. It has to do with Lydia. I know it does. With something that mattered a lot to her. "Kristina, what did my sister say Lydia was doing when she was taken?"

"Confronting Ilse about something or other," Kristina replied absently, her gaze on the window.

Oh boy. "About what? Any ideas?"

"I heard someone say Ilse had put all our names on the stupid saloon petition. Lydia was death on that thing. Maybe that's why."

Like the rolling of dice in Allison's head, the tumbling ideas clicked into place. "Oh, shit," she whispered softly.

"What do you think they meant by it?" Wesley breathed to Dylan as they made their slow way north toward the abandoned soddie.

"To cause trouble," Dylan whispered back.

"Yeah, of course," Wesley agreed, "but why take them?"

"They hate me for hanging that kid last spring and they hate Jesse for breaking up their nest in Colorado. What more do you need to know?"

"Blaylock threatened Cody as well, but didn't take Kristina," Wesley pointed out.

"So? She wasn't there."

"She was alone practicing in the church all afternoon. I heard it. It would have taken nothing to grab her, but they didn't."

"Are you trying to make a point, Fulton?"

Wesley nodded, the movement barely visible in the darkness. "If they took anyone else's woman, you and Jesse would have sat down and puzzled it out. They took yours and made you react without thinking. I bet it was intentional."

"Would you shut up," Jesse hissed. "We're almost there."

Wesley's words struck a chord with Dylan, but he couldn't quite fit the pieces together over the more pressing worry about Lydia's safety.

Addie looked pitiful, hunched up on the floor, her arms around her knees as though to protect her unborn child from whatever evil these criminals intended to inflict on them.

Lydia crouched beside her. "Are you hurt? They dropped you pretty hard."

Addie lifted her face from her knee, stunning Lydia with her determined, angry expression. Her breath heaved between her tense lips in little pants. "So far I think I'm all right."

Lydia opened her mouth to speak, but a grating voice outside the window interrupted her.

"Think they'll take the bait?"

"Hell yeah," another gruff male tone growled. "They'll be combing the prairie for hours, fumbling around in the dark. The rest of them will be sitting ducks."

"I still don't like this plan," a third, softer voice spoke into the night. "Slaughtering women and children just isn't right."

"Which is why you aren't going," Blaylock said. "Randall, if you weren't my last remaining son, I'd string you up myself. You're as weak as your mother. Just sit here on your ass and guard these two. Think you can manage that?"

"What choice do I have?" the young man asked bitterly. "We're miles from civilization, not counting that rotten town, and all the horses are leaving shortly."

"You don't need horses, idiot," the rough voice replied with a guffaw. "Between the boss's hurt leg and his bad arm, he can't ride anyway, and the last time you sat a horse, you fell off, remember? Landed right on a horse apple." Roaring with laughter, the gruff-voiced man stomped away.

The soft voice did not answer, and two footsteps, one soft, the other uneven, wandered away from the window. In the pale moonlight, Lydia saw Addie's eyes grow wide. "Oh, God. They're using us as bait to lure the men away from town," she whispered.

Lydia nodded.

"We have to do something. At least warn them."

"How?" Lydia demanded in a furious hiss. "They threw away my gun. If I had that, I might be able to do something, but I'm unarmed."

"You may be, but I'm not." Addie reached into her boot and drew out a thin, wicked-looking blade.

"You know how to use that?" Lydia demanded, "Or did Jesse give it to you as a present?"

"Once, a man threatened me… and this baby." She waved her hand in the direction of her belly. "That man will not be bothering anyone again." Her eyes narrowed to slits and her jaw locked. "Don't mistake me for a soft, city-bred girl, Lydia. I'm half wild mountain woman and half Kiowa Indian. I know how to fight, and I'm not afraid to do it."

Her fierceness brought a wicked smile to Lydia's lips. "Then we have reason to hope. Put that away until we need it, and let's figure out a plan."

"Billy," Allison said in her softest voice, "I need your help. Can you come with me?"

"Are we going outside, Miss Allie?" Billy Fulton's thick lips twisted in confusion.

"That's right, Billy. We forgot some folks and it's not right. You and I are going to go get them."

"I'm not good with a gun, Miss Allie. They scare me."

She laid a hand on his bulky arm. "I know, Billy. I'll carry the gun. I need you to be sure no one is sneaking up behind us, okay?"

He nodded. Allison cast a longing glance at her son, now cradled in Becky's arms, and on her stepdaughter, asleep beside them on the pew. She lifted her eyes to receive Kristina's solemn wave from the balcony. Then she and Billy slipped out into the darkness, ducked between two buildings and headed toward the east edge of town.

"Damnation!" Dylan roared and Jesse uttered a fouler curse at the sight of the abandoned soddie and its decaying barn, still empty save for the spiders that had taken up residence. No sign of a camp or any human habitation in ages.

"I don't understand," Rob muttered. "I just don't understand. What else could they have done? Set up camp on the open prairie?"

"If they did," Jesse answered grimly, "good luck finding them."

"Are there no other homesteads or structures that could be turned into the foundation of a makeshift camp?" Dylan asked.

"Plenty." Wesley stalked toward them, crushing prairie grass under his feet. "Gentlemen, I don't think this kidnapping was anything less than a calculated attempt to lure us out of town. Yes, they'll have their revenge on the sheriff and his deputy, but we've also left the rest of the women mostly unguarded."

A murmur rippled through the posse.

"What do you suggest then, Wes?" Dylan demanded. "Do you mean for us to abandon Ilse, Lydia and Addie to their fate?"

"Wesley, you've been my best friend since we were born." Even in the dim lamplight, Dylan could see the redness of Jesse's eyes. "I've lost one woman I loved. Please don't ask me to lose Addie too."

"Of course not," Wesley insisted. "I would never suggest such a thing. I think... I think we need to split up. So send half of the men home. We jumped in too fast, committed too many men. Half of us should still be able to take down a small camp of robbers if, in fact, they're still all at their camp."

"Good thinking, Wes," Dylan agreed.

Lydia's heart pounded so hard, she feared her ribs might crack, but she slowly nodded. "That just might work." She met Addie's brown eyes and saw shocking cold sternness there.

"If I'm going to die, I'd rather die fighting."

"We might not die," Lydia pointed out.

"Don't," Addie urged. "We have to try, but you know what the odds are. No false hope, Lydia."

She's right, Lydia admitted to herself. Her breath caught. *How many more breaths do I have left? How many heartbeats?* She closed her eyes against the sudden sting. "Don't give up. Give it all you've got. For your baby. For Jesse."

"For Dylan," Addie replied. Lydia nodded. "I'm glad to have known you, Lydia Carré. It wasn't long enough, but you were a great friend."

"I'm glad to have known you too, Addie," Lydia replied. "I still have to hold on to hope. It's my way, but should anything happen, remember, you and your baby come before me. Promise me."

"I would like to argue that with you, but I can't." Addie broke eye contact, staring at the floor. At last her composure seemed to give way. Her shoulders shook and her inhalation held an echo of a sob.

Lydia reached out and gripped her arm.

From a short distance, voices rose in discord, shouting. A woman screamed, and then a brief, sharp explosion cut off the scream into eerie silence.

Creeping between the buildings in the dark was something Allison had never considered doing. No one had ever dared her. No one had ever encouraged such a wild feat. *And yet, here I am, a grown woman, a wife and mother, slinking through the shadows like a naughty child... right up to a building I've never dared approach in my life.*

"Ooooh!" Billy said, pointing. "I know this place. Miss Julie lives here."

"Miss Julie?" Allison raised her eyebrows.

"Uh-huh. She's my friend. I go and talk to her. Sometimes she lets me go in her room, but I'm not supposed to talk about it." He giggled.

Well there you have it, Allison thought. She sighed and crept up to the front of the quiet three-story building. Even in the moonlight, the garish red paint seemed to glow, and the gilt name, *Chester's Saloon*, caught the faint illumination and flashed. Though the bar had been closed down, lights shone from inside, and the sound of women talking spilled into the street.

Allison heaved a sigh and knocked on the door.

"We're closed," someone shouted.

"I know," she called back. "That's not why I'm here."

Skirts swished inside and a moment later a mature woman with fading gingery hair appeared in a halo of light. "What do you want? You can't shut down the saloon, you know."

"I know that," Allison snapped. "I had nothing to do with it. Please, I need you to listen to me. We're all in danger."

"What danger?" A round face framed with long, dark brown curls appeared beside the older woman.

"Miss Julie!" Billy cheered, waving at the pretty brunette.

"Oh, hi, Billy," she replied, smiling.

"I assume Chester is out with the posse?" Allison guessed, focused on the danger.

"Yep," the redhead confirmed.

"Well, so is everyone else. I mean, everyone. All the able-bodied men in town have run off and left us. We've gathered at the church for safety, but it occurred to me that no one thought to warn you."

"Thank you for letting us know." The woman attempted to close the door.

"Wait," Allison said. "Listen, I don't think you all should stay here. It's easier if we all stick together."

The redhead's jaw dropped. "You're... inviting us into the church?"

Allison nodded. "Lydia would have wanted it that way."

"What happened to Lydia?" Another young woman, this one blond, pushed past the older woman onto the porch.

"She was kidnapped, along with two other women," Billy said loudly.

"Billy." Allison shot the young man an exasperated look. "Please keep your voice down. If anyone is creeping up on us, we don't want to let them know where we are."

"Lydia was kidnapped?" The brunette stared in horror.

"Yes, that's why the posse was formed." Allison studied the floorboards.

"Well, that's just terrible," the blond said, and from the tone of her voice, she meant it.

"Yes, it is. So the men have gone to fetch them back, but we don't want them to come home to a slaughter scene. Will you join us?"

"Please come, Julie," Billy said softly, holding out one blunt-fingered hand to the brown-haired prostitute. She regarded her companions and then stepped out onto the porch, laying her slender fingers on his palm.

"All right," the redhead conceded. "My name is Ruth. I'll be right back with anyone who wants to accept your invitation."

Allison nodded.

Ruth turned back into the saloon.

"Oh, Ruth?"

The woman turned her head and glanced over her shoulder.

"Can any of you shoot?"

A wide grin broke across Ruth's face.

"You know what would be nice?" Becky asked Kristina, stroking one hand over Melissa's hair.

"What's that?" Kristina stared in fascination at the infant sleeping in her lap.

"When Dylan and Lydia come back, let's surprise them."

"How?" Kristina wanted to know.

"Well, I know they're getting married, but their planning time got all shot to pieces with this robber business. After all this time, I would hate for them to miss out."

"I imagine," Kristina told her friend, "that they'll want to get it done immediately. Not waste a second."

"Exactly!" Becky tucked one knee up onto the pew so she could face Kristina more fully. "And when they do, how would it be if we had the whole wedding waiting for them. Music, food, dress and all?"

"It's a grand idea," Kristina admitted, "but how would you figure on accomplishing it?"

"Oh, trust me, I have a plan," Becky smiled. "We can talk it all out right now and be ready to jump into action in the morning. Are you interested?"

"Tell me more."

Dylan watched as Rob led half his posse back into the tall prairie grass, James Heitschmidt at his side.

"I'm surprised you stayed," he said to Wesley, who stood beside him. A little further off, Jesse paced nervously.

"I know James will watch over them," Wesley replied, "but if I came home without Lydia, my wife might not speak to me for a month. Besides, I had another thought about where they might be holed up, and it's not too far from here."

"You know a place I don't, Wes?" Jesse, passing by, cut in.

"How do I know whether you know it?" Wesley replied. "You did all your courting aboveboard… when you were here." He leveled a wholly inappropriate smirk on his friend, which Dylan attributed to tension. "I, on the other hand, know a few spots to be alone, should the need arise. There's a ruin of a house, about a half-mile east of here. I've been there. It wouldn't be much since it's not much bigger than this soddie, but it would be a place to start searching."

"Take me there," Dylan urged. *Hold on, Lydia. I'm coming.*

"Did they leave?" Addie hissed.

Lydia glanced out the windows. "Ten men on horses just rode south."

"Typical," Addie muttered. "Even injured, a proper leader leads." She shook her head. "Pitiful."

"Don't underestimate him," Lydia urged. "He's faster than you'd think with that injured leg, and he's also cunning as hell."

Addie grinned. "So are we." She tucked herself further into the corner of the room, along the wall adjacent to the door. Her smile faded and that look of icy tension chased across her features once more. "Ready?"

Lydia dipped her chin in acknowledgment, took a deep breath and called, "Mister! Hey mister!"

The door of the abandoned cabin opened a crack and a long, thin nose poked into the room. "Did you need something?" asked the soft-voiced man.

"My friend is sick. You know, expecting and all. She needs to eat something or she's going to throw up and then I'm going to throw up..."

"Let me see what I can find," the soft voice said. "I'll be right back. Ask her to hold on."

"Miz Williams?" a voice called from the balcony.

"Yes?" Kristina called back softly.

"Someone's out there."

Kristina's heart began to pound. She rose slowly and made her way up the stairs to the choir loft, where an elderly man—Jacob Fulton, one of Wesley's great-uncles—sat on the organ bench, peering out into the darkness.

"Any idea who it might be?" she asked.

He shook his head. "Can't tell from here, but they're moving around in the shadows, real creepy-like. He pointed.

Kristina squinted and her heart sank as the moonlight flashed on the barrels of drawn weapons. A tiny pinprick of light flared in the darkness and then resolved into a bigger light.

"Oh, Lord protect us," she prayed. Then she called down to the congregation below. "There are people out there with guns and torches, and they're behaving in a way I don't think our family members would. Be ready. If you're not able to fight, keep your head down… and while you're there, pray. We're in serious trouble." Kristina's stomach swooped and knotted with tension. *I wish Allison was here. She's much better at taking charge. God, help me. I'm so scared.*

From outside, a gruff male voice called, "Come out, come out wherever you are…"

In answer, Kristina leaned over the organ bench and called in the direction of the window, "Get out of here. Go on. Get."

Jacob grabbed Kristina and pulled her back from the window seconds before the leaded image of the crucifixion exploded into colored shards.

From below, more glass shattered as a member of the congregation took a shot at the shooter.

"They're armed!" She could barely hear one of the criminals shout over the ringing in her ears and the pounding of her heart. "They're ready for us."

"They're a bunch of old men and girls," another replied. "We can take 'em."

"Of course we can," the first man agreed, "but let's not lose our heads. Even a girl with a gun can get lucky."

"This is it," Kristina spoke over the balcony. A child, awakened by the gunfire, began to wail, which in turn woke more children.

Please, God, not this. We need to hear what they're doing out there, not listen to a lot of babies cry. Of course, once the crying began, there was no stopping it.

Sensitive to sound, Kristina longed to clap her hands over her ears. Her tension ratcheted up higher. *I can't do this. Allison, where are you?*

The sound of gunfire echoed between the buildings. Allison cursed under her breath. "I knew something like this was going to happen, damn it."

"Looks like you guessed right," Ruth replied.

"I wish to God I'd been wrong." Allison crept along the alley, where it emerged beside Lydia's café, and peered out.

"How many?" Julie hissed in her ear.

"I can see six," Allison replied, "but there may be more I can't see."

"What are they doing?" Another woman, whose name Allison couldn't remember, whispered from the back of the group.

"Aiming guns at the church windows," Allison replied. "Ladies, it looks like I've brought you into a hornet's nest. If you wanted to go back to the saloon… or to run off at this point, I wouldn't blame you. This is about to get really ugly."

"What are you going to do?" Ruth demanded.

"My sister, my best friend and my children are in there. I have no choice," Allison replied succinctly.

"I'm staying," Ruth said, laying a hand on Allison's shoulder. "I know the women in this town don't think much of us, but I won't forget what you did tonight. Let's see if we can give these ruffians something to think about."

Allison smiled sadly. "You're a good woman, Ruth. Thank you."

"What do I do?" Billy asked.

"I don't know," Allison replied honestly. "Pray?"

He nodded, taking the suggestion seriously.

Allison crept out into the street, keeping in the shadow of the café. Focused on the church, none of the robbers noticed her stealthy movements. Selecting one of the men near the front door, who carried a flaming torch, she took aim and waited.

The door of the farmhouse slowly swung open and a man stepped in. Short, thin and possessed of a truly epic nose, he appeared neither fearsome nor threatening. Lydia almost felt sorry for what they were about to do. *Almost.*

"Here you go. Sorry, all I could manage was porridge. We're a bit low on supplies and… wait, where is she?"

He stared around the room in consternation, and that moment of shock proved to be his undoing. Quick as a flash, Addie wrapped one arm around his waist and with the other, laid her knife against his throat, pressing just enough for him to feel the bite of the blade. The porridge fell with a clatter, the moist contents oozing into the rotting floorboards.

Lydia approached and plucked his gun from its holster, aiming it casually in his direction. "Let's take a walk, shall we?"

"Don't shoot at random," Kristina urged. "Make sure you have a clear target. Our supplies of ammunition are not unlimited." *Am I doing this right? Am I saying the right things? I have no idea.* Though she felt like her guts were about to expel themselves, Kristina forced her face and voice to a certain expressionless calm. Around her, women jiggled fretful babies and hushed fussing toddlers. Pandemonium was quickly building up inside the church, which she felt certain would do nothing but distract the baker's dozen individuals crouched beside the windows, waiting for their chance to do something, anything to alleviate the situation.

Will Watson, who had insisted, despite being no more than twelve, that he was big enough to help, aimed a rifle through a broken image of the Garden of Eden and squeezed the trigger.

A yell from outside revealed the child had hit his target, but to what end, Kristina couldn't know.

A bullet whizzed back through the spot where Will had just been, flew across the sanctuary and embedded itself in the opposite wall.

Kristina bit her lip until the metallic tang in her mouth reminded her to ease up. She wiped the blood from her chin, not certain what to do or say next. *God, please, help us!*

"Those bastards," Allison snarled. The men in front of the church seemed to be piling what looked like newspaper against the wooden structure. "I know what that torch is for."

A shot rang out inside and one of the men stationed near the windows dropped to the street, clutching his shoulder. One of his companions returned fire.

Allison took a slow, deep breath and focused her attention on the torch. "You won't be burning up my babies." With infinite care, she squeezed the trigger.

The bullet flew straight and true, cutting through his thick, dark hair and lodging in his brain. He fell without a sound, the torch extinguishing itself as it rolled over and over the red bricks of Main Street, until it came to rest, harmless now, against the trunk of a stunted oak tree. The report of the rifle drew the other men's gaze her direction, and several weapons flashed in the moonlight. Only then did Allison realize her mistake. While she'd made herself hard to see, the front of the café offered little cover. She dropped to the ground under a hail of fire, only to see the flash of pistols and shotguns all around her. More robbers cursed and shouted, falling to the street.

Distracted by the sudden appearance of multiple shooters, the criminals didn't notice Allison inching her way back into the cover of the alley. From there she found another target, a tall man in a ragged leather vest, and sent him his just rewards... directly above the garment's top button.

Gunfire exploded out of the windows of the church. *Now they don't know where to look,* Allison thought with grim satisfaction. *They'll be sorry they took on Garden City. We're no town of citified, civilized dandies.*

A deeper shadow blocked out the moonlight and Allison rolled to look directly into the unblinking eye of a shotgun's muzzle, and beyond it to a bald head with a huge mustache. She gulped. *So this is how it ends.*

The look and smell of the robber camp made Lydia wrinkle her nose in disgust. *What a bunch of filthy pigs.* It seemed being disarmed and having two weapons trained on him had rendered their guard completely docile, though Lydia didn't exactly trust it. Neither, it appeared, did Addie. Though she'd stepped back to allow the man to move, her knife still flashed in the starlight.

"Oh, God," Addie said, sounding revolted.

Lydia dared a quick glance and her stomach swooped at the sight of Ilse Jackson—or what was left of her—sprawled in the dirt with her skirt hiked up to her waist. Blood oozed slowly from a hole in her temple. The blue eyes, devoid of their usual sly animation, stared blankly into the night sky.

Addie gulped twice and then vomited.

Lydia barely managed to suppress her own urge to retch. She quickly averted her eyes from her one-time rival's ignominious end.

Blaylock limped out of his tent and stormed unevenly toward the three "Randall, what on earth? Why are these women out? Have you lost your mind?"

"No, sir, Mister Blaylock," Lydia replied, voice calm but hands shaking. "He's lost his gun. Luckily for me, I found it." She waved the weapon his direction before training it back on his son. "Now, if you'd like your remaining family member not to die in the dirt, I suggest you step right over here into the house. He'll be joining you momentarily."

Blaylock's eyes skated to Addie, who leaned forward weakly, hands on her knees, staring at the mess she'd just made. Lydia couldn't see the knife anymore. *Hope she didn't drop it. We need every advantage we can get.*

In a sudden explosion of movement, Blaylock whipped his pistol from its holster—fast despite the awkward fumbling across his body—and fired. The bullet tore through Randall's belly and out his back, grazing Lydia's hip as it flew. The youth crumpled with a groan. His fall revealed Lydia's silver-haired nemesis, standing cocked at an awkward angle, his right arm in a dirty sling. His left hand wavered and wobbled with the unaccustomed weight of the gun, but at only a few paces, even the poorest shot would certainly not miss.

"You bastard!" Lydia cried. "How could you kill your own son?" *This ends now!* She lifted the stolen pistol and took aim at Blaylock's head, knowing as she did so that she'd never get him before he got her. *So we both die. At least Addie will be all right.* Time seemed to slow as Lydia squeezed the trigger.

A flash of gold drew James' eyes to the alley beside the café. It only took a glance to reveal his sister-in-law's yellow hair and lush figure sprawled on the brick street. Another glance as he raced in her direction revealed a bald man aiming a weapon directly into her face. *I'll never make it,* he realized sadly.

All around him, the rest of the returned posse fanned out. Strange women armed with all manner of weapons stepped from the shadows, drawing closer to a motley assortment of criminals huddled near the door of the church, back to back, still fighting to a man.

Ignoring the scene before him, James ran toward Allison, trying to aim his pistol while running. The stranger hovering over her laughed, shaking his head. He pulled back the hammer on the shotgun slowly, his sneer showing he was intentionally torturing her.

A sudden whir of movement came to an abrupt halt against the man's bald head. Something dull and blacker than the night connected hard with white, shiny flesh. The man seemed to vibrate from the blow, and his knees slowly buckled. Before he could even hit the ground, James finally managed to steady his hand and fire a shot. The man's throat exploded in a gush of red and he toppled to the earth, revealing the familiar features of Billy Fulton, a large cast-iron skillet clutched in both his hands.

"You saved me, Billy," Allison said in a soft, trembling voice.

Billy lowered the frying pan and extended one hand to Allison, helping her gently to her feet.

"If you don't hit ladies, you shouldn't shoot them either," the young man intoned in all seriousness.

Allison smiled and then threw her arms around him in a tight squeeze.

"What's happening?" James asked.

"The kidnapping was a ruse," Allison replied, her voice muffled in Billy's coat. "They wanted to lure you all away so they could attack us, and that was how they planned to get revenge on the town. I had a bad feeling, so I made everyone gather in the church where those of us who can shoot could protect more people."

"You're a smart girl, Allison Fulton."

"I know it," she replied with her usual lack of subtlety, though with considerably less confidence than she normally displayed.

"But then, why are you out here in hand to hand combat? Why aren't you inside? Where's Rebecca?"

"James," she said with a sigh, "I'm sure your wife is safe inside, but this is no time for telling stories. Nothing against Deputy Fulton, but he looks a bit out of his depth over there."

James glanced and cursed. The young lawman had the knot of robbers at gunpoint, but the wild look on his face could be seen from across the street.

"All right. Later, then. Get somewhere safe, Allison, would you?"

"You watch yourself, Heitschmidt," she shot back. "We have no idea how many there are. This fellow here," she waved at the corpse," is proof we can't relax yet."

He took the advice with a grim nod.

A clearing ahead showed once-plowed land that had not fully reverted to nature. The decaying wreck of a small house sat moldering against the backdrop of the endless prairie, surrounded by a flock of patched and dirty tents. The wind blew through the camp, carrying the stench of unwashed bodies, rotting food and human waste.

"Looks like we found it," Jesse said, his voice so tense it sounded ready to snap.

"Looks like it," Dylan agreed.

"I don't like this," Wesley commented. "It's too quiet."

"It does seem abnormally still," Dylan agreed. "Okay, everyone. Move forward but slow and easy."

They surged ahead, cutting through the tall grass. Every rustle and snap seemed like an announcement of their presence. They crept into the camp, searching for signs of movement, listening hard for conversation, respiration, anything, but the eerie silence remained unbroken until…

"Randall, what on earth?" a familiar male voice snarled. "Why are these women out? Have you lost your mind?"

"No, sir, Mister Blaylock."

Oh, dear Lord, that's Lydia, and she sounds mad as hell, so she can't be badly hurt.

"He's lost his gun. Luckily for me, I found it. Now, if you'd like your remaining family member not to die in the dirt, I suggest you step right over here into the house. He'll be joining you momentarily."

The night seemed to take a deep breath, which then exploded into gunfire.

Forgetting stealth, Jesse raced forward, Wesley and Dylan at his heels. They burst into the yard, among a low stubble of half-grown prairie grass, just in time to see an unfamiliar young man crumple to the ground, leaving Lydia and Blaylock, pistols drawn, facing each other with matching expressions of grim determination. Though Blaylock's right arm hung useless in a sling and his left hand wavered, at this distance, he still could not miss.

As the two slowly took aim, another figure moved beside them. Addie, drawing up to her full, diminutive height. She thrust her hand forward. Silver flashed. Flashed. It revealed itself to be a slender blade as it landed and sank deep into the side of Blaylock's neck. At the same moment, Lydia fired and fell to her side, dodging a bullet that never flew. Blaylock released a gurgling howl and collapsed to his knees, his hand on his neck as a dark red stain spread across his snowy white shirt.

The men drew up short, staring in astonishment at Lydia and Addie.

Jesse broke through his surprise first, racing to his wife and crushing her in his arms. "Addie, Addie..." the wind carried his murmur back to the ears of the men.

Dylan stepped forward, approaching Lydia and extending a hand to help her to her feet.

"Dylan, you have to go. Get back to town. They've sent the band to attack..."

"I know," he said softly.

"You do?" Her eyes gleamed in the darkness.

He nodded. "Wes figured it out. We sent half the men home to see what was happening."

"Well, there's no one left alive here," Addie said, her voice cold. "We should go back. See if we can help."

"Ilse?" Wesley asked.

Lydia shook her head.

Addie wriggled out of her husband's grasp and smoothed the dead woman's skirts down over her bare privates and legs. She murmured a few words Dylan couldn't understand over the corpse.

"We can come back for them in the morning, with horses," Wesley suggested.

"Sounds good," Dylan agreed. "Shall we get the ladies out of here?"

Nods greeted the suggestion.

"It's a bit of a long walk back to town," Jesse pointed out. "Are you up for it, Addie?"

"Jesse, right now I'm so mad I could probably walk until I got to the sea without getting tired," his wife replied. "I'm still not made of porcelain, you know."

"Thank God for that," her husband said. His laugh sounded a bit wild, but the relief in it echoed through the clearing.

Addie might be angry enough, but I'm starting to feel exhausted, Lydia realized, by the time they'd covered half the distance back to town. She wavered and Dylan wrapped a strong arm around her waist. *Good thing he's so powerful. I'm far from light.*

He offered no protest, merely helped her over uneven spots and other unseen obstacles until every step blended with every other.

Lydia's feet went numb. She felt almost as though she were floating rather than walking. *Without Dylan to support me, I'd probably lie down in the dirt and sleep until morning, the cold be damned.*

Garden City appeared like a mirage on the horizon, bathed in a soft, pink glow. Lydia tried to smile at the sight, but her frozen, exhausted face refused to cooperate.

Main Street also seemed strangely quiet, but enough noise emanated from the church to render the scene less eerie. *Or perhaps that's the sunrise restoring hope.*

From their left, Rob Fulton ran out of the jail. "We got 'em, Sheriff," he hollered, waving his hat in the air. "The women figured out they were coming and holed up in the church, and then Allison went and got the whores from the whorehouse. They almost had the lot rounded up by the time we got here. They managed to kill half, and the other half are locked up in the jail."

His eyes fell on Lydia and Addie, weaving like drunkards as they stumbled on the uneven bricks. "They okay?"

"They're both fine. Just tired." Jesse chuckled. "What a couple of tigers. Say, Sheriff, do you think…?"

"Take her home," Dylan replied. "I'm sure she's done in."

Without a word to Rob, only a tip of the head Lydia's fatigued brain almost didn't take in, Dylan walked her across the street to the café, opened the front door, and guided her up to her apartment. Tenderly, Dylan unlaced her boots and tucked her into bed. Lydia dozed off the second her head touched the pillow.

Chapter 12

"Well, well, well," a sly voice spoke into the fog. "Sheriff Dylan Brody asleep at his desk. Tsk tsk."

"Shut up, Jesse," Dylan muttered. "Why are you so wide awake?" Rubbing his aching eyes, he glared at the younger man, who seemed to be bouncing on the balls of his feet with excitement.

"You're getting soft, old man," Jesse teased.

"Let me guess, you caught a few winks in your nice, warm soft bed, with your nice, warm soft wife in your arms. You didn't trek all night through the prairie and then sit your ass down on a rock-hard chair and stay awake six more hours. If you had, I bet you'd be much less chipper right now."

Jesse shrugged. "Semantics. Listen, boss, why don't you head out? As you said, I'm wide awake and ready to take over. If I'm not mistaken, you also have a warm, soft woman who could use some comforting."

"We're not married yet," Dylan grumbled.

"Didn't stop me," Jesse pointed out. "Also, you're not fooling anyone. Get out of here."

"Whippersnapper," Dylan muttered as he hauled himself out of his chair. Ignoring Jesse's suggestion, he stumbled to his tiny, one-room house and crashed into his bed with his boots still on.

Bang! Bang! Bang! "Lydia, wake up!" Becky shouted, her voice muffled by the door. "What's a lady to do to get some cake around here?"

Lydia groaned. "I'm staying closed today, Becky. Go away."

"Not on your life," her friend called. "Get up. I have a surprise for you."

Only then did Lydia's foggy brain recognize that Becky's knock had come, not from the outer door of the café, but from her apartment.

Hauling herself to her feet, she confronted the grinning blond, who stood in her living room.

"Cake? Are you joking?"

"Not at all," Becky replied.

"What are you up to, Rebecca Heitschmidt?" Lydia demanded.

"I told you, it's a surprise," Becky replied, grinning until the corners of her eyes crinkled. "You once told Esther spice cake was your favorite, so make up a nice big one, okay?"

"I have no idea what you're talking about," Lydia groused.

"Good," Becky said, turning on her heel. Then she stopped and turned around to face her friend again, reaching out to grab the taller woman in a tight hug. Her rounded belly pressed hard against Lydia, the bump squirming between them. "I'm so glad you're home safe and sound. I was worried about you."

"I was worried too. We overheard the robbers saying they were luring the men away to attack the town."

"They tried," Becky admitted, "but between Kristina keeping everyone safe inside the church and Allison coming after them from behind, they didn't stand a chance. Then James and Rob led half the posse back into town, and it was over. None of us even got hurt, except for Allison, who has some scrapes on her hands."

"We lost one." Lydia examined her stockings, noting a hole where her big toe protruded, her skin unusually pale against the black fabric.

Becky sighed. "I heard. Poor Ilse. I didn't like her, but I didn't wish her ill."

"Me either. She was selfish and misguided, but not really a bad person. Is Cody preparing the funeral?"

Becky nodded. "For three days from now."

Lydia's lips twisted into a sad frown. "I hope I can eventually remember her, pretty and sassy, putting her pert little nose in everyone's business. She made a pitiful corpse."

"Don't think about it," Becky urged. "Get dressed. Hurry. You have a cake to bake. Remember, make it big, and frost it up pretty."

"How big?" Lydia demanded. "Who's paying for it?"

"The biggest you can make in half a day, and never mind the costs. It's covered, no matter what."

Still puzzled, Lydia shooed her friend out of the apartment and stripped off her clothes. Noting quite a quantity of blood on her dress did little for her composure, and the ache of her bullet-grazed hip snapped the remaining thread. Choking sobs rose up in Lydia's throat, almost cutting off her breath. She sank to the floor in her torn bloomers and sweaty, dirty chemise and cried like she hadn't cried since her parents' deaths.

"Well?" Kristina demanded, "what did she say? Did you have to tell her anything?"

Becky shook her head. "She looks a little lost, but I think she's going to do it. Now, did *you* do what *I* asked?"

Kristina held up the length of fabric to which a paper pattern had been pinned. "Just finished. Are you sure I'm up to this?"

"Of course," Becky assured her. "You have nimble fingers. Just follow my directions and don't fret. I'll do the detail work."

"Okay," Kristina agreed, sounding doubtful. "I'm not very good at sewing, you know."

"You just don't want to pay attention to it, but for Lydia?"

"For Lydia, I'll try. Can we talk about music to keep my mind off it?"

"Of course," Becky agreed with a laugh. It sounded strained. *It would be to be a while before life got back to normal.*

A quiet knocking roused Dylan after not nearly enough hours. "Who is it," he called.

"It's Cody," the pastor's softly-accented voice replied. "May I come in?"

Grumbling, Dylan made his way to the door and yanked it open.

"You look terrible," Cody said.

"Glad to know I'm consistent," Dylan quipped weakly. "Come on in, pastor, but I can't promise much hospitality."

"You don't need to," Cody replied. "I'm here to warn you. There's a plot afoot, and you're involved. I don't think you can get out of it, so you might want to, you know, take a bath. Change into clean clothes."

"I've had about all I can take of secret plots," Dylan commented, stomping to the area along the rear wall that served as a kitchen.

"I'm sure that's true," Cody agreed, trailing after him, "but this one isn't dangerous, at least I don't think so. See, last night, when they were hiding out in the church, the ladies decided it was high time you and Lydia got married."

"I agree," Dylan said as he filled a kettle and lit the stove. "Maybe now that the robbers are gone, we can get around to planning it."

"Well, um, you won't have to."

Dylan stopped scooping grounds into the coffee pot. "What exactly do you mean, preacher?"

"I mean that Mrs. Heitschmidt and my wife have taken it upon themselves to marry you two... this afternoon. They're making a dress. Can you imagine my Kristina sewing?" He chuckled.

Dylan gave him a sour look.

"They've fooled Lydia into baking her own cake, but if you don't clean up and put on a nice suit, you're going to look mighty silly. I felt like I needed to warn you."

Dylan sighed. "Cody, I feel like I've been rode hard and put away wet. The last thing I want to do is some fancy party making."

"I know," Cody replied, looking sheepish. He ran his hand through his hair, loosening the black curls from their pomade. "I wouldn't suggest it myself, but if married life teaches you anything, it's that you don't fight women over the small things. They're all feeling their oats today, and it's best if we let them have their way."

Dylan frowned at the kettle, willing it to boil faster. "Oh, all right. I guess the result is the same either way."

"It is, and it means the next time you sleep, it will be beside Lydia. Having a wife is pretty nice." His expression softened into a private smile.

Ah, that does sound good, Dylan thought. Though tired, Dylan's sex responded to the memory of his and Lydia's previous passionate encounters. *Okay, maybe this plan has merit.* "I'll take a bath, preacher. Thank you."

"I'll be by to collect you at 4:30. The wedding is at five."

Dylan nodded and poured the boiling water into the coffee pot.

"Oh, and sheriff?" Dylan looked up from his brewing coffee. "It's three-fifteen. You might want to get a move on."

Dylan scrunched his face in answer.

"Smells great in here," Allison said, letting herself into the kitchen of the café. With one arm she clutched her son to her chest. With the other, she led little Melissa.

"For some reason, your sister wanted me to make a big spice cake. I just finished it. Do you know what it's for, Allie?"

"Yes," Allison replied, and her tone of voice drew Lydia's gaze. The blond woman had a teasing smirk on her face.

"What is it?" Lydia demanded.

"Come with me," Allison urged, gesturing with her head.

Lydia took in her friend's appearance. "You look might fancy. Should I change?"

"No," Allison said. "Not yet. Come on. Leave the cake. We'll be back."

Bemused, Lydia trailed after them, through the dining room and out into the chilly street. Allison turned left and angled across the street. A gust of cold autumn wind cut through Lydia's dress. Baby Peter began to fuss.

"Hurry," Allison called over her shoulder. "It's too cold to be out like this for long."

"Where are we going?" Lydia demanded, hoping for a clue.

"The vicarage," Allison replied.

Well, that tells me nothing. Thankfully, the small house lay only half a block from the café. Lydia and Allison had arrived quickly at the door and hurried inside. The parlor, much smaller since the interior walls had been added, seemed far too crowded with women. Kristina immediately grabbed Lydia's hands and maneuvered her into an armchair.

"What's happening?" she demanded. Becky pulled the pins from her messy semblance of a bun and produced a brush as though from thin air.

"We're getting you ready," Kristina informed her.

"For what?"

"You'll see," Allison teased. She sank onto the sofa and unbuttoned her blouse, positioning the baby on her breast.

"Am I late?" Addie asked. "Sorry, I was still tired." The plump curve of her growing baby pushed out the front of her dress almost past the point of decency.

"No ill effects, Addie?" Lydia asked, momentarily distracted from her puzzlement.

"No," the tiny redhead replied. "Nor from my homecoming either." She giggled at her own naughtiness. "The little one is still tucked away safe and no signs of trouble." Lydia could see that, though Addie's words sounded light, tension crumpled the corners of her eyes.

"I would like it very much if someone would tell me what was going on," Lydia commented.

"You and Sheriff Brody are betrothed, right?" Becky asked around a mouthful of hairpins.

"Yes, why?"

"Well, you won't be for much longer." Kristina pulled a length of butter yellow satin out of a black garment bag.

"What?" Lydia tried to rocket out of the chair.

Becky pushed her back into the seat. "Not the best way to phrase it, Kristina," she said. Grabbing a section of Lydia's hair, she began braiding it. "Okay, we're close enough now. You can find out."

"We didn't like that your wedding planning time got interrupted by... all this," Allison said.

"So, what, you did it for me?" Lydia guessed.

Heads nodded.

Lydia's throat burned and her eyes stung hard. "Goodness. I don't know whether to laugh or cry."

"Well, take it from us married ladies," Kristina said, "either one is possible, and either one is fine. How's that hair coming, Becky?"

"Getting there," Rebecca replied. "Give me ten. Lydia, when James and I married, I got so nervous, I almost fainted. I wanted to spare you that. Did we come close?"

"After everything that happened yesterday," Lydia informed her friends, "a little thing like getting married isn't going to cause much more than a flutter."

"I'm with you there," Addie agreed. "I'm ready to retire from crises for good. How about you?"

"Definitely," Lydia agreed.

"So, um, do you need someone to... explain your wifely duties to you?" Kristina asked, her face flaming to match her hair.

"Oh, er, no thank you." Lydia's own cheeks burned. "I know what I need to know."

"Not that they're duties, you know," the pastor's wife added. "Being married is really nice."

"Oh, I know," Lydia blurted. "I mean... that is..."

"Don't worry," Addie urged. "Not everyone behaves themselves like a pastor. As long as you get married, it doesn't much matter."

"I agree," Lydia said.

Dylan stood at the front of the church, Jesse, James, Wesley and Rob arrayed behind him, all dressed in their Sunday best, washed, shaved and ready. Sweat moistened the sheriff's palms and he shifted his weight from one shoe to the other.

Kristina poked her head in the door and then scuttled up the staircase to the choir loft, where she took a seat on the organ bench. Moments later, glorious music bellowed from the pipes, defiantly cheerful after such a terrible night.

She set a tempo perhaps a bit fast for processional music so that when Sarah, Rob's sweetheart, walked into the room in a red gingham dress, she walked a bit unevenly.

Behind her, Allison a baby in one arm made her way up the aisle. A quick scan of the congregation revealed Melissa sitting with the Spencers, Allison and Rebecca's parents. Rebecca came next, smiling, arrayed in scarlet, a cleverly cut gown that concealed the curve of her advancing pregnancy.

Dylan couldn't help but smile to see Lydia walking in arm-in-arm with Addie. *Those two are stuck for life, like sisters,* he thought. *I'm so glad they both came out of it safe.*

Sunlight poured through the broken stained-glass windows and illuminated the bullet holes in the walls. *We've come through a lot, but we're still here. Still ready to face the future together. Hope lives on. Love lives on.* Suddenly, the wild plan to go along with this spur-of-the-moment wedding seemed, not strange, but perfect.

His gaze settled on the woman he loved. Her dark hair gleamed in the late-afternoon sun. Her eyes glowed with the light of love that lit up her face brighter than the sunset outside. Dressed in a simple, yellow gown that set off her olive skin to perfection, she looked like an angel, come down from heaven to lead him to salvation.

She drew near and he reached out one hand and clasped hers, accepting all that their future together would mean. She took that final step that placed her directly beside him, and at the peace of their love settled over the congregation.

Epilogue

In the end, it took far less time to clean up the church than it did to clean up the frightened and wounded spirits of the little town on the prairie. While nearly everyone survived the attack, something was lost. Innocence, trust. The knowledge that their world was safe and everything would be fine.

Still, life went on, the way life always does.

Addie and Jesse's baby arrived right on time, a healthy—if tiny—girl with a shock of reddish hair and plump cheeks no one could resist kissing. She could have been named for a record of most-kissed baby. She grew up healthy and happy, with three annoying younger brothers who kept her humble.

Allison and Wesley's son was the first of six children they had together, along with Melissa. As time passed, the connection between them grew, as did their patience with and affection for each other. Despite their rocky start, they developed into a mature and enviable relationship that quite set the tone for other marriages in the town.

Cody and Kristina never did have children, but they truly didn't mind. In later years, they said the whole church was their family, and not having small fry to contend with left them time to be more involved in the community. They felt no regret.

Becky and James's daughter, born only a week after the Wests', quite charmed the town... until she learned to walk. It was only then that they realized two mild-mannered parents could produce a hellion. They managed her, but only just. Still, they loved her, and each other, with a joy and gratitude that would never end.

Billy Fulton married a former saloon girl named Julie, and if she had to handle managing the family, well, he provided for her and loved her better than any other man could have done. Eventually, she came to be accepted in the town, starting with Allison and her friends, of course.

The rest of the saloon girls eventually moved on, and what happened to them, no one ever knew. Allison told everyone she hoped they were happy. She meant it.

And as for the sheriff and his bride… two years after the attack on Garden City, Lydia shocked the town—and herself—by proving the doctors had been wrong. Her typhoid fever had not rendered her sterile. The discovery, at five months into the pregnancy, that she was expecting caused a flurry of nerves on the part of her husband, that resolved in a healthy delivery of a big, chubby and adorable son, and three years after that, another.

And in this way, though it didn't banish the memory of evil, love did heal wounded hearts, restore shattered lives and bring back a measure of peace so that Garden City, Kansas, once again became a place people were proud to call their home on the High Plains.

Author's Note

Garden City, Kansas is a real town—a cattle town on the High Plains of Western Kansas, with brick streets downtown, a few stunted trees, and a wind that never stops blowing. Nowadays, it's an interesting mixture of quaint and modern, but back in 1889, it was a new town, only a couple of decades old. The timeline I've created deviates a bit from historical accuracy (the town actually sprang from one man's vision in the 1870s rather than being incorporated from an existing settlement), but I've worked hard to maintain the accuracy other than that.

And the Fulton family really was the foundation of the town. Fulton Street is still a main commercial thoroughfare named in their honor. However, the Fultons mentioned in this story are my own creation, not based on the historical family at all.

Dear reader,

We hope you enjoyed reading *High Plains Passion*. Please take a moment to leave a review, even if it's a short one. Your opinion is important to us.

Discover more books by Simone Beaudelaire at https://www.nextchapter.pub/authors/simone-beaudelaire-romance-author.

Want to know when one of our books is free or discounted for Kindle? Join the newsletter at http://eepurl.com/bqqB3H.

Best regards,
Simone Beaudelaire and the Next Chapter Team

You might also like:

Keeping Katerina by Simone Beaudelaire

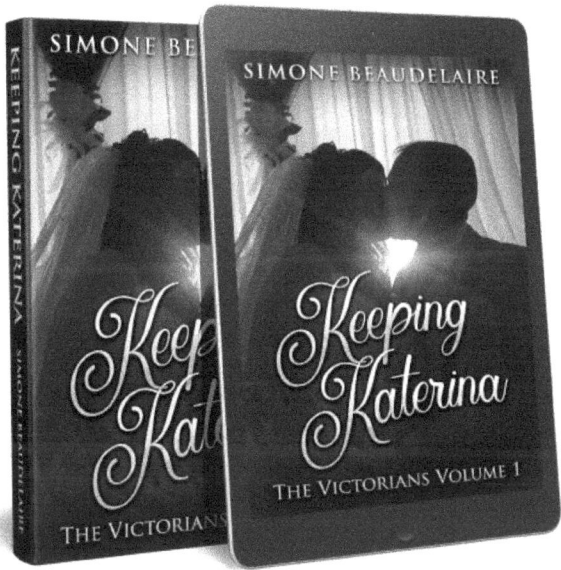

To read the first chapter for free, head to:
https://www.nextchapter.pub/books/keeping-katerina-regency-romance.

Books by Simone Beaudelaire

When the Music Ends (The Hearts in Winter Chronicles Book 1)
When the Words are Spoken (The Hearts in Winter Chronicles Book 2)
Caroline's Choice (The Hearts in Winter Chronicles Book 3)
When the Heart Heals (The Hearts in Winter Chronicles Book 4)
The Naphil's Kiss
Blood Fever
Polar Heat
Xaman (with Edwin Stark)
Darkness Waits (with Edwin Stark)
Watching Over the Watcher
Baylee Breaking
Amor Maldito: Romantic Tragedies from Tejano Folklore
Keeping Katerina (The Victorians Book 1)
Devin's Dilemma (The Victorians Book 2)
Colin's Conundrum (The Victorians Book 3)
High Plains Promise (Love on the High Plains Book 2)
High Plains Heartbreak (Love on the High Plains Book 3)
High Plains Passion (Love on the High Plains Book 4)
Devilfire (American Hauntings Book 1)
Saving Sam (The Wounded Warriors Book 1 with J.M. Northup)
Justifying Jack (The Wounded Warriors Book 2 with J.M. Northup)
Making Mike (The Wounded Warriors Book 3 with J.M Northup)
Si tu m'Aimes (If you Love me)

Lightning Source UK Ltd.
Milton Keynes UK
UKHW012114280720
367329UK00005B/112